Let's Get Lost

Praise for *Let's Get Lost*

This surprising retro-speculative romance from Steven Ramirez (author of *Tell Me When I'm Dead*) finds the son of renowned scientists adrift—and caught up in science-fiction and horror scenarios—after his parents' untimely death. What began as a sort of coming-of-age narrative about a college grad in the 1960s quickly evolves into a spirited, genre-crossing story that will keep readers riveted until the exciting conclusion.

— BOOKLIFE

Let's Get Lost relies on science instead of magic as its driving force to invigorating effect. And the prose is elegant yet understated, featuring rich narrative flourishes, dry humor, and period-specific details. The narrative arc is at once surprising and satisfying, fulfilling the expectations set up early in the story but taking several unexpected turns. Cliffhangers are used to great effect, lending the tale a note of urgency. *Let's Get Lost* is a playful, charming fairy-tale romance novel that is elevated by the creative risks it takes.

— FORWARD CLARION REVIEWS

Author Steven Ramirez has crafted a rollercoaster of emotions, blending elements of romance, suspense, and existential reflection in a well-balanced narrative that gives both intellectual and emotional stimulation in equal measure. Adam's cleverly mirrored journey from heartbreak to self-discovery is both relatable and inspiring, resonating with anyone who has grappled with life's uncertainties but giving that ever-present sense of hope that humanity often clings to. Overall, *Let's Get Lost* is a captivating tale that I would recommend to fans of accomplished romantic dramas everywhere.

— READERS' FAVORITE

Books by Steven Ramirez

LITERARY FICTION

Let's Get Lost

HELLBORN SERIES

Tell Me When I'm Dead

Dead Is All You Get

Even The Dead Will Bleed

HARD TO KILL SERIES

Brandon's Last Words

Faithless

SARAH GREENE MYSTERIES

The Girl in the Mirror

House of the Shrieking Woman

The Blood She Wore

OTHER BOOKS

Chainsaw Honeymoon

Come As You Are: A Short Novel and Nine Stories

Come As You Are: A Novella

LET'S GET LOST

A Modern Fairy Tale

STEVEN RAMIREZ

glass highway

Copyright © 2024 by Steven Ramirez.

All rights reserved. No part of this publication may be reproduced, distributed, or transmitted in any form or by any means, including photocopying, recording, or other electronic or mechanical methods, without the prior written permission of the publisher, except for brief quotations embodied in critical reviews and other specific noncommercial uses permitted by copyright law. For permission requests, contact the publisher at stevenramirez.com/permission.

Glass Highway

Los Angeles, CA

stevenramirez.com

Publisher's Note: This is a work of fiction. Names, characters, places, and incidents are a product of the author's imagination. Any opinions expressed belong to the characters and should not be confused with those of the author. Locales and public names are sometimes used for atmospheric purposes. Any resemblance to actual people, living or dead, or businesses, companies, events, institutions, or locales is coincidental.

Let's Get Lost / A Modern Fairy Tale / Steven Ramirez.—1st ed.

Hardcover: 978-1-949108-25-5

Paperback: 978-1-949108-26-2

EPUB: 978-1-949108-27-9

Kindle: 978-1-949108-28-6

Audiobook: 978-1-949108-29-3

Library of Congress Control Number: 2024903728

Edited by Rebecca Millar

Cover design by Damonza

For my parents

'Who's going to believe a talking head? Get a job in a sideshow.'

— HERBERT WEST, *RE-ANIMATOR*
(1985)

Let's Get Lost

CHAPTER 1

What Am I Here For?

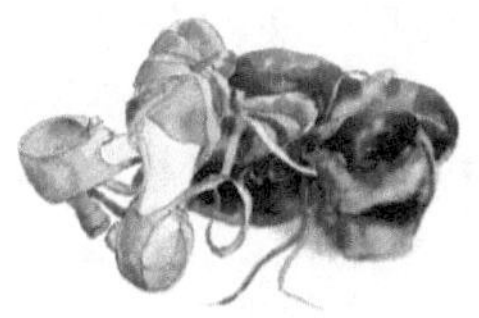

This is the story of a young man called Adam West. Not the actor, mind you. Adam was an agreeable chap who read physics at Cornell because he wanted to follow in his parents' footsteps. But he wasn't very good at it. This is not to imply he was a dimwit. Far from it. He was... Oh, what's the word? *Distracted*. And it didn't help that his beloved mother and father were killed before he left university. They were the chief scientists at Bland Corporation, working on Lord knows what, and had been there many years.

Jon West was a gifted scientist and the son of the illustrious Aaron West, who served as Bland's chief scientist until his death in 1940. Adam's mother, Miriam Hoffman West, was a brilliant researcher whose intellect outshone her husband's. Together, they ran the science division and assumed their son would join them as a junior scientist after obtaining his master's degree. They also believed he would get his PhD and take over the division one day after his parents retired. That was the plan, anyway. Alas, none of it came to pass.

The accident happened on 2 January 1960, the day John F. Kennedy announced his candidacy for the Democratic presidential nomination. There was a terrific explosion in the physics lab where Jon and Miriam worked. The story goes that the star-crossed scientists were killed instantly, burned beyond recognition. There were other casualties too. Eight assistant researchers, a cleaning woman – who went by the nickname 'Gertie' after leaving prison in Bedford Hills – and some poor sod from the canteen who had only just arrived with coffee and pastries.

Due to the thickness of the concrete, the damage was confined to the immediate area. Shattered glass carpeted the room and scorch marks adorned the walls like an abstract painting by Willem de Kooning. Most of the equipment was destroyed. The double doors leading to the corridor were nowhere to be found. Some in the department conjectured they were sucked into a black hole, never to be seen again. One survivor offered a more mystical explanation, claiming the doors had never existed. He said life was an illusion and he was from the planet Neptune. They sent him to Bellevue Hospital for evaluation.

After an exhaustive inquiry that involved feeding stacks of punch cards into a gloomy IBM computer, the hastily assembled task force delivered their report to the CEO, who everyone affectionately referred to as the Old Man. The results were less than satisfactory. Their findings were inconclusive, which someone managed to spell as *inconclusie*. The team were convinced that whatever happened had something to do with quantum mechanics. Considering that quantum mechanics had been the nature and focus of the scientists' work, the CEO was incensed and threatened to sack everyone, including Mr Dawkins, the canteen manager.

The task force didn't take their leader's warning lightly. After a worrisome night – involving copious amounts of alcohol and several attractive ladies – they returned to the office refreshed. They found some more punch cards in a dusty drawer in a back room and fed them into the bewildered computer.

This time, a new hypothesis began to take shape. It was likely the disaster occurred at the subatomic level. How it resulted in the destruction of an entire laboratory, however, was anyone's guess. Still, the computer left them with a dark warning. Had the explosion occurred a little to the left, it would have destroyed the very fabric of the space-time continuum.

Upon reading the new report, the Old Man made good on his threat and sacked the task force straight away, telling them in no uncertain terms they 'screwed the pooch.' Moreover, he called them 'dilettantes', a word his wife taught him at dinner after reading *Madame Bovary*. Next, he warned every CEO from New York to Chicago that those gits were not to be trusted with anything more challenging than delivering coffee and pastries. In closing, he stated they had no idea how to spell *inconclusuff*. But he wasn't finished.

As a testament to his superior physical prowess, the CEO took a fireman's axe to the IBM computer. The machine died a miserable death, spewing thousands of half-digested punch cards into the air. Some say if you stand in the middle of the data centre and close your eyes, you can still hear the gentle whirring of the tape drives and a tiny child's voice whispering, 'You sick bastard!'

At the will reading in Manhattan, Shlomo Engel, the West family solicitor, let it be known that Adam had inherited 'the whole megillah.' The list of spoils included his parents' estate in Long Island, numerous holiday properties around the country – including a beachfront mansion in the Hamptons – sixteen automobiles, a collection of priceless European art and a sizeable investment portfolio, which at present-day value ran into the millions. He was also the proud owner of a pied-à-terre in SoHo, purchased in 1937.

If anyone else had fallen headlong into this Carrollian fairy tale, they would have elected never to work again. But not Adam. Like most Americans, he sought purpose and wanted his life to mean something. And so, alone and depressed, he graduated from Cornell. But rather than continuing his studies, he prepared to enter the working world.

Sadly, no friends or family came to celebrate his achievement. Only the solicitor was there to congratulate him. Adam knew of an uncle he could have invited – a hermit living in the Hudson Valley – but since childhood, he'd been warned the mysterious relative was a nutter and was to be avoided.

Since childhood, he had looked forward to joining his parents at Bland and staying there until the day he retired with a healthy pension and a gold-plated pen-and-pencil set. Hopefully, by then he would have married and given his doting mother and father the grandchildren they deserved. But Jon and Miriam were dead. Adam didn't have a girlfriend, much less a wife. And even with his enormous wealth, his future looked bleak at best.

Compelled to honour his commitment to the late scientists – and also because he owed them money – the Old Man offered the grieving graduate a job in Bland's marketing department. Not knowing the first thing about misleading people, Adam accepted with the knowledge that his dream of becoming a scientist would most likely never come to pass.

Though he had a job now, there was another problem.

Bruce Donovan, the firm's VP of Marketing, disliked Adam. Not because of his personality – the executive hadn't yet met him. No, it was because he'd been hired without the VP's knowledge. Also because there was only one open position in the department, the first in over a year. Bruce had promised the slot to his good friend Tito Ladrón, a Cuban immigrant who worked as a copywriter in the firm's Miami offices. As a result, Tito felt obligated to despise his rival as well.

Adam was unaware of any corporate intrigue. Otherwise, he wouldn't have flirted with Jenny. If a sensible man were to look at the situation with a critical eye, it would be clear any other woman on the planet – including the late Gertie – would have been preferable, dating-wise, to Bruce Donovan's fetching daughter.

Adam did flirt with her, however. Well, not intentionally. It was more of a fish-out-of-water affair. Vice President Nixon comes to mind. Like Eve, it was all the girl's fault. But instead of an apple, she offered him a kosher pickle. He was a sucker for the tender cucumbers swimming in tangy brine. Especially when accompanied by a corned beef sandwich slathered in Reuben dressing and horseradish, which one could find easily at Katz's Deli on the Lower East Side.

Jenny knew instinctively the way to a man's heart. And more importantly, she always got her way.

CHAPTER 2

Good Bait

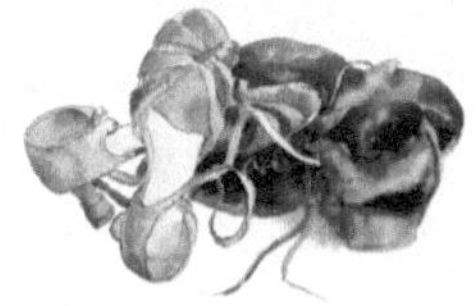

Jenny Donovan was nineteen, three years younger than Adam. Pretty and petite, she adored Audrey Hepburn and copied her timeless bob. She often wore capri pants with flat shoes except in winter. Her favourite film was *Roman Holiday*. She had been in love with Bobby Darin until the day he married that troll – her words – Sandra Dee.

After making her debut at sixteen, the girl was regularly courted by eligible university men who all had middle names beginning with J. They were invited to the house in Great Neck, where they spoke of trust funds, summers in Martha's Vineyard and sailing in Newport. As the only child of Bruce and Lilith Donovan, Jenny, too, was wealthy and spoiled and made sure everyone knew how unimpressed she was with the endless parade of pretenders.

At one point in her junior year of high school, she considered attending university. She knew her parents would support her whatever her decision. But they were traditionalists and often expressed the opinion that a woman's job was to get married and raise children. Not that she was against that sort of life – she looked forward to having a family one day.

Several of her friends decided on college, not because they wanted a career. They would read fun subjects such as art, history and music. If they met their future husbands in the bargain, all the better. None of those interested Jenny enough for her to devote four years to them, and she had no desire to become a teacher, one of the few career paths open to women. She was terrible at maths and science. Besides, she had plenty of suitors to keep her busy.

The only reason she'd bothered with Adam was to annoy her father. Nightly at the dinner table, he complained about an odd young man with no discernible skills who, like a lame shelter animal, had been foisted on him by the cunning CEO. What was worse, the dilettante insisted on eating pickles at his desk and telling physics jokes in the canteen. To wit...

'A photon checks into a hotel and says to the bell-hop, "I didn't bring any luggage. I'm travelling light."'

As Bruce continued his tirade, an idea began to form in Jenny's fertile mind, one that could prove beneficial to her current dilemma. Cosying up to her dad, she asked him for the troublesome employee's name, which he spat out like spoilt milk.

'Adam West,' he said.

. . .

Never one to procrastinate, Jenny set out the next morning. Wearing a stylish beige jumper beneath her warm cashmere coat, she travelled to New York's Lower East Side, via a car service, in search of Kosher pickles. The trip took a little over an hour.

Upon arriving, she found herself in a place whose pavements were packed with bearded men in black Borsalino hats and chattering women wearing tichels, some carrying little ones on their hips. Everyone spoke a blend of English and Yiddish. There was something curiously inviting about the neighbourhood. Despite having shop fronts, merchants preferred selling their wares outside, which made walking tricky.

Beginning at the Bowery, the privileged girl from Great Neck made her way east on Delancey Street, taking in the sights and sounds. Boys in yarmulkes waved to her, perhaps impressed with her admirable posture and steady gait. At first, she ignored them. But after three blocks, she warmed up to the townsfolk and stopped here and there to inspect fresh fish, dishes and women's clothing.

Presently, she felt a tug on her coat, and when she turned round, a little girl with blue eyes and curly blonde locks looked at the young woman with her palms raised. In one hand lay something black, shiny and round.

'For me?' Jenny said.

An exasperated mother of around thirty took the girl's hand. 'She's doing this all the time, giving things to strangers.'

'Aw. What's her name?'

'Hannah.'

Crouching, the young woman smiled at the child. 'Hannah is a very pretty name. I'm Jenny.'

The girl whispered something to her mum, and the weary woman sighed.

'She says you need that.'

When Hannah offered it again, Jenny took the object and examined it. It was a glass eye, the type used for stuffed animals. She looked at the generous little giver, quite serious.

'I can only accept this if I give you something in return. Wait here.'

Jenny slipped the treasure into her coat pocket. Glancing round, she spotted a man selling bagels nearby. She purchased one and gave it to the girl, who was delighted.

No longer cross, the woman clasped Jenny's hand. 'A lebn af dayn kop.'[1]

The cherubic girl waved goodbye as she and her mother disappeared into the crowd of daytime shoppers. Remembering her mission, Jenny started off again. At length, she discovered Essex Street Pickles and purchased a jar, depositing it in her yellow straw bag. Luckily, her driver had followed and waited at the kerb to collect her. Soon they were on their way to Bland's offices.

Jenny arrived around lunchtime. According to her father, Adam West liked to walk to the automat for a sandwich and jelly. Earlier, she'd got her hands on a staff newsletter and recognised Adam amongst all the other men in suits and hats. As he made his way through the crowds of lunch-goers towards the lobby entrance, she stepped in front of him.

'You look awfully strong,' she said. 'Do you think you could open this for me?'

Adam was concerned the vending machine would run

out of cherry Jell-O. Still, he sympathised with the attractive girl in the adorable beret and ankle boots, and he thought it wise to help her. It never occurred to him to ask what she was doing with a jar of pickles in the middle of a busy lobby. After giving the cap a quick twist, he handed it to her.

'Wow, thanks,' she said.

'Simple physics. Which reminds me of a joke. A neutron walks into a bar and says, "How much for a whisky?" The bartender tells him, "For you, no charge." Um, that was the joke.'

'I don't get it.'

'See, because neutrons don't carry a... It's not one of my better ones.'

Giggling, she took his hand. 'Come with me.'

'Where are we going?'

'You'll see.'

'But—'

'Don't be a scaredy cat.'

A brisk wind came up, stirring the leaves, as she led him down Avenue of the Americas towards Rockefeller Center. At West Fifty-Second, they made a sharp left and continued to the middle of the block, where he spotted a narrow walkway. She gave him a conspiratorial look and brought him to a secret garden – a pocket park – nestled between two tall buildings. The path turned to cobblestone, and inviting park benches stood under the bare London plane and honey locust trees. The sound of traffic had faded. Now there was only birdsong and the chittering of squirrels.

'Isn't it breathtaking?' she said.

'How did you know about this place?'

'Oh, I... Someone brought me here once.'

'Seems like the perfect spot for a kiss... I don't know why I said that.'

She offered her hand. 'I'm Jenny Donovan.'

'Adam West. Wait, my boss's name is Donovan.'

'What a coincidence! I'm his daughter. And it's nice to meet you.'

She sat on a bench and placed her bag between them. Opening the jar, she offered him a pickle. Though he would've preferred a meal, he didn't regret missing lunch. Being with this peculiar girl with the Audrey Hepburn hair was like a dream, but he wasn't sure he should be there, considering who she was.

He tried remembering other girls he'd dated at Cornell and couldn't recall any of their names except one – Millicent Taylor. She came from a family of doctors and was meant to become a psychiatrist. They met at a party. After two cups of spiked punch, she told him she'd had a dream about a trickster who, as it turned out, looked quite like Adam. She claimed it was the reason she approached him. After three more drinks, they attempted some mischief in his car, but gave up because he couldn't work out how to unhook her brassiere. Flushed and frustrated, she left, informing him he wasn't a trickster at all but a dull-witted boy who would never understand women. He responded by admitting, without a modicum of irony, that she would make an excellent doctor someday. She slapped him.

The cucumbers were crisp, and the chewing noises attracted a few sparrows. They sat in silence for a while, Adam pondering over this unexpected adventure and Jenny trying to understand why she'd become less confident about her mission. She had planned to lead the young man on with dinners, films and Broadway shows. As their relationship blossomed, he would be invited to her house. All so that she could receive her well-deserved reward.

Knowing how much her dad detested the young man, he would agree to buy her the Rosso Corsa Ferrari California Spyder she longed for. As soon as he handed over the keys, she would unceremoniously dump her boyfriend, insisting he gave her a headache. It was a perfect scheme, yet there was something so bloody appealing about Adam. Was it the turned-up shirt collar? Or the way he blushed when she mentioned her knees? Or perhaps it was because he was handsome with his straight blond hair forever falling over his left eye whenever he turned his gaze towards her. *I'm not a monster. Why not give him a chance? Then we'll see...*

'Kiss me,' she said as he reached for another pickle.

'What?'

'You said so yourself, it's the perfect spot.'

'But we're not even—'

'Adam, if you don't kiss me right now, I'll never know if... That is, we'll miss our chance.'

'Gee, are you sure?'

'Yes.' Adjusting herself on the bench, she laid a gloved hand on his shoulder and closed her eyes.

Images of fiery doom ran through his head like a herd of wild bison, the worst being her father chasing him through Central Park with an axe, followed by thirty generations of Donovans carrying pitchforks and torches. And then he gazed at her full, eager lips. They were perfect and he wanted to taste them.

'Any time, mister.'

Adam removed his hat and taking Jenny's face in his hands, pressed his lips to hers. The feeling was magical – disorienting. He slipped his arms around her to prolong the moment. Divine. Where did she come from, this girl with the pickles? Like a lost angel, she'd descended from the sky into his life.

His cologne was subtle and fragrant, and his lips fit wonderfully on hers. She saw her red sports car driving away on its own into the mist of a tomorrow that might never come. And, without bidding it goodbye, she melted in his arms like a snowman in spring.

How was it possible? Somehow she, Jenny Donovan – conductor of men – had fallen hard for the awkward, self-effacing junior executive in the expensive Brooks Brothers suit. She was, as the saying goes, smitten as a kitten. Someday, she would get her little red Spyder. But in the meantime, she had Adam.

And although he didn't know it yet, Adam had Jenny.

---

1. 'Life on your head.' A Yiddish blessing.

CHAPTER 3

It Could Happen To You

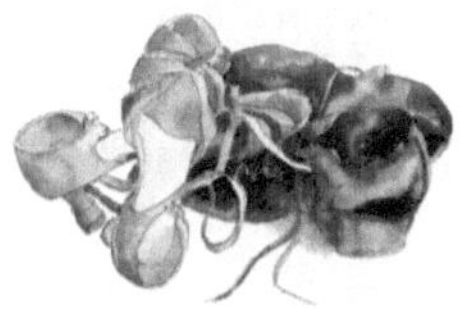

Bruce Donovan laid down his fork and gazed at his family. It was Thursday night and Adam had been invited once again to join them for dinner at their home.

'I've come to a decision,' Bruce said.

Often when Jenny's father opened a conversation with those words, it had to do with attempting a diet or threatening the media with bodily harm via the telly for picking on poor Dick Nixon. Everyone laid aside their cutlery and placed their hands on their laps. Under the table, Jenny squeezed her boyfriend's hand. For weeks, she'd implored her dad to give Adam more responsibility. Weary of the feminine frontal assault, Bruce gave in.

'Adam, I'm putting you in charge of Bland's new ad campaign.'

His daughter pretended to be surprised. 'Oh, Daddy, that's wonderful!'

'I'd like to kiss you now,' Mrs D said to the startled young man.

The woman's eyes smouldered with passion. Stroking

the stem of her wine glass, she winked as she ran her tongue under her upper teeth. Later, she would insist the two martinis she'd consumed before dinner had gone to her head, when really it was the Valium.

Distracted by Jenny's finger drawing a heart on his palm, Adam failed to comprehend any of it. He was sure his boss had asked him to wash and detail his Oldsmobile at the weekend. In the meantime, the VP waited for a reply.

'Thank you, sir.'

'Don't thank me yet. It's going to be hard going. You have no idea.' He laughed like a French inquisitor at an auto-da-fé.

Jenny pecked her boyfriend's cheek. 'I'm sure he'll do great. Won't you, honeybunch?'

'You'll start on Monday,' Bruce said. 'I'm moving you into the office next to mine.'

Mrs D stirred her wine with her little finger and addressed her untouched vegetables. 'Kiss you very, very hard.'

Before witnessing any further embarrassment, her husband pushed away from the table and stood. 'If you'll excuse me, I have to make some calls.'

His wife reached for the cut-glass decanter. She topped up her goblet and, ignoring the wine-stained tablecloth, toasted her husband's disinterested backside as he marched to his study. Too excited to eat, Jenny took her boyfriend by the hand and led him into the garden. Their housekeeper, Mary Malloy, emerged from the kitchen and discreetly cleared the table. She had heard the drama and, as always, felt sympathy for Mrs D.

It was early March and though cold outside, the fairy lights created an atmosphere of warmth and promise. Adam removed his grey herringbone jacket and draped it over his girlfriend's smooth, bare shoulders, which he desired to nibble at. The moon was full. He heard a screechy cry and thought it might be a barn owl. They stood beside the stone fountain, her head nestled against his shoulder. Unsure what he'd signed up for, career-wise, he tried to think of a good physics joke to lighten the mood.

'Looks like you're on your way, mister,' she said.

'I'm excited and all. But I thought your dad didn't like me.'

'What do you mean? You don't give more responsibility to people you disapprove of. That's dumb.'

'I guess.'

'Listen, about my mother. Sometimes, she—'

'It's all right.' He looked towards the dining room where the morose Mrs D sat alone, finishing her wine.

'In the morning, she'll claim she doesn't remember anything.'

'I know. Jenny...'

'Come with me.'

She took his hand and led him to a little alcove hidden by a tall screen. Inside, there was a wooden sectional with dark grey cushions. Getting the picture, he tried kissing her, but she grabbed his belt and began undoing the buckle.

'I want to see it.'

He stopped her. 'We've talked about this, angel face.'

Pouting, she withdrew her hand and glowered at the sectional. '*You've* talked about it, you mean. I don't see what the big deal is. Why can't I touch it?'

'Because... Well, because we're not married. Which reminds me. Did you hear the one about the—'

'What does marriage have to do with anything?'

He turned her towards him and placed a finger under her chin. In the moonlight, she looked sixteen. He had the urge to protect her. From her family. The world. Life in general. Was that wrong?

'I like you a lot,' he said.

'Oh. I see.'

'And I don't want to do anything to ruin what we have. Besides, if things went too far, it would be Dickie Somers all over again.'

'Who's Dickie Somers?'

'Just a guy I know, but that's not important right now. What about your father?'

'Daddy's too busy to notice anything I do.'

'And your mom?'

'Are you being serious?'

'Look, you're young. Someday you'll appreciate—'

'Okay – golly.' Scrunching her nose, she toyed with her pearls. 'You're not at all like the other boys I've dated.'

'Thank you.'

'It wasn't a compliment. You need to be more adventurous. Take a chance once in a while. Do you understand what I'm trying to say?'

'Sure. You want us to have sex as soon as possible.'

'It's all I ever think about.' She took hold of his belt again. 'Let me see it – one time. I promise I won't touch it.'

He brought her hand to his lips. 'Aren't you afraid of getting pregnant?'

She walked her fingers past his ear. 'You could wear one of those thingamabobs.'

'Tell you what, I'll think it over.'

'Really? Well, don't think too long. Or I might have to find a new boyfriend who isn't afraid to...'

With his crestfallen look, he reminded her of a man who had missed his train during a blizzard. She pressed her lips together and shook her head. What was the matter with her, anyway? Adam was sweet. Unlike the others, he never mentioned money. She was pretty sure he'd never even set foot on a boat. Okay, so he wasn't in love with her – yet. There was plenty of time. *Grow up, Jenny.*

'I'm sorry,' she said. 'You didn't deserve that.'

'It's all right. Let's pretend it never happened.'

Bravely, she took his hand. 'You're probably starving. I'll fix you a sandwich.'

'Are there any pickles?'

All this talk of sex had given Adam a proper hard-on. As they made their way through the dining room, he slipped a hand into his trousers pocket and adjusted himself to the right as his tailor had advised. The truth was, he had thought a lot about having sex with his girlfriend. He was no doubt more obsessed than she was. But that's not how things worked. There were girls you had sex with and girls you married. He thought about his flatmate at Cornell.

Dickie Somers had done a summer internship at The Bank of New York, where his father worked. Soon after starting, he met a girl from the typing pool and they began dating. By autumn, she was pregnant because one time he'd neglected to wear a johnny.

She came from a working-class Catholic family, and after her dad found out, he demanded the young man do the right thing. Dickie's family were Lutheran. His vice-president father had planned for him to begin working full time at the bank after graduation. Now, he advised his son to marry the girl and find a job elsewhere.

In the end, Dickie did get married. They moved into her parents' house whilst he finished university. The last Adam heard, his friend had got a job in advertising. They had two beautiful children and as it turned out, he loved his wife very much. Though everything worked out for his old flatmate, Adam had no intention of getting a girl preggers. Then another thought. Did Jenny have sex with those other men she mentioned?

He hoped Mrs D was no longer in the vicinity. When he heard the sound of sobbing upstairs, he knew he was safe. All he wanted was to eat his sandwich, return home and have a quiet wank before going to sleep. He'd been given a chance at something big. And he wasn't about to squander it by getting in hot water with his boss.

Because Adam West was on his way.

CHAPTER 4

Close Your Eyes

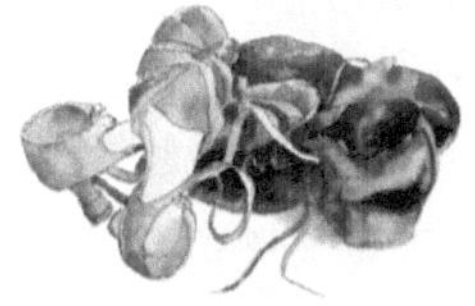

It was after midnight and Jenny couldn't sleep. After Adam had gone home, she tried comforting her mother, assuring her that her behaviour at dinner wasn't so bad compared to Jenny's eighteenth birthday party last summer. Her parents had invited her high-school girlfriends and a selection of eligible young men from Columbia University. It was meant to be a fun evening.

The sweet smell of night-flowering jasmine was intoxicating as everyone gathered in the garden, where a jazz combo played songs made famous by Frank Sinatra and Ella Fitzgerald. Food was set out buffet style and her dad had hired a barman for the evening. Jenny wore the black chiffon tea-length dress her aunt had bought her in the city. Though it fit her perfectly, she didn't like how she looked. Her father reminded her his sister had spent a great deal of money on it. To ease the pain, he got her the black suede stilettos she'd seen at Bergdorf Goodman.

Jenny had her eye on a particular chap called Roger Davies. His father's forebears were English and his mother's French. He was loaded but didn't like talking about money.

Whilst the others traded stories of skiing mishaps and randy adventures on the European continent, this young man spent the evening listening to everything Jenny had to say. At one point, she pictured herself dating him exclusively. Perhaps they would become serious. He wasn't bad-looking – if you ignored the wonky tooth. And though lacking a humorous side, he was polite and respectful.

Her mother had got sloshed again and wandered woozily through the crowd, making inappropriate comments directed at the young men. Most ignored her, including her husband. But when she tried ordering a fifth martini, he deposited her in the sitting room where Jenny and Roger were in the middle of an intimate conversation. They didn't notice Mrs D until she got to her feet and grabbed Roger's genitals. As he recoiled, his hand – the one with the class ring – caught her cheek and sent her reeling. The girl shrieked and her dad came running, followed by other guests.

'What happened?' Bruce said.

Glancing at Jenny, the young man cleared his throat. 'She fell.'

'Don't just stand there.'

The two men helped her up and led her to the two-seater where Jenny's mother collapsed, unsure of what had happened. Her husband pulled out his handkerchief and dabbing her cheek, whispered something. When Roger saw the blood, he blanched and turned away.

'I *won't* go to bed!' Mrs D said. 'This is a party and I'm entitled to be here.' Then to her daughter, 'Don't waste your time with him. It's like a Weiner Whistle down there.'

Chortling, she waved a dismissive hand at the red-faced young man and passed out. Mortified, Jenny escorted Roger to the garden, where she hoped they could salvage what was left of the evening with dancing. Apologising, he gave her a story about an early squash game and left her standing there in the black chiffon dress she detested.

None of the other young men would come near the birthday girl. Her friends formed a protective circle, where they discussed how unfairly she'd been treated. One of them, Shelley Jacobs, vowed to swear off men as a result. But it was a hollow promise since Jenny knew her best friend was a lesbian. Still, she appreciated the gesture and hugged the girl like a sister.

Now alone in bed in her peignoir, Jenny thought about Adam. She hadn't felt this way about anyone since Roger Davies. Like him, her boyfriend was a good listener. But unlike that other quiet young man, Adam at least tried to tell jokes, corny as they were.

Something occurred to her. They'd been seeing each other for several weeks. Yet she knew nothing about him other than his parents had died and, like her, he was an only child. Would he be capable of providing for her should they decide to get married?

He dressed well and had plenty of money for their frequent dates. But she had never seen his flat which he said overlooked Central Park. Could it be he *was* rich? If so, he didn't show it. He never liked talking about himself and always steered the conversation around to her. He once said she fascinated him and the words gave her a funny feeling. Though she'd experienced the sensation before, they intensified whenever she was around Adam.

Once at summer camp, she and Shelley had what could be best described as a fumble. They were fourteen. She remembered the experience as being pleasant, though she was in no way attracted to the other girl. They had taken a boat out to the middle of the lake. No one else was about except the loons with their melancholy yearnings. It started with dirty jokes, something Jenny enjoyed but only with her best friend. Soon, the talk turned to movies. Shelley described an Italian film she saw with her cousin.

'And all the girls had their bazooms hanging out.'

When they were done laughing, Shelley confessed that watching the scene had brought on a funny feeling.

'Funny how?' Jenny said.

'I dunno. All tingly. You know, down there.'

'That happened to me during *From Here to Eternity*. The part where Burt Lancaster and Deborah Kerr are kissing on the beach?'

'Sure. Have you ever touched yourself?'

'When I take a bath, I guess,' Jenny said.

'That's not what I meant. Other times, like in bed?'

'No.'

'I have. Ever since that darned movie. You should try it.'

'Let's go. It's almost dinnertime.'

'You're scared. That's okay, I was too. Hey, I've got an idea. Close your eyes and I'll show you. And if you don't like it, I'll stop, okay?'

'I don't know, Shel...'

'Scaredy cat, scaredy cat – time to be brave.'

'Are you sure?'

'I'm an old hand at this.'

'Ha ha. You realise I'm not...'

'Shh, I know.'

'Okay, but just for a minute.'

Jenny lay on her back on a cushion and, with her pulse racing, closed her eyes. It was so peaceful out here. A cool breeze rocked the boat, and the lapping of the water made her a little sleepy. She could feel Shelley's warm hand slipping under her shorts. Her fingers were gentle and the way she massaged her was tender.

'How's it feel?' her best friend said.

'Good, really good. It feels like... No, stop it!'

As promised, Shelley stopped. Jenny sat up, her face flushed, and adjusted her shorts. She looked over and the other girl was wearing a Cheshire Cat grin.

'What's so funny?' Jenny said.

'You've been initiated. You'll do it all by yourself from now on without any help from me.'

'Will not.'

'Will too, scaredy cat.'

That was five years ago. Jenny could still hear Shelley's words. *Will too, scaredy cat.* Like other nights, she imagined Adam naked in bed with her, touching her all over with his firm hands. Taking his time, he made his way down, starting with her breasts, and she thought she would lose her mind. She heard herself babbling something, words she'd been too afraid to say to Shelley. *Don't stop, don't stop, please don't stop...* She cried a little afterwards and cradled her teddy with the missing eye.

'I want you, Adam,' she said.

CHAPTER 5

Well, You Needn't

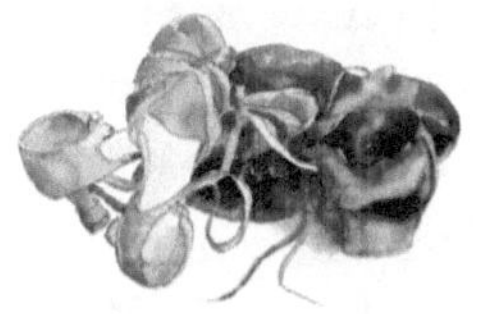

It was almost April, and Adam had less than three months to come up with a new marketing campaign for the science division. The project's code name was Gold Medal in honour of the upcoming Summer Olympics in Rome. Though the details hadn't been hammered out yet, the Old Man insisted on seeing a timeline with milestones. He liked milestones because they allowed him to sack people who didn't hit their numbers. Otherwise, he would have to read lengthy performance appraisals he felt lacked story structure.

At his boss's urging, Adam met with the senior account manager at Bland's advertising agency located on Madison Avenue. The smiling crawler was happy to be of service and assigned two people to the project. Using a template that had been honed over the years, the agency documented the steps, which included defining goals and objectives, identifying the target audience, developing a unique selling proposition and creating a budget and timeline.

Of course, they promised there would be the coveted milestones. Later, they would help the junior executive secure the relevant marketing channels. They assumed he would handle the core messaging and theme. Their client didn't know what those were but assured them he would.

The agency's efforts took less than a week and after they were finished, Adam had everything he needed. When the day came to show the CEO, everyone met in the twentieth-floor executive conference room, which a former intern had dubbed the *Camera stellata*, or the Star Chamber. Appreciative of the reference, the young man enlisted the agency to present the project plan. The seasoned pros used colourful flip charts as visual aids. Like a trained dog, an assistant turned to the next one each time he heard the annoying clicker, which the presenter pointed at him like a derringer.

So far, all went smoothly. Adam wished Jenny could see him in action, although his only job was to sit there and learn. He sneaked a glance at the Old Man to ensure he was engaged and was stunned to find him asleep. Panicking, he whispered to a junior advertising executive to whisper to the assistant to whisper to the senior account manager to pick up the pace. The CEO's executive secretary had a better idea. She poked her boss in the ribs with her fountain pen. It wasn't the first time.

The last milestone featured a *New Yorker*-style cartoon of an Olympic sprinter crossing the finish line with his hands high in the air. The senior account manager explained that full-page adverts could be taken out in the *Wall Street Journal*, the *New York Times* and other prestigious newspapers. But it was up to the junior executive to decide since he was in charge of the project. The young man appreciated the obsequious agency rep respecting his authority and was about to end the meeting, but then, things took an unexpected turn.

'What about magazines?' Bruce Donovan said, tapping the ash from his cigarette.

Ignoring Adam, the senior account manager responded. '*Time*, *Fortune* and *Popular Mechanics* are always good choices. Of course, you know this already, Bruce. It's why you pay us.'

The VP roared in laughter and everyone joined in except Adam. All at once, he felt very small – like Alice – as the senior account manager continued down this unwelcome path, suggesting the creation of radio adverts featuring the likes of Yul Brynner. He didn't stop there. The agency could produce television spots and air them on shows such as *Gunsmoke* and *Bonanza*. None of these ideas were mentioned in previous meetings.

Adam pictured himself as a four-year-old sitting at the children's table with his food cut up for him whilst the adults enjoyed a proper meal. With each new agency suggestion, he felt the cold, grasping fingers of corporate seniority and entitlement snatching the project out from under him. But why? He hadn't done anything wrong.

The Old Man was giddy and, to Bruce's chagrin, praised Adam – not the agency – for all the excellent suggestions. Thanking him, the young man tried again to end the meeting before anyone else could undermine him. But before he could get the words out, the junior advertising executive with the red hair saw an opportunity to impress his boss by ad-libbing a suggestion.

It was an idea he'd formulated the previous night whilst watching television in his flat and eating a Salisbury-steak ready meal. If he had bothered to run the idea past his superiors, he would have been spared the most brutal bollocking of his life.

Beaming, the ginger announced that Bland should

consider purchasing airtime on *The Twilight Zone*. The show was edgy and skewed towards a younger demographic. His voice rising like the Duke of Mantua singing 'La donna è mobile,' he held up a hand-drawn chart to demonstrate the potential positive effect of increasing Bland's market share with people aged under thirty. After concluding his monody, he awaited the showers of kudos he surely deserved.

There was no applause. He had miscalculated and was greeted with icy stares, none worse than those which came from his boss. Solemnly, the CEO informed the troublemaker that despite his writing ability, Rod Serling was a Jew and likely a communist. Moreover, Joe McCarthy missed his chance by not investigating the writer-producer in the fifties. The Old Man reminded everyone he and the missus preferred real Americans like Lorne Greene.

'But he's Canadian,' the junior ad executive said before his teammates could salvage his sinking ship of a career.

As a result of his impertinence, the senior account manager ordered the junior executive to leave the meeting. Later, he was removed from the Bland account and assigned to Manischewitz. He managed to secure a TV spot on *The Twilight Zone* around the High Holidays, which came a cropper. Not long after, he left the agency to pursue a career as a television actor but ended up doing commercials for laundry detergent.

'Anyone else have any bright ideas?' the CEO said.

Everyone, including the ad-agency executives, declined to make eye contact. Nodding wisely at his secretary, the Old Man lit a fresh cigar and marched out of the room.

'And that concludes our presentation,' Adam said.

CHAPTER 6

Little Girl Blue

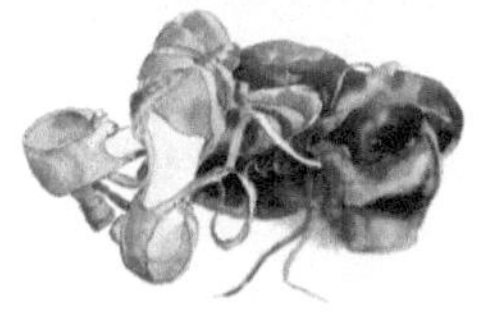

For days, Adam basked in the Old Man's praise. Recognition at last. Determined not to disappoint the CEO, he travelled to Cambridge to visit Bland's science division. The trip was bittersweet. Seeing the tree-covered campus after so many years brought back haunting memories of his parents and boyhood visits to their lab. They were a reminder of how much he missed them. Tearing up, he imagined he could feel their presence.

The department heads had organised elaborate presentations on their latest projects in the hope that, once again, the science division would regain their footing. Over the past two quarters, their budget was cut. The last time that happened was during the war. After a decade of economic growth, the heady days of rising payrolls and exuberant spending were coming to a close. And the science division suffered the consequences.

Despite a looming recession, the Old Man diverted more of the company's cash to the consumer division. The board questioned his decision because it flew in the face of all the economists' dire warnings. Standing his ground, he shared his flawless logic.

'People will always need toasters,' he said.

Relieved, the board agreed and to demonstrate their confidence in their CEO's visionary leadership, gave him a generous bonus with the proviso that he do something to promote the dwindling science division. Though the Old Man considered them glorified boffins, he agreed.

Everyone met in a conference room similar to the one in New York. Commemorative glass nameplates were arranged around the massive table like place cards at a dinner party. Beside each lay a black leather-bound Stamford notebook emblazoned with the Bland logo. And next to it, a Parker 51 Aerometric fountain pen and a green Murano ashtray.

The male scientists dressed alike in Kuppenheimer grey flannel suits and silk bow ties, making it difficult to tell them apart without the nameplates. Besides a black intern who might have been twelve, the only other female in the room was the chief scientist, Dr Irenka Lewandowska. She wore a Digby Morton tweed jacket and dress but no hat. At five foot eleven, she was nothing short of stunning.

Adam thought she looked familiar but couldn't recall where he'd seen her. As the day wore on, he sneaked glances, hoping a word or a gesture might jog his memory. Her profile was as beautiful as the rest of her. Thick, dark eyelashes, a Roman nose and full red lips. An image of Delacroix's *La Liberté guidant le peuple* popped into his head, making him blush.

For nine hours, the group covered weighty topics such as theoretical probability, quantum mechanics, robotics and space exploration. Writing nonstop, Adam did his best to keep up. The last presentation was given by the director of the Department of Theoretical Physics, Dr Paul Gibbon, who delivered an enlightened dissertation on the possibility of time travel. He began with Einstein's theory of special relativity and its application to quantum mechanics. Then he touched on the Grandfather Paradox and the concept of parallel universes.

'As I'm sure everyone knows, this concerns a time traveller who goes into the past and kills his grandfather before he can have children. But then, the time traveller would never exist and couldn't go back in time. But if that's true, he *would* exist and could accomplish the task after all.'

Dr Gibbon concluded the talk with the notion that if time travel were possible, it must include parallel universes. In other words, a man could never murder his actual grandfather. The best he could hope for would be to kill a version of his relative. Furthermore, constructing a time machine would require exotic matter, which has a negative mass. The last time he checked, there wasn't a lot of that lying around. This last remark earned him a round of sustained laughter from everyone except the intern, who patiently wrote in her notebook.

Adam's eyes were glistening when the presentation ended at five o'clock but they were tears of ecstasy. Dr Lewandowska smoothed the wrinkles from her dress. Her manicured nails were the palest of pink. He sat slack-jawed as she adjusted her demure gold bracelet and fixed her eyes on him – and him alone – whilst addressing the room.

'What an illuminating presentation, Dr Gibbon,' she said. Then to the group, 'Dobra, wszyscy, bardzo dziękuję.[1] You have made our guest very welcome.'

Her cultured Polish accent was delightful and Adam

wished he spoke the language. She led everyone in a round of applause and encouraged the junior executive to stand. He had practised a joke for the occasion but chose to save it for the cocktail reception. Instead, he clapped along with the others.

Like waves crashing on the coast of Maine in winter, the applause roared in his head. A single thought played in his mind like the 'Cor Anglais Solo' from Dvořák's *New World* symphony. It was something he had never felt anywhere else since leaving university. *This is where I belong.*

Outside in the corridor, Dr Lewandowska approached him, accompanied by the intern. She was a serious girl with café-au-lait skin and hypnotic green eyes behind black frame glasses. Her coat was unbuttoned, revealing a starched white shirt and a pleated blue plaid skirt, which came to right above her knees. Her black shoes were of the practical variety.

'I hope you found the presentations useful,' the chief scientist said.

'So very interesting. Thank you again, Dr Lewandows-ka.' He waved his notebook. 'I wrote down as much as I could, and I have a cramp now.'

She ignored his weak attempt at humour. 'May I introduce you to Claire de La Lune? She's spending the semester as my research intern.'

They shook hands. The serious girl looked nervous, as if afraid of being recognised.

'I've asked her to show you around. I hope to see you later at the reception?'

Giving him a curious smile, she left him alone with the intern, who didn't appear to be in much of a hurry. She was pretty and slender with straight, brown hair held in place by silver hair clips. Her nails were short but tidy and her eyebrows were prominent.

Adam's eyes drifted down to her smooth, bare legs. 'Are you interested in time travel?'

'We should get on with it,' Claire said and, buttoning her coat, walked away.

---

1. 'Okay, everyone, thank you very much.'

CHAPTER 7

Just Friends

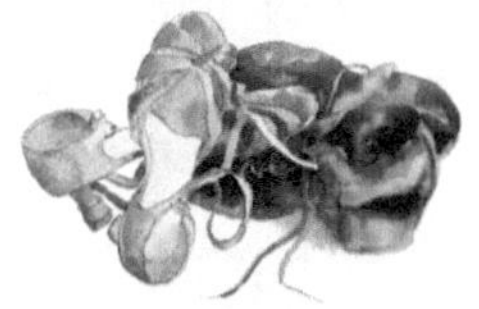

Though spring had arrived, it was chilly. Making his way across campus, Adam recognised many of the buildings he'd seen as a child. The stately elms and maples were bare but for a scattering of green buds here and there. The entire way, Claire chattered about the history of the campus, pointing out landmarks and the occasional feral cat.

There was a park bench in a little grassy alcove and he asked if they could stop. On the way, they passed two young women in business suits. One narrowed her eyes at his serious guide and whispered something to her friend, who nodded. Claire hadn't noticed but Adam did.

She sat beside him, studying his face. It was something she often did with strangers, trying to discover clues on how to conduct herself. As a rule, she wasn't comfortable around people regardless of colour – especially men. Except for her father, they were usually loud and said things of little value. Perhaps this one was different.

When he noticed her counting on her fingers, she blushed. He seemed enraptured by his surroundings and she thought she detected a glimmer of longing in his eyes. Observing him gave her butterflies, a sensation she'd never understood. Whenever it happened, she would recall a particular phrase from Higginson's 'Ode To A Butterfly.'

> *And yet the soul of man upon thy wings*
> *Forever soars in aspiration...*

'Have you been here before?' she said.

'When I was a kid. I used to visit my parents over there.'

He pointed at the familiar International-style building that housed the physics laboratory and was set off amongst a smattering of ash trees. The frontage was black steel with large glass panes glowing with light from the afternoon sun. Broad concrete steps led up to the entrance. This had been his parents' professional home and was where they died. Claire looked too, as if seeing the neat, uncluttered structure for the first time.

'I heard about what happened,' she said. 'Were you very close?'

'My mother used to call me Ace. After Ace the Bat-Hound? It was because I loved comic books, especially Batman.'

She sighed. 'I never got to see those. Being the only child of academics, you can imagine. Instead of fun stuff, I was reading Aristotle, Plato and Marcus Aurelius.'

'You never went to the movies?'

'They took me to see *Cinderella* for my seventh birthday. I liked the songs.'

'How old are you?'

'Seventeen.' She got to her feet. 'Shall we?'

A tabby bounded over and got between them, stopping in front of Adam. He bent down and stroked its back.

Purring, the animal rubbed against his leg and for the first time, the serious girl smiled.

'He likes you. Did you have pets growing up?'

'They weren't permitted inside the house. I used to be allergic, but I outgrew it. One time I tried taming a squirrel who lived in our garden. But he bit me and I had to get rabies shots.' He showed her the faded scar on his hand.

'Sounds painful.'

'Twenty-three, to be exact.' He pointed at his abdomen. 'All given here.'

'How old were you?'

'Eight, I think.'

The animal scurried off, and they began walking again, passing a low, flat building that housed the canteen. A group of men and women wearing laboratory coats walked down the steps, carrying paper cups and arguing about the potential number of parallel universes.

'Come on, I'll buy you a cup of coffee,' Adam said and veered off.

'All right.'

The dining room was enormous with a polished black marble floor and tables and chairs made of birch. A series of white saucer pendant lamps illuminated the interior and on the walls there were black-and-white photographs of ground-breaking inventions such as the electron micro-scope, the first car phone and the pop-up toaster. The oppo-site wall was glass and afforded a stunning view of the campus.

After getting their drinks, they found seats in an orange booth by a window and removed their coats. Adam hadn't created the diversion because he was interested in talking to Claire, although he found her attractive. After all, she was a kid and a little strange. No, it was because he dreaded seeing where his parents lost their lives.

'Are you from this area?' he said.

'New Orleans originally.'

'I've never been.'

'It's beautiful – especially the music.'

'How did you end up here?'

'Good grades. The last time I was tested, they said I have an IQ of two hundred and twenty-five.'

'That's impressive.'

Surprised by his reaction, she sipped her coffee. 'Most men are intimidated when I tell them. Anyway, Dad joined the faculty at Harvard and we moved to Boston. I'm starting there in the fall.'

'What does your mother do?'

'She teaches English at a private school in Boston. My parents thought an internship would be good for me. I applied to twelve different programmes.'

'That's a lot. Why so many?'

'Because twelve is an abundant number. Do you know what that is?'

'It's a number where the sum of its proper divisors is greater than the number itself.'

'Exactly right because one, two, three, four, and six equal sixteen. Do you like to dance?'

'Excuse me?'

'I've never tried, but I thought later, at the reception, we might—'

'I'm not much of a dancer. It was my parents who...' Then when he caught her look of disappointment, 'Hey, but we could try.'

'Gosh, I was sure you'd say no.'

'People can surprise you,' he said.

He pulled a shiny new half-dollar from her ear. It was one of the few magic tricks he knew and it delighted her.

As they approached the physics building steps, he noticed a bronze plaque on a plinth. It stood inside a well-maintained circle, which was geometrically accurate. Soon, a lawn of lush green grass would replace the barren soil. With his hands on his knees, he read the inscription.

DEDICATED TO DR JON WEST AND
DR MIRIAM HOFFMAN WEST.
IN RECOGNITION OF THEIR PIONEERING WORK AND
DEDICATION TO THE FUTURE.
SCIENTIA IPSA POTENTIA EST.
MARCH 11, 1959

'It is a real shame,' Claire said.

After signing in at the security desk, Adam followed the intern to the lift bank, where they rode to the top floor. He was disappointed to discover the floor tile he remembered as a child had been stripped down to the concrete and given a polyurethane coat. The cream-coloured walls hadn't been painted in what seemed like years and the fluorescent lighting, though functional, gave off a harsh, greenish glow. The effect made him think of hell as designed by highway technicians.

She continued walking. 'Not much to look at. I was told we should see Dr Gibbon.'

He recalled the physics laboratory was at the end of the hall. On the way, they stopped at a steel door. The nameplate read DR PAUL GIBBON. DIRECTOR, THEORETICAL PHYSICS.

'So, how does Boston compare to New Orleans?' he said.

'The restaurants aren't as good.' She shot him a nervous glance. 'I would knock but I'd smash my hand.'

Shrugging, he pulled the brushed metal door lever down and they walked in. The reception area was spacious with discreet lighting and plenty of potted ferns. A middle-aged secretary wearing a dark green dress with a high ruffled collar sat typing at a sleek steel-and-glass desk. There was a black-and-white mural of the Hudson Valley on the wall behind her. And to the side, an inner office oak door with a ribbed glass window.

'I believe Dr Gibbon is expecting us?' Claire said.

The secretary continued working without making eye contact. 'That's right. Have a seat.'

There was a comfortable-looking olive leather sofa next to the entrance. The intern sat first, crossing her legs and placing her small hands on her lap. Adam was about to join her when the second door opened and the director emerged.

'I thought I heard voices. Thanks for stopping by.' He shook his guest's hand and nodded towards the intern. 'I hope our little girl did a good job of looking after you.'

'As a matter of fact, she—'

'Excellent.' Then to Claire, 'I'll take it from here. Run along now.'

Casting her eyes down, she left the room quietly. Adam resented Dr Gibbon for treating her like a common servant. But before he could comment, the director ushered him out, telling his secretary they were headed to the laboratory.

'I want to get your gut-level impression of today's presentations,' he said in the corridor. 'I hope they were helpful.'

'I don't even know where to begin. The calibre of people working here is—'

'I like to think we are the best and the brightest.' Then in a stage whisper, 'In spite of what the Old Man might believe.'

The director swung open one of the double doors leading to the physics laboratory where Jon and Miriam West had perished. Adam's gorge rose in his throat.

'Shall we?' Dr Gibbon said.

CHAPTER 8

Siboney

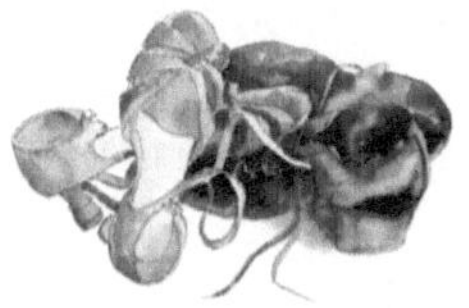

The science division had arranged a cocktail reception in the Dome Room of the Lenox Hotel in Boston. Adam was dazzled as he walked into the second-floor ballroom. After checking his coat, he made a slow circle, taking in his surroundings.

The storied ceiling was gilded and contained a ring of pendant lamps shining brightly onto the rich carpet. A bar stood in the corner and sprinkled round were tall cocktail tables covered in tablecloths that matched the walls. One area was cordoned off with enough instruments for an eight-piece band, including a grand piano. In front of that was a dance floor.

Scientists, business executives and administrators filled the space, chattering in small groups. Adam's eyes wandered as he looked for someone familiar. Catching sight of Dr Lewandowska, he hurried to the bar. The bowtie-wearing barman handed the chief scientist an old-fashioned glass filled with clear liquid. She extended her slender hand towards the smiling junior executive.

'I'm glad you came,' she said. 'Can I offer you a drink?'

'What are you having?'

'Wódka.'

'I guess I'll try that.'

The barman produced a clear bottle with a striking blue label that read WYBOROWA VODKA. Adam laid his notebook on the bar. Raising his drink, he and Dr Lewandowska clinked glasses.

'Do nas,' she said.

He repeated the phrase, unaware it meant *To us*. After taking a sip, he smacked his lips. The drink was peppery and sweet at the same time, unlike any vodka he'd ever tasted.

'Interesting.' He took another sip, enjoying the warm feeling in his stomach.

'It's made from rye, not potatoes. I understand Dr Gibbon brought you into the lab? If I had known, I vould have said something. I hope it vasn't too traumatic for you.'

'I'll admit I was nervous. But once he showed me around, I felt better – relieved, in fact. Thank you for your concern, Doctor, but it's something I needed to do.'

'I'm glad it vorked out.' She waved to someone at a nearby table. 'You must excuse me.'

She opened her black clutch purse and removed a brass hotel key. The number 423 was stamped on the bow. He nearly dropped his glass as she handed it to him.

'Come to my room in one hour. There is something I vant to discuss with you.'

Before he could respond, she disappeared into the crowd and joined a group of men debating the recent defections of several Bland scientists. From the snatches of conversation he could hear, he gathered they left to work for

NASA. Not knowing what else to do, he finished his drink and ordered another.

He was about to walk off when a woman's hand tugged on his sleeve. He turned to find Claire. She wore her hair in a bouffant and had on an unusual pale pink sleeveless cocktail dress. Her false nails were a paler shade of pink and matched her lipstick. Instead of heels, she wore black ballet flats.

'You didn't recognise me, I'll bet,' she said. 'I left my glasses at home.'

'I love your outfit.'

'It's Maxwell Shieff. He calls it a petal dress. My mom purchased it on a trip to Los Angeles but never wore it.' Laughing self-consciously, she pointed at her shoes. 'I was supposed to wear heels, but I kept tripping.'

'You look gorgeous.'

She got butterflies again but didn't think about the poem this time. Instead, she turned towards the group of musicians who were assembling on the stage. All wore shiny black suits with slim red ties. A Latin singer in a red, low-cut halter neck dress stepped up to the microphone. The band began with the smouldering habanera 'Siboney.'

'Shall we?' Adam said, taking her hand.

'Sir?' It was the barman. 'Your notebook.'

'Hang onto it, will you?'

On the way to the dance floor, Dr Gibbon pulled him aside. 'Are you sure you wouldn't rather dance with one of the other young ladies?'

Adam gazed across the room where a small group of smartly dressed girls looked at him with expectation. He glanced at Claire, who was swaying to the music.

'Excuse us, Doctor.'

When he was twelve, Adam's mother decided he must

learn to dance for his own good. His parents were excellent dancers. His birthday was coming up and she was determined to throw him a party and invite a few girls. The idea terrified him. But seeing how serious she was, he acquiesced. Once a week on Fridays, they would practise in the sitting room before dinner.

Though she was a busy woman, she arranged to work a half-day each week. They didn't own many records and she purchased a new one every Friday on her way home. Those were some of his happiest memories, just him and his mother dancing to Frank Sinatra and Tony Bennett, Ella Fitzgerald and Peggy Lee. Occasionally, she threw in some Tito Puente.

With everyone watching them, Claire felt awkward and suggested they forget about it. But the brass and the timbales were raising the temperature in the room, and she surrendered to her newly discovered passion as her partner led her across the floor. The effect was dizzying and for a delicious few moments, she didn't know where she was. All the books and the museums and the art – they were nothing compared to what she felt now.

Gliding across the floor, she happened to glance at the exits. She couldn't be sure of what she saw because she wasn't wearing glasses. There was a brief shimmer, followed by a rippling of the air itself. Now, an elderly black woman wearing an identical petal dress and pale pink lipstick stood in the doorway. She gazed at the girl as if she knew her. Then, Adam spun Claire round, and once again she was caught up in the music. When she turned to look, the woman was gone.

As if waking from a dream, she noticed they were surrounded by other dancing couples. With the first song long over, she realised they'd been at it for nearly an hour. It seemed like minutes. Adam held her firmly and she felt safe in his arms. Then he twirled her in magical circles she hoped would never end. It was only after the band stopped for a break that everyone made their way off the dance floor. Floating on air, she returned with him to the bar where he retrieved his notebook and ordered her a cherry Coke.

The barman gave the girl a sidelong glance. 'And for you, sir? More of the same?'

Adam ignored the sarcasm. With another vodka in hand, he walked Claire out to the balcony, hoping to show her a view of the city. But outside, only a brick wall greeted them.

'If you crick your neck, you can see Boylston Street,' he said.

Leaning over the railing and going up on tippy-toes, she did her best. 'I think I see a streetlight.'

They stood facing each other. He was much taller and she had to look up. More than anything, she wanted to be kissed. Then, covering her mouth, she giggled as if drunk.

'That was amazing! Thank you.'

'My pleasure. I had fun too.'

She poked his arm. 'You told me you couldn't dance.'

'I said I wasn't much of a dancer.'

'Are you kidding? You were incredible. Can we do it again?'

'Sure. Wait, what time is it?'

She referred to her silver Timex. 'Almost nine.'

'I have to go. Listen, you were wonderful out there.' He stroked her cheek with the back of his hand and kissed her forehead. 'Goodnight, Claire.'

He left her on the balcony. She watched as he wove his way through the ballroom towards the cloakroom. Dr Gibbon tried getting his attention but Adam pretended not to notice. Claire knew what she felt was a crush because she'd read about those in Jane Austen novels, notably *Mansfield Park*. But instead of being sad, she savoured the feeling. In a way, it was comforting to know she could experience things the way other girls did.

'Goodnight, Adam,' she said.

CHAPTER 9

Teach Me Tonight

Adam still couldn't remember where he'd seen Dr Lewandowska before and the feeling plagued him. Why on earth did she ask him to her rooms? It couldn't be for sex – she was decades older. Besides, she was the chief scientist. Why would a woman in her position risk losing her job over a... His mind reeled.

What, Adam? An affair? A tryst? An assignation? Une liaison? A fling? Okay, enough. It's none of those things. Oh my God, what if she wants to offer me a position?

That must be the reason. During the brief time they spent together, Dr Lewandowska had recognised the scientist in him. Why else was she so concerned about him visiting the physics lab? It was because he would be working there every day and she wanted his assurance he could handle it. He couldn't wait to speak to her.

He examined the room key whilst waiting at the lift bank. A passing bellhop who wore his little round hat rakishly stopped in his tracks and stared. His lips breaking into a foolish grin, he arched his eyebrows like a vaudeville

51

performer. Adam wished the doors would open and he pretended to ignore him.

'Hot date?' the plebeian said.

'What?'

'That, my friend, is Judy Garland's suite. You must be pretty darn important.'

'I guess.'

'You're an actor, am I right?'

The doors opened and relieved, Adam stepped into the lift. This was perhaps the worst conversation he ever endured, except for the time he had been accosted on the street by a madwoman claiming she awakened in a bathtub only to find one of her kidneys was missing. As he pressed the button for the fourth floor, the insolent bellhop saluted him and broke into hysterics.

'Good luck!'

Before he knew it, he was standing in front of Room 423. Should he knock? *No, stupid. She gave you a key.* Embarrassed by his own silliness, he let himself in. The suite was breathtaking. He felt he'd walked into a posh flat on Manhattan's Upper East Side. A crystal chandelier bathed the room in a soft, welcoming glow. Opposite him, a wood-burning fireplace crackled. The large windows offered a magnificent view of Boston's Back Bay area.

The bedroom door was open, and he could see the chief scientist's tweed jacket lying across the king-size bed. A silver tray with a bottle of Wyborowa vodka and two glasses was on the nightstand. He removed his hat and coat and laid them on a chair.

'Hello?' he said. 'Dr Lewandowska?'

'In here.'

He made his way to the bathroom and stumbled. Inside,

he found lots of Italian marble. The chief scientist was about to turn on the shower. And she was naked.

'You're late,' she said, her back to him.

His cheeks burning, he spun round and started out the room.

'Hand me the soap, vill you?'

Like a lady's maid, he crossed to the sink and laying his notebook on a shelf, grabbed a fresh bar still in its wrapper. As he handed it to her, she pulled him close.

'Better get undressed. It vould be a shame to ruin your suit.'

'I don't understand.'

'You studied physics, correct? Let me explain to you chemistry.'

Whether it was the effects of the vodka or the scent of Chanel on her breasts, he was aflame. The wall melted away, revealing Radio City Rockettes dancing to a Broadway show tune. Jenny tried to break through the line but was swallowed up in a sea of legs in fishnet stockings. Tearing off his clothes, he climbed into the shower. After doing everything they could think of in there, they moved to the bedroom.

Half a bottle of vodka later, he lay on his pillow, exhausted yet exhilarated with the music from the ballroom playing in his head. Claire's pretty face appeared, and he dismissed it like a pet who'd wandered into the room. Then panicking, he sat up.

'We didn't use any protection!' A vision of Dickie Somers appeared, his arms folded, winking at him.

She played with the hairs on his chest. 'It's fine. You have your father's chin.'

'You knew my father?'

'Everyone did.' She poured them each a drink and made herself comfortable under the duvet.

'Wait, did you and he...'

'I vanted to.' She patted his cheek. 'He only had eyes for your mother.'

For God's sake, Adam. You're in bed with a beautiful woman. Make some small talk.

'How did you end up at Bland?'

'Let me see. I earned my doctoral degree in 1936.'

'Ah. Which university?'

'The Sorbonne. Vhen I returned to Warsaw, I got a job at Lilpop. I stayed until 1939. September, to be exact.'

'Oh, right, when Hitler invaded.'

'Friends of mine had gone to America. They begged me to leave. I took their advice before it vas too late.'

'What about your family?'

'They stayed. Someone in the State Department vas friends vith your father and sent him my CV. Vhen Dr West read it, he decided to sponsor me. I've been at Bland ever since.'

'Dr Lewandowska—'

'Irenka.'

'Why me? I mean, why this?'

She finished her drink and set the glass on the night-stand. 'You don't remember me.'

'I've been racking my brain.'

Scrunching under the sheet, she snuggled next to him and clung to his arm. 'You vere ten. It vas—'

'Snowing.'

'See? You do remember. You vere such a handsome boy. And sad, too, in your little tailored suit and bowtie. Your father and mother introduced you to all the team members.'

'Didn't you used to wear glasses?'

'Gówno. That you remember.'

'So, I was ten, which would've made you...'

She pretended to slap him but lit a cigarette instead. 'I vas thirty-one. No more math.'

Taking away his glass, she climbed on top of him. Aroused, he got ready for another mad, fantastical trip to a land without words. Kissing him, she prepared to mount him. He stopped her and looked into her eyes.

'Irenka? What happens next?'

'You return to New York, of course, vhile I carry on here. Neither of us breathes a vord to anyone.'

'I...'

She gave his nipple a painful pinch. 'It's vital that you not say anything. Understand?'

He stroked her hand. 'I can do that.'

CHAPTER 10

In The Wee Small Hours Of The Morning

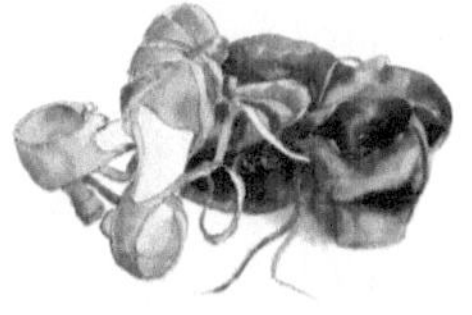

It was after midnight when Adam left the hotel and the streets of Boston were deserted, unlike Manhattan. A town car idled at the kerb, waiting to whisk him to New York. He lay against the soft black leather and glanced at the late-edition newspaper lying beside him.

A front-page article explained how NASA planned to launch the Explorer 8 satellite in November. Their aim was to determine upper atmospheric densities regarding altitude, latitude, season and solar activity. He wondered if that was the project the former Bland scientists had been hired for.

His trip would take three hours. He'd close his eyes awhile. Unable to get Irenka out of his mind, he thought about his crazy night. First, dancing with the indefatigable Claire and now this. The chief scientist was smart, sexy and exciting. He suspected he might have feelings for her. So what if she was twenty-one years his senior? She was a mature woman who knew what she wanted. A creature beyond temper tantrums and silly girl fantasies and...

'Shit,' he said.

Jenny floated in front of him like a hungry ghost. Her hair and clothes were in disarray from the earlier Rockette rumble. Adam would have to tell his girlfriend the truth, that's all, without mentioning names. She needed to understand that in business, men and women, they... That was no good – it implied deceit.

'You see, Jenny,' he said. 'Sometimes, two people meet and there's chemistry. There's no logic to it. That is to say, I didn't plan to... It just happened.'

She was sitting next to him now, her eyes innocent pools. *'You mean like it did with us? Don't you remember the pickles?'*

'That's different. I think what you have is an infatuation – like a crush.'

'You're saying I'm a child who doesn't know the difference between real feelings and puppy love?'

'I'm saying with more experience, you'll see there are relationships that can last forever.'

'But I wanted ours to last forever.'

'I'm not sure I feel the same. Oh, don't cry. You're a beautiful, desirable girl with a good family. You'll have no trouble finding someone who will—'

'I don't want someone, Adam. I want you. Why can't it be you? Who is she, anyway? Someone you met at the office?'

'She, um, she doesn't work for Bland. I knew her before. Recently, we decided to pick up where we left off. It's no one's fault.'

Folding her arms, she gazed out the window. *'You're a terrible liar.'*

'One day when you're older, you'll understand what I'm talking about. Something like this comes around only once. And you can't— You have to take a chance.'

'This is how you decide to heed my advice?'

'Because we get one life. What's the point of wasting it?'

'*Wonderful. So now I'm a waste of time.*'

'That came out all wrong.'

'*I still think you're a liar,*' Jenny's apparition said and departed in a simmering ball of ectoplasm.

The driver had heard rumours of madness running in the West family, and here this git was, living proof. He couldn't wait to be rid of the loony so he could hightail it to the garage to tell the lads.

Instead of going to his flat, Adam instructed the driver to drop him at the office – he would deal with his girlfriend later. It was time to think about the campaign. He reached for his notebook and, stupefied, realised he must have left it at the hotel. Fine, he would work from memory. As he approached his desk, he saw the note scribbled in his diary.

Dinner with Jenny

He imagined an evening at 21 with Irenka. Unlike his girlfriend's couture, the chief scientist would wear a suit – and she'd smoke. Instead of food, there would be bottles of Wyborowa vodka on the table. None of that mattered, though, because the sex afterwards would be incredible.

With no other choice, he would have to cancel tonight's date. Too much work – Jenny would understand. In the meantime, he'd mollify her with a gift. He knew how much she liked Godiva chocolates.

Outside, the streets were quiet with only the occasional police siren. He threw his coat and jacket on the two-seater and loosened his tie. Next, he sharpened three No. 2 pencils and cleared his desk of everything except a yellow legal pad. As he jotted down some warm-up phrases, he pictured Irenka glistening and naked. Furious, he jabbed the pencil point into his palm and, ignoring his throbbing erection, got to work.

Everything the Bland scientists had shown him was about the future. And what a future it was. Thanks to the company, there would be more leisure time. Everyone would live past one hundred. It wouldn't be long, relatively speaking, before people colonised Mars. Indeed, anything was possible, technology-wise. Anything...

Someone knocked at around five. Snapping awake, Adam wondered how long he'd been asleep. The door creaked open and a big-boned woman wearing a name tag that read BEULAH pushed her trolley through.

'Y'all fixin' to stay?' She had flat brown hair and spoke with a twangy West Virginia accent.

'I was just leaving.'

'Fine, then. I'll redd up the office soon's ya go.'

He had no idea what she'd said and prayed she meant him no harm. One thing was clear – she wanted him out tout de suite. He gathered his clothes and papers and left the unpleasant woman to her duties.

What he needed most was a shower, a shave and fresh clothes. On the way out, he thought he heard her mutter something. He couldn't be certain but it sounded like, 'Man who works this late must be in a mess o' trouble.'

Ignoring the unwelcome observation, he rode the lift downstairs, said goodnight to Earl, the elderly lobby guard, and hailed a cab. On the way to his flat, he reviewed his notes. There were seventeen slogans in all. Three had stars next to them.

 * Discover the future made Bland.
 * Bland knows what's going to happen.
Do you?
 * It's easy to predict the future. Think
Bland.

His stomach did a somersault. These were terrible and he had a meeting with Bruce Donovan later that morning. As dawn broke over Manhattan, he gazed at the towering piles of rubbish on the pavements and the vendors and panhandlers getting an early start. A dog trotted past and urinated on a discarded easy chair.

'I've screwed the pooch,' he said to the taxi driver, who was used to hearing worse.

CHAPTER 11

Take Five

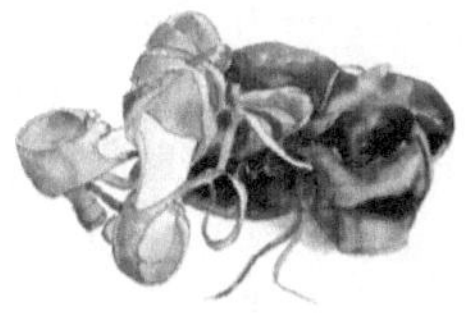

Adam arrived at his office with enough time to consume three cups of strong coffee and half a cheese Danish. He'd managed to sleep for two hours and felt somewhat refreshed. Looking over his notes again, he hoped the three slogans would look more promising in the light of day. They did not. Taunting him, they lay on the page like pungent curses delivered by the Wayward Sisters. Indeed, his muse had failed to appear, having been held up in customs.

Hoping for inspiration, he tried rewriting the phrases and found he was doing nothing more than substituting one word for another. He hadn't felt this much anxiety since walking into his 'Condensed Matter Physics' final after a rowdy night of drinking with Dickie Somers. It was the one and only time he ever failed an exam.

At two minutes to nine, he stood at the desk of his boss's executive secretary, Miss Lamb. The stern woman was past forty. She wore a grey suit with black kitten-heel court shoes and no jewellery. Her dyed raven hair was pinned in such a way as to lift her eyebrows into a permanent astonished sneer. Hypoglycaemic since puberty, she snacked throughout the day – fruits and nuts, mostly. Her weight never fluctuated. She typed at 213 words per minute – three words shy of the record set by Stella Pajunas in 1946.

Miss Lamb lived with her mother in Hoboken. Every Thursday night, they played bridge at her mother's friend's flat. She had no hobbies but liked to read. Military history, mainly. On Saturday mornings, she met an old high-school friend, Penny something or other. They would spend the weekend travelling up and down the New England coast, searching for antiques neither could afford. In the autumn, they bought pies at roadside stands. Penny had never married either.

The secretary paused from the memo she was typing and gave the young man one of her legendary judgemental looks. This would be an excellent time for him to say something.

'Um...'

'That's not a word, young man.'

He coughed into his hand. 'I have an appointment with Mr Donovan.'

Sighing, she checked her boss's agenda. Sure enough, Adam's name was in the nine o'clock slot in her handwriting. She folded her hands and attempted a smile, which only served to terrify him.

'You may go in,' she said.

Like other senior executives, Bruce Donovan enjoyed a corner office that afforded a view of Avenue of the Americas, which New Yorkers insisted upon referring to as 'Sixth Ave.' The boss was on the phone with the director of Personnel. Adam used the opportunity to pour himself a glass of water. He took a seat and waited for the call to finish.

'Are you sure?' the VP said into the phone. 'Because I'd heard they were opening up some new positions. No, I can't say who told me. You'll need to— What?' Glancing at the junior executive, he lowered his voice. 'I don't want to ask the Old Man. Why can't you confirm... Fine. Thank you.'

He slammed the receiver into the cradle and closed his eyes. Adam thought he should reschedule the meeting. His boss didn't speak for what seemed like minutes. Maybe he forgot he had a visitor.

Bruce reached into his inside jacket pocket and removed the silver cigarette case his wife gave him seven anniversaries ago. They had gone to Europe that year. Jenny had just turned twelve, he remembered. It was a wonderful trip. Never mind the general strike in Paris. The memory calmed him as he lit a cigarette.

'What have you got for me?' he said, praying the answer was zilch.

The young man shifted in his chair. 'I, I've been working on some ideas I think you might—'

'Do you smoke, son?'

'No.'

'Got something against tobacco?'

Adam stared at the Dunhill cigarettes lined up smartly like little waiters with gold collars. *Take one, fool. He's trying to bond with you.* Unsure, he reached out his hand. His boss stood and, flicking open a sleek gold lighter, lit it.

Taking a small puff, the young man nodded. *This isn't so bad.* Feeling adventurous, he took a stronger drag, which brought on a choking fit. Bruce handed the novice the water glass. Grateful, Adam left the cigarette burning in the ashtray and worked his way through his note cards.

After listening to the junior executive's inferior ideas, the VP folded his hands on his desk, confident the tosser was out of his depth. He reminded the employee that besides coming up with catchy slogans, there were roughly 487 other tasks to be completed if they were to make their deadline. He recited the first 50 from memory. By the time he was done, Adam's head was spinning.

'How am I supposed to do everything by myself?' he said.

Bruce sat back and blew a perfect smoke ring. Adam noticed he didn't wear a wedding band but had a distinctive onyx pinkie ring.

'Good point. In better times, I would've assigned you a team. But as you know, thanks to the Old Man, we're short-staffed.'

The junior executive stared at the open cigarette case, willing its occupants to transform into living, breathing marketing assistants.

'Couldn't I at least have one person?'

Knitting his brow, his boss made a *hmm* noise. He pulled out a full-colour organisational chart from a desk drawer and laid it on the blotter. Tucking his tongue into the corner of his mouth, he ran his index finger across and down the page. Adam recalled fondly that Jenny did the same thing with her tongue whenever she worked a crossword puzzle.

'There is a team member who might be available,' Bruce said. 'I believe I can let you have Del Dillard.'

'Is he any good?'

'The best.'

The VP wore the poker face that had won him a hundred simoleons at last week's game. Relieved, Adam got to his feet and shook his boss's hand.

'Thank you!'

'Be sure to ask him about the Bland Is Better campaign of 1934,' Bruce said without a hint of duplicity.

CHAPTER 12

You're Driving Me Crazy

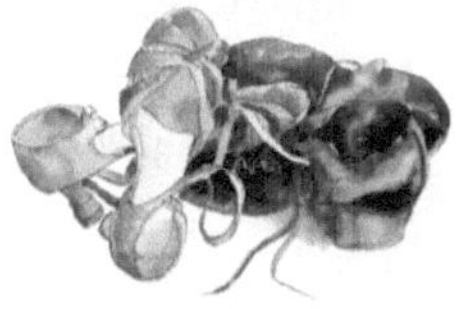

Del Dillard was English and on the wrong side of fifty. He'd been passed over for promotion so many times, most employees thought he'd expired and become a spirit. Whenever anyone spotted him on the street, they would tell their co-workers there'd been another 'Del Dullard' sighting.

Rumour had it you could often find him at Shanty's, a disreputable tavern not far from the office. There, he would consume gimlets and regale anyone in earshot with the story of his one great triumph, the Bland Is Better campaign of 1934. And he always began the same way.

'That was the year of the Dust Bowl, you know.'

Del was a born raconteur, his presentation honed to perfection thanks to his membership in the Cambridge Footlights in his university days. His voice was resonant like Dylan Thomas reciting his poetry whilst on a raging bender. By the time he finished, there wasn't a dry eye in the house. With great humility, he would end the recital with his trademark flourish, 'That was a cracking campaign.'

The barman, who had worked at Shanty's since 1946,

had seen the performance no fewer than 9,000 times. He used to think about doing to the Englishman what he'd visited upon the Nazis at Anzio but chose to get out his aggression by frequenting peep shows in Times Square.

Adam couldn't wait to give Del the good news, but when he arrived at the empty office, his heart sank. Everything was immaculate and untouched. The chair looked as if it had never been sat in. The desk was clear with only a green blotter, a banker's lamp and a brass pen-and-pencil set with the Bland logo. A framed marketing award hung on the wall without a speck of dust on the glass thanks to Beulah's redding up.

It was after five-thirty and Adam assumed his new teammate had gone home for the day. He was supposed to have dinner in the city with Jenny, anyway. Hopeful he would see the Englishman in the morning, he left the office to change clothes. He hadn't made much progress on the campaign but he had an assistant now. Nothing could stop him.

He'd planned to break the news to his girlfriend that he was in love with a mysterious woman. But that same afternoon, he received a plain package delivered by courier. Inside was his journal and a typed note.

<pre>
          Thanks for everything.
          Don't bother calling.
</pre>

Shaken, he closed his office door and wept. What had he done? The answer, of course, was nothing. Unaccustomed to flings with independent women, he let himself become entangled in a scenario that called for cool detachment. But the bald truth was far worse. Irenka had used him like a dog with a chew toy.

. . .

Adam and Jenny ate dinner at Delmonico's in Lower Manhattan. She had on a black Givenchy cocktail dress, a precursor to what Audrey Hepburn would wear in *Breakfast at Tiffany's*. Other women cast sidelong glances and she knew they envied her. Good. After the salad, she raised a glass of cherry Coke and toasted her distracted boyfriend.

With the disappointing end to his brief affair behind him, Adam was ebullient. He began by telling Jenny about his new assistant. She choked on an ice chip. For a full minute, she tittered like someone with the hiccups, causing disapproving heads to turn. Her subsequent braying got on his nerves.

'Is something wrong?' he said.

She dabbed her eyes with her serviette and took a big sip of water. 'It's nothing. I thought you said your assistant's name was Del Dillard.'

'It is.'

She fanned herself and reaching across the table, took his hand. 'So, this isn't a joke?'

His collar felt tight, as if he were being strangled by his Hermès tie. He thought he saw a fly doing eye-high kicks in his lobster Newburg. When he opened his mouth to speak, his voice sounded like a *Looney Tunes* character – he couldn't recall which one.

'Is there something I should know?' he said.

If Jennifer Louise Donovan was anything, she was loyal. But her family came first – always. Sensing a conflict between her father and her boyfriend, she decided it was wiser to avoid a situation where she would be forced to take sides. She focused on his crooked tie.

'I didn't mean to embarrass you,' she said. 'The Grenadine went to my head. If Daddy assigned... What was his name again?'

'Del Dillard.'

'Then I'm sure everything will be fine. He wants you to be successful, right?'

'Right...'

So as not to make eye contact, she concentrated on cutting her steak. She wasn't sure how long she could keep up the pretence as she struggled to understand her father's motivation. Growing up, the Englishman had been a frequent topic of conversation in the Donovan house. Her dad let it be known he'd tried repeatedly to fire Del but the Old Man wouldn't hear of it.

The firm's leader grew up listening to stories about the legendary Bland Is Better campaign as told by his father, the previous CEO. Del Dillard was an institution, for crying out loud. Okay, so he was English and possibly queer. But, by golly, if Dad liked him, it was good enough for the Old Man. And if he had anything to say about it, which, as the CEO he did, the Limey would retire someday with a full pension and a firm handshake.

Sullen, Adam picked at his food. Jenny was hiding something. Rather than pursuing it, he brought up a topic he knew would please her. The next Press Week was scheduled for autumn and would feature famous fashion designers such as Oscar de la Renta, Bill Blass and Roy Halston Frowick – better known as Halston. He was aware his girlfriend had attended the semi-annual event since she was sixteen and suspected she wanted him to accompany her.

They danced after dinner. Both were well taught and as they moved about, people made room. When Jenny was a teenager, she had gone to Arthur Murray and so far, there wasn't a dance step she didn't know. Each time Adam spun her, the dress came alive. Her slender arms extended, she practically floated over the floor. Seeing her this way made him realise how much he cared for her.

At length, he excused himself to go to the gents. On the way, he remembered their earlier conversation. Still sore over the Del Dillard business, he pulled aside his waiter and advised him not to bring up dessert. Getting the wrong idea, the Brylcreem-haired server gave him a suggestive wink and nudged the customer like the poorer half of a Borscht Belt comedy duo.

'Can't wait to get 'er home, eh?'

'Just bring the cheque,' Adam said.

CHAPTER 13

You Can Depend On Me

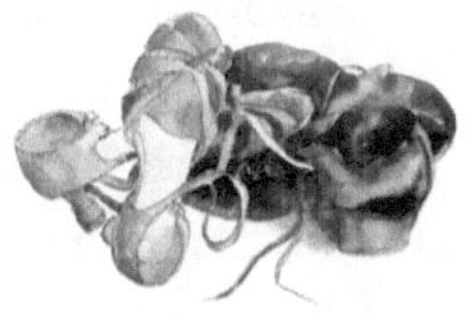

Adam made several frustrating attempts to locate Del Dillard, including some detective work at the cigarette stall in the lobby. This required purchasing ample amounts of chewing gum to compensate the shopkeeper for his time. After two frustrating hours travelling between floors, he bumped into a colleague he recognised, who informed him he could most likely find the elusive marketer at Shanty's. He was surprised that Adam was surprised.

The young man ran through the lobby to the pavement and pushed through crowds until he reached the notorious establishment. The exterior was dreadful. As if anyone needed help understanding the building's true purpose, a neon sign blinked like a nearsighted astronomer. Bar, it said. Hideous yellow-and-orange awnings hung on either side of the entrance. Adding to the atmosphere of neglect, an air conditioner teetered ominously over the front door.

Inside, the place smelt of stale beer and urinal cakes. It was just gone eleven in the morning and there were only a few scattered customers. The Englishman had been there since nine and was already on his sixth gimlet when he got a tap on the shoulder. Burping, he craned his neck and squinted at a dapper young man who resembled an insurance salesman on the verge of a big score. He thought the stranger was a hallucination and returned to his drink.

'I told the constable I didn't kill anyone,' he said, slurring his speech. 'Besides, anything you say won't make a difference. Like Falstaff, I'm damned to hell. Now piss off.'

Undaunted, Adam took a seat at the next barstool. The long-suffering barman, who wished he still had that length of piano wire, placed a cocktail serviette featuring a dirty joke in front of the customer and slid over a bowl of unshelled peanuts. He hoped the appearance of this shiny new salaryman was a sign from God his days of torture were at an end.

'Coffee,' the young man said. Then to his co-worker, 'I'm Adam West and you've been assigned to work with me.'

Del gulped his drink and signalled the barman with a bent finger he tried straightening by shaking it, but without success.

'Another, my good man. And this time, try adding some alcohol.'

The Englishman dabbed his lips with his serviette and belched like a Liverpool docker. He was surprised to see the stranger again and sniffed.

'You've made a mistake.'

'No mistake. Mr Donovan told me—'

'Donovan!' Del's resonant voice echoed off the dim, sticky walls of the nearly empty bar, causing a framed photo of Jake LaMotta to tremble. 'Man's an insect. Haven't you read Kafka?'

Pulling at his collar, the junior executive glanced around the room and leant over. 'He's our boss.'

'He may be yours, young Pip. I, on the other hand, am the supreme master of my destiny. I go where I please and do my best to avoid oversized cockroaches. Now, if you'll excuse me.' Then to the barman, 'Put this on my tab – not the coffee.'

He stood, brushed off his suit jacket and fell like a sack of mud face first on the floor. The indifferent barman leant over to see. Adam tried assisting the Englishman, but he weighed well over fourteen stone and was supremely immovable.

'Help me,' Adam said to the bemused bartender.

Together, they managed to wedge Del into a booth. Whilst the barman went in search of a first aid kit, the young man grabbed a stack of serviettes from a dispenser and pressed them to his co-worker's swollen, bleeding nose. In a few seconds, the Englishman pushed away his volunteer nurse's hand.

'Enough! Who did you say you were again?'

'Adam West.'

'Haven't I seen you on the telly?'

'No, that's— We have less than three months to complete this project and it's going to be a lot of work. So we better—'

'What are you prattling on about?'

'The campaign. Didn't they tell you?'

'No one said anything to me. Not a single member of the den of vipers you call a department has asked for my advice or counsel since Truman was sworn in.'

'I didn't know.'

'You, young man, have been deceived.'

The barman returned with a glass of water and a plaster. He left both on the table and scurried away before Del could order another drink.

'What do you mean, deceived?' Adam said.

The Englishman took a big gulp of water and grimacing, choked it down. 'Oh, haven't you heard? I'm Del Dullard. Not worth the paper I'm written on. I had one good campaign in me. 1934. That was the year of the Dust Bowl, you know.'

Before he could utter another word, the barman returned with a liverwurst sandwich and pushed half of it into the Englishman's gob. The taste pleased the customer and he consumed everything on the plate.

'Where was I?'

The junior executive glanced at the barman, who pretended to cut his throat with his finger.

'I was telling you about the project,' Adam said.

'Ah, yes. Another campaign, I take it? What is it this time? "The Future Is Bland"? I say, that's not half bad.'

Adam thought it over. *The Future Is Bland.* Of course. In four simple words, it was everything he had struggled to articulate. Already, he could picture the adverts. Flat television screens. Computers the size of your palm. Girls in flying cars. *Why am I thinking about girls?* Robot servants. Bullet trains with girl conductors in tight little outfits – gah!

'You appear to carry a lot of baggage,' the Englishman said, finishing his water.

'I was reacting to your slogan. It's—'

'Brilliant?'

'That's the word I was going to use.'

'Excellent. Then, I'll help you.' He wagged his stubby, irregular finger. 'But no interference from you-know-who. Do I have your word?'

'Of course. Anyway, you report to me. Now can we return to the office?'

'Soon as I use the loo,' Del said. 'Oh, and one more thing. Could you be so kind as to pay my tab? There's a good lad.'

Yesterdays

The VP set the presentation for 16 June which, coincidentally, was the day Paramount Pictures planned to release Alfred Hitchcock's psychological horror film, *Psycho*. It was also the day Karl Hiller was scheduled to die by electrocution at Sing Sing.

The infamous serial killer liked to strangle his female victims, then carve up the bodies using his daddy's hunting knife. He objected to any comparison between him and Ed Gein and referred to the latter as an amateur. At his sentencing, he announced he was looking forward to meeting Old Sparky.

For the weeks leading up to the big day, Adam and Del spent hours working on their pitch. They built everything on the as-yet-to-be-revealed top-secret slogan, *The Future Is Bland*. The junior executive was reluctant to ask the scientists in Cambridge for help, fearing he might be forced to speak with Irenka. He tried going through Claire de La Lune. Thrilled to hear his voice, she promised to ring him with news.

A few days later, the chief scientist contacted Adam.

Her tone was cordial and suggested they might have met at a conference during the Eisenhower years and done nothing more untoward than exchange business cards. The sound of her voice made him long for her. Steeling himself, he asked her for the favour. To his surprise, she agreed.

'I don't understand,' he said. 'Why are you helping me?'

'The science division is in trouble. Besides, ve are professionals, are ve not?'

He confessed that he missed her. After listening to him moon, she told him when he could expect the materials from Cambridge.

'I miss you too,' she said before hanging up. 'Goodbye.' Women were a mystery, he felt – much like black holes. And Silly Putty.

A week later, the scientists sent over mock-ups of the exciting projects they were working on. A diorama from the theoretical physics department depicted an ordinary sitting room complete with furniture and a drinks trolley. A chamber with little blinking lights around the doorway stood in the centre and beside it, a scientist in a laboratory coat fiddling with the dials. On the other side, a man with blond hair wearing a hat and contemporary clothes had emerged from another chamber into a futuristic landscape of glass buildings and flying automobiles. He resembled the junior executive.

So far, the work was going splendidly. Adam had been concerned Del would spend the remaining weeks in a bacchanalian haze. But the Englishman surprised him, having quit drinking altogether. Often, Adam found him chatting up Miss Lamb, who seemed to enjoy the attention. Every day at lunch, Del took a brisk walk down Sixth Avenue.

Eager to get in shape, the young man joined him. On a

warm spring day, trees bloomed and the air was filled with birdsong. As they passed the entrance to the pocket park, Adam was reminded he hadn't seen Jenny in days. He missed her and promised he would ask for some time off after the presentation.

'I'm worried about you,' she said on the phone one night.

It was the Monday before the big day. Adam was at the office going over the order of the flip charts for the umpteenth time.

'I'm fine.'

'Have you eaten dinner?'

'Del left to pick up something.'

'And he's working out?'

'I don't know why you were worried.'

She didn't say anything for a long time. Then like Ophelia, she sighed.

'Is something wrong?' he said.

'I didn't want to say anything. Since you weren't coming to dinner last week, Daddy invited a man I've never met.'

'Oh? Who is he?'

'Tito something. He's from Cuba and works in the Miami office.'

Adam didn't like where this was going, competition-wise. He pictured a smooth-talking, dark-haired mambo dancer with puffy glittered sleeves and maracas. The man could be a spy sent by Castro to infiltrate US businesses and bring about the fall of capitalism. Or worse – he owned a restaurant.

'What was he doing at your house?'

'I don't know. But they seemed friendly. He brought Daddy a box of Cuban cigars. He said he wanted to repay him for getting Tito his job.'

'I thought those were illegal. Did the guy say anything to you?'

'Let me think. He complimented me on my dress. Oh, and he was fascinated with my shoes. He knew they were Renazzos. Anyway, Daddy kept saying how he wished he had another opening so Tito could put in for a transfer.'

'Okay, look. I'm sure it's fine. I have to get to work. I'll call you tomorrow.'

'Adam? I have a bad feeling about that Cuban.'

'Gotta go.'

Del walked in with the food and set it out on the desk. There were roast-beef sandwiches, chips and coffee. The young man dug through the bags and, disappointed, looked up.

'You forgot the pickles.'

'Sorry, old chap. The deli man distracted me. Poor sod's got an enormous goitre. Looks as if he's grown an auxiliary head. I expected it to make a prediction.'

Though he was fond of the Englishman's zany stories, enough was enough. 'I thought we might road-test the presentation with the Cambridge scientists.'

Del gave him the greasy eye. 'Nonsense, my boy. We'll spring it on 'em and watch as their eyes roll up in their heads as if, like Halley's comet, they'd been catapulted headlong into the abyss.'

'Um, sure. But what if they don't—'

'Like it? They'll lap it up like a good custard.' He took an enormous bite of his sandwich. 'What do you say tomorrow we partake of a nice hot dog? I've recently made the acquaintance of a purveyor of said delicacy over on Lexington Avenue. Fellow by the name of Skeech.'

Since going on the wagon, the Englishman couldn't get enough of the food for sale on every street corner – bagels, pretzels, doughnuts and hot dogs piled high with sauerkraut. Despite consuming a massive number of calories each day, to his delight he lost weight. He didn't wheeze after taking more than a few steps. During his annual physical, the company doctor informed him his at-rest pulse was under seventy. And as a bonus, he no longer suffered from high blood pressure – a modern miracle.

Del examined the little time traveller as Adam rearranged the index cards on the bulletin board.

'Hm, the Protean Man,' he said.

He thumbed through the posters the scientists had sent over. Each was mounted on Fome-Cor and resembled film lobby cards.

'Well, well, well. Seems my past has caught up with me.'

Getting no reaction, the Englishman removed a poster from the stack and brought it over. The young man turned round to find a colour studio photo of Irenka in three-quarter profile. The chief scientist looked into the camera, her arms folded, catchlights in her eyes. She had on a black suit and a silk blouse, which was the palest of pink. Her lips were a luminous red. Adam dropped the box of drawing pins, spilling them on the floor.

'What's she – I mean *that* – doing here?' Adam said.

'One can never tell with foreign women. Perhaps she wants to remind everyone who runs the science division.'

Crouching, Adam picked up the drawing pins whilst his teammate propped the photo against the wall.

'What did you mean, your past has caught up with you?' Adam said.

'Hm? Oh, that. Happened ages ago.'

Flushed, the jilted lover put aside the box and confronted him. 'Explain.'

'Steady on. We had a brief encounter.' Then on the junior executive's confusion, 'Un coup d'un soir? Una botta e via? Eh? Blimey, I shagged her, didn't I?'

'You had sex?'

'Been known to happen. Of course, I wasn't as chubby in those days. Hardly weighed twelve stone. My God, man. Why are you sweating?'

'It's nothing. Um, how did it happen? Where did you—'

'Curiouser and curiouser, eh? I suppose one should expect such eager interest from so callow a youth. Very well, I shall elucidate.'

Del made himself comfortable at Adam's desk and fiddled with a No. 2 pencil. Shoulders slumped, his sullen audience of one sank into the guest chair.

'Let me think.' The Englishman tapped his temple with the pencil. 'This would've been 1940 in the spring. Ah, yes. All coming back to me now. It happened at the company meeting. The Old Man wanted to make a splash and put us up at the Park Sheraton. The lovely and demure Dr Lewandowska was new and quite fetching. Smart too. Studied at the Sorbonne.'

'I know. But why would a scientist—'

'I believe what you're attempting to say is why would such a magnificent creature with a mind like Einstein ever deign to spend a modicum of time with a loutish Englishman with no prospects? Have I got it right?'

'That's not at all what I— I mean, why would a scientist be interested in someone who works in marketing?'

'Ah, I see your point. I suppose it was because I used to be charming. Did I ever tell you about my days in the Cambridge Footlights? No matter. We were introduced at a cocktail reception. Irenka didn't know too many people.

'She was rather a shy bird in those days. I spoke a little

Polski thanks to my flatmate at university. Come to think of it, the copious amounts of free vodka may have played a small part.'

Adam covered his mouth. 'I'm going to be sick.'

'Somehow or other, we ended up in my room. Hadn't exerted myself so much since my rugby days. Surprised our sweaty bodies didn't go hurtling into the room below like meteors on the moon.'

Adam bolted out of the office with a hand over his mouth. Barely noticing, Del gazed at the chief scientist and sighed like Zephyrus admiring Venus.

'That was a cracking campaign,' he said.

CHAPTER 15

Fin De L'Affaire

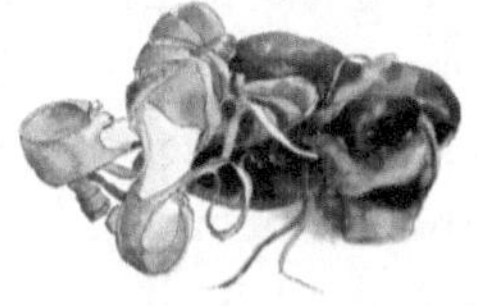

Del called in sick in the morning. Adam thought he might be faking. After obtaining his home address from Personnel, he took a taxi to see the Englishman at his flat in Chelsea. The cab dropped him in front of a converted brownstone on a tree-lined street near the park. There was no lift. Arriving at the fifth floor, he knocked. Silence, then music – a haunting solo violin. He banged on the door, which triggered a thunderous rebuke.

'If you don't bloody well sod off, I'll give you a proper bollocking!'

As the door opened, he found Del holding a violin and bow. He was in his bathrobe with his knob hanging out. *Well, he's not Jewish.*

'Are you all right?' the young man said.

'Matter of opinion, I'm afraid.' Then when his visitor didn't move, 'Entrez-vous?'

The flat was small and surprisingly neat. The sitting room featured light-coloured walls lined with packed book-shelves and a polished parquet floor. No telly in sight but

89

there was a Crosley radio on a side table, the wood in perfect condition.

On the wall hung a black-and-white photo of rugby players in a scrum, their bums to the camera. The heavy curtains were drawn to reveal an enchanting view of the park. Del directed his guest to the floral sofa and turning away, fastened his robe.

'You thought I was having you on, I'll wager,' the Englishman said without rancour.

'No, I... I was concerned, is all.'

Adam spotted a violin case and beside it, a music stand with an open book. His host put away the instrument. Touching his stomach, he winced.

'Been practising "The Devil's Trill Sonata" to take my mind off the pain.'

'I didn't know you played.'

'Since I was three. Never went professional. Why are you here? Ah, yes. You were concerned.'

'What's wrong with you?'

'Bit of food poisoning, I suspect. Damned roast beef. I've a mind to confront that two-headed Hydra at the deli.'

'But we both ate the same thing and I'm fine.'

'That's because you had the mustard. Mine was mayonnaise, remember?' Del grabbed his stomach again and sank into an occasional chair.

Getting to his feet, Adam entered the kitchen and filled a glass with water. Everything was neat and tidy, like the sitting room. The dishes were washed and the counter clutter-free. Curious, he opened the cupboard doors one after the other. Not a drop of spirits in the place. Relieved, he returned and handed his friend the water, which the Englishman greedily drank.

'Much obliged,' Del said. 'Can I offer you some tea?'

'I'll make it. You rest.'

After a few minutes, the young man walked in with a tray containing a lovely blue-and-white teapot depicting a countryside scene and two matching cups and saucers. He poured out and handed a cup to Del, who added milk. For a while, they admired the view of the park.

'You were right,' Adam said. 'I thought you were avoiding me.'

'Why ever would I do that?'

'I behaved badly when you mentioned Dr Lewandowska.'

'I've been thinking it over. I reckon you've tasted the forbidden fruit too?'

'I really can't talk about it.'

'Never fear, Lothario. Your secret is safe with me. Besides...' He gestured at the room. 'Who would I tell?'

'I'm seeing Bruce Donovan's daughter, Jenny. Maybe you know her?'

'I had the pleasure of meeting the young lady once when she visited our offices. Charming girl. Well done, you.'

'She doesn't know I—'

'Oh, I see. Bit of sneaky beaky, eh? My advice is don't tell her unless your plan is to get at her father.'

The young man squirmed. 'I have no intention of doing that. It's just... I feel guilty.'

' "So full of artless jealousy is guilt, it spills itself in fearing to be spilt." Hamlet, Act Four, Scene Five.'

'English Lit wasn't my best subject. What does it mean?'

'Simply that guilt isn't good for you. Men like having sex and that's all there is to it.'

'You make it sound so simple.'

Del rolled his eyes. 'Because it is. Put away the memory

and – what do you Americans say? – save it for a rainy day. Everything will be tickety-boo. There is one caveat. Don't tell the girl. It'll only make her cry.'

'That's good advice, thanks. More tea?'

'Cheers. How did you meet the young woman?'

'It was the pickles. Well, not only that. She radiates this sort of light I can't... Guess I'm kind of stuck on her. I don't know why I ever—'

'The male of the species has but two muscles,' the Englishman said. 'One is the heart. You can guess what the other is.'

Adam set aside his cup and wiped away a tear. He was embarrassed, yet with Del, he didn't feel uncomfortable. He had an irrational urge to sell his flat and move to Chelsea. He and his friend could have tea together and play chess. He didn't understand how someone so smart could end up being the target of everyone's jokes. The more he thought about it, the more he hated Bruce Donovan – and Bland.

As the dream faded, he wished he was in Cambridge working in the physics lab. More than anything, he wanted his parents to be proud of him. Finishing his tea, he stood and shook the Englishman's hand.

'Will you be all right?'

'In time. Thank you, Adam. You've succeeded in lifting my spirits. Sometimes, I think of all those years...'

'Don't let it bother you. Bland doesn't deserve you.'

'On that, we agree. They don't deserve you, either. Why do you work for them? There are other jobs, surely.'

'Technically, I don't need to work. I came into a lot of money last year.'

'Won the lottery, did you?'

'My parents died.'

Del looked at the floor. 'I seem to have put my foot in it.'

'I was supposed to be a scientist. Now, I just want to be useful.'

'You are, my friend. More than you can imagine.'

'Thanks. You are too.'

'I'll see you tomorrow morning, fresh as a daisy. There's a wonderful kosher restaurant round the corner. I plan to ring them later to send over a generous bowl of chicken soup.'

'Always makes me feel better,' Adam said and left.

CHAPTER 16

How Long Has This Been Going On?

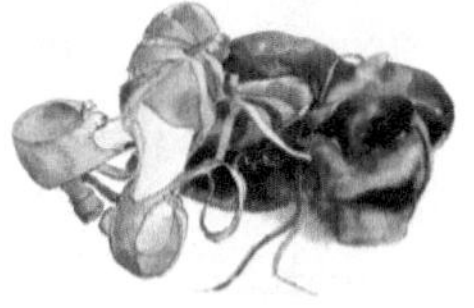

It was Thursday, 16 June, the day of the big presentation. *Psycho* premiered in two movie theatres in New York City and earned an impressive fifteen thousand dollars. Meanwhile at Sing Sing, Karl Hiller's execution had been postponed, thanks to some legal manoeuvring.

Disappointed, the serial killer made the best of the situation. He would use the extra time to complete his novel, a flaccid imitation of Nabokov's *Lolita*, as seen through the eyes of the killer's first victim, a young housewife from Terre Haute. It was rumoured Doubleday had expressed an interest.

The week prior, the ad agency's senior account manager rang Adam, offering again to take charge of the presentation. The junior executive declined, recalling what happened the last time. He thanked the unctuous agency rep, insisting he had everything under control.

As a courtesy, Adam invited him and his staff to attend. The senior account manager was pleased at the offer and promised to be there. After ringing off, he was said to have uttered the prescient phrase, 'Your funeral,' within earshot of his secretary.

Arriving in a new grey suit, Del was the picture of success. He'd purchased an alligator belt and pomaded his freshly trimmed hair. Adam marvelled at the transformation since meeting him that first day at Shanty's. He couldn't wait for things to get underway.

They had done several dry runs and committed the presentation to memory. The Englishman played with the clicker during a break, pretending it was a remote control. Watching him, Adam realised he'd overlooked something important.

There was no one to flip the charts! His mind racing, he wondered if the department had any interns. They did not. For a fraction of a second, he considered Miss Lamb, but dismissed the thought with a shudder.

Sensing his teammate's distress, Del left the room. He returned minutes later, accompanied by a slim young man in an ill-fitting suit. His hair was dark and curly and instead of a handkerchief, he sported a white pocket protector bursting with writing instruments. Adam gawped at him.

'Who's this?' he said.

The Englishman removed a bit of lint from the timid man's jacket. 'Found him in the canteen. His given name is Leonard. I forget the surname.'

The unwelcome guest extended a clammy hand. 'Yevstigneyev.'

'I don't care,' Adam said. Then to Del, 'What's he doing here?'

'He used to work in accounting. They sacked him last week. Now he spends all his time downstairs hoping to hear about a new position. I thought we might employ him to...' The Englishman waggled the clicker.

'I don't know if—'

'What choice do we have, mon ami?'

'Fine.'

They spent the next hour practising. The clicker's sound annoyed the ex-accountant due to his tinnitus, causing him to miss his cues. But after a while, he got the hang of it. Keen to impress his mentor, he added a little flair, flicking his wrist each time he heard the signal.

Adam felt confident but would have preferred to do a dress rehearsal with the scientists. Nevertheless, he trusted Del's instincts. The man was a seasoned marketer and knew what he was talking about. Though the story about Irenka had put him off, he was glad the Englishman was on his team. Then a chilling thought popped into his head as he collected his index cards.

What if the chief scientist was in the room? He might be all right if he could avoid eye contact. But how long could he keep that up? What if she asked him a question? He couldn't help imagining kissing those inviting lips again and hurried out of his office to see Miss Lamb.

'Excuse me,' he said.

Keying furiously on her IBM Executive typewriter, she ignored the irritating young man the way she would a gnat. He took a moment and, clearing his throat, raised his voice. 'Miss Lamb? Can you stop that for a minute?'

His voice carried and others poked their heads out of their offices. No one ever had the temerity to speak to the imperious executive secretary in that manner before. Secretly, some admired the junior executive's gumption.

Taking her hands off the keyboard, she glowered at him. The audacity. The sheer rudeness. Now she would have to spend her entire lunch hour devising a way to punish him.

'It's urgent that I see the list of attendees for my presentation,' he said.

They locked eyes. Clearly, the whippersnapper meant to see this through. Pressing her lips together, she yanked open her desk drawer and handed him three typed sheets of paper.

'Thank you.' He began walking away.

'I need that back,' she said and resumed her typing.

Adam closed his office door and pored over the document, wishing the infernal woman would choke on a Brazil nut. Rather than alphabetical, the attendee list was sorted by division, department and title. He ran his finger down the names until he came to the science division. The only person on the list was Dr Paul Gibbon.

Relieved, he sank into his chair and kissed the framed photo of Jenny and him taken at Copacabana, where they'd danced the night away before a crowd of admirers. It was the first time a band begged *them* for an encore. His phone rang. He guessed it was Miss Lamb wanting her damn list.

'Mr Donovan wants to see you,' she said and rang off before he could respond.

He heard voices as he approached the VP's office. Inside, a slim, dark-haired man, who was shorter than him, rose from the guest chair. He wore a blue, double-breasted suit with a yellow silk pocket square and a gold collar pin. His perfect teeth were blindingly white.

'I'd like you to meet Tito Ladrón from our Miami office,' Bruce said.

Shaking hands, Adam noticed the stranger's were manicured. A little embarrassed, he withdrew his.

'Tito writes Spanish copy for us and is here for the day. I invited him to see your presentation.'

'Why? I mean, that's great. I could've used a copywriter. But with all the belt-tightening around here...'

'It's a pleasure to meet you,' the Cuban said. Admittedly, his accent was pleasant. 'Bruce – Mr Donovan – has told me a lot about you. I understand you attended Cornell?'

'I wanted to become a scientist. Some things happened that—'

'Shame about your parents. You have my condolences.'

'Thank you. Are you from Miami originally?'

'I came over from Havana.'

'Well, I've never been, but I hear it's beautiful.'

'It is. Not the same, though, since... I'm sure Mr Donovan doesn't want us talking politics at the office.'

'Of course not. If you'll excuse me, I need to check on the conference room.' Then to his boss, 'Was there anything else?'

'Nope. Oh, and best of luck. We're all rooting for you.' The VP winked at the simpering copywriter from Miami.

'Thanks,' Adam said. Then to Tito, 'Nice meeting you.'

CHAPTER 17

My Shining Hour

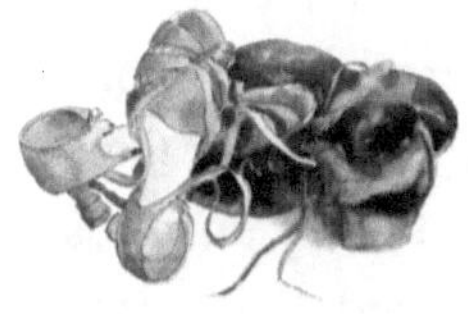

The catering staff had just finished setting up the coffee and pastries, and the flip chart stand was in place. All the models and dioramas had been arranged around the perimeter. Adam laid his index cards on the podium and stood near the windows overlooking the street. He thought about dinner at the Donovan house where they would celebrate his triumph. Tito wasn't so bad. It was silly him worrying.

Del marched in, seemingly pressed for time. 'I need a favour.'

'Anything.'

'Seems my nerves have gone a bit jangly. Thought I'd nip out for a fag. Shouldn't be long.'

He strolled past the dioramas, his hands folded behind his back, and stopped at the time-travel display.

Adam checked and rechecked his watch. 'We have less than fifteen minutes.'

'Everything will be fine.'

'But what if you get stuck somewhere? You're responsible for half the presentation.'

'Were anything to happen – and I assure you it will not – you've got it under control. Remember, you're Theseus come to slay the Minotaur.'

'I forget, who's the Minotaur?' Then sotto voce, 'You mean Mr Donovan?'

'It's Bland. Listen. They devour those who attempt to navigate the corporate labyrinth on the way to a doubtful victory. Many have been sacrificed to the beast, myself included. The whole bloody business is a chimera.'

'A what?' Concerned, Adam walked up to him. 'Say, is everything all right?'

Del regarded his friend with affection. 'I envy you your youth.'

Taking the young man's face in his hands, the Englishman kissed him on the lips. Then he gave him a smart salute and like an RAF lieutenant, turned sharply on his heels.

'If anyone asks,' Del said, 'I'll be in my office.'

Dr Gibbon wandered in early and, finding Adam, pumped his hand. 'Glad I caught you. I just wanted to wish you luck. I've been called into another meeting.'

'That's fine, Dr Gibbon. And thank Dr Lewandowska for all the excellent materials.'

'I will. It was our pleasure.'

On his way out, the scientist moved from display to display, admiring his team's handiwork. When he got to his time-travel diorama, he paused.

'That's odd,' he said and, grabbing a pastry, walked out.

Adam looked out across the sea of faces that filled the conference room. People, some of whom hadn't seen each other in a long time, talked and joked. The smarmy senior account manager had brought his entourage from the ad agency. The VP of Marketing and the Cuban sat next to each other. They spoke in whispers, throwing knowing glances at their young colleague and sniggering like children at Catholic school.

The Old Man walked in with his executive secretary at one minute to eleven. As she escorted him to his seat, the chatter stopped and everyone sat upright. No sign of the Englishman. The junior executive froze like an ice lolly.

When he made eye contact with Leonard, the ex-accountant nodded his encouragement. Several attendees coughed. Through a blue haze of cigarette smoke, Adam happened to glance at the time-travel diorama and noticed the figure – Future Man – was missing.

'Let's get this show on the road,' the CEO said.

Adam grabbed his index cards and stared at the doors, willing Del to materialise like the ghost of Hamlet's father. Meanwhile, the clock on the wall ticked away the seconds. He imagined himself as Future Man. But instead of stepping into a wondrous world of a better tomorrow, he discovered he'd arrived in a charred landscape of ruin where there was wailing and gnashing of teeth. Accepting his fate, he adjusted his tie.

'Good morning. Thank you all for coming. Before I begin, I want to express my gratitude to Del Dillard for the... F-for...'

His head pounding, he stared at all the cigarettes burning in ashtrays and gripped the podium with both hands. The Old Man squinted at him through his cigar smoke.

'What's the matter, son?' he said.

Adam regarded him with vacant eyes. 'Del doesn't smoke.'

Something hurtled past the windows, startling the attendees, and the room erupted in a chorus of gasps. Unaware of what happened, he assumed his audience was making another joke at the Englishman's expense. Did they dislike the man that much? His friend was right, the lot of them were vicious like the Minotaur. Outside, car horns blared below on the street. Several attendees ran to the windows and looked down. Adam thought he heard someone scream outside.

The discomfort in the room was palpable but the young man carried on. Del would have. Those who were standing returned to their seats. Glancing at Leonard, Adam pressed his clicker. His assistant snapped away a blank flip chart with a flick to reveal the new campaign slogan.

Elaborate artwork depicted a pristine city set against a bright blue sky dotted with flying cars. A monorail looped its way amongst tall buildings that seemed to kiss the clouds. The pavements were filled with happy white-collar workers going to their fulfilling jobs. The metropolis was surrounded by verdant parkland. And below in bold print...

THE FUTURE IS BLAND

Adam gestured grandly the way he'd practised. 'This is our slogan. Now, I'll go through each component of the campaign...'

No one listened. People murmured, some pointing at the windows. An executive with a crew cut rushed in and approached the CEO, whispering urgently. The Old Man jabbed his finger at the door and the man hurried out. The audience squirmed and fidgeted as distant sirens wailed from every direction. Then, as if deprived of oxygen, they fled as one, like frightened bats in a fruit orchard.

Alone except for Leonard, Adam stared at the empty conference room, the cigarettes still burning in their ashtrays. The familiar clacking of Miss Lamb's low-heeled shoes made him look up. Soon, the executive secretary was in the doorway. Instead of her usual air of superiority, her face was drained of colour and he had the impression her dark eyes were floating in space like eerie black opals.

'What is it?' he said. 'What's happened?'

She bit her lip. 'It's... It's Del, he...'

Gathering her strength, she managed to look him in the eye. Impatient, he pointed his clicker at her and pressed it repeatedly – anything to keep her going. Quailing, she choked back a sob.

'He's fallen,' she said.

CHAPTER 18

If You Could See Me Now

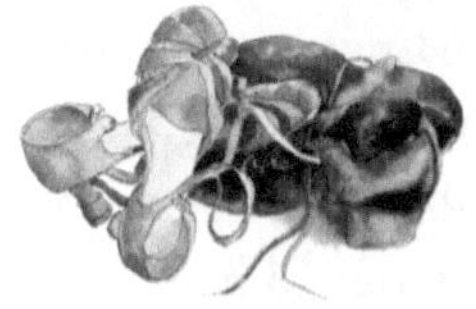

Rubberneckers crowded round in a horseshoe pattern, trying to get a glimpse of the grisly accident scene. Policemen had stopped traffic in both directions and were putting up wooden barriers. An ambulance, two fire engines and several patrol cars crowded the street.

Adam pushed his way along the pavement, where he found his boss speaking to a plainclothes detective. Behind them, a body with a sheet over it lay in an ever-widening pool of blood. One hand was exposed, clutching something. He tried to see but a police officer with a low forehead shoved him back.

'Where do ya think you're goin', pal?' the plonker said.

'That's my friend.'

'If you wanna pay your respects, you can visit him down at the morgue. Now, screw.'

Two ambulance attendants carried away Del's body. As they placed the stretcher into the vehicle, something fell and rolled over the kerb. In a few minutes, the vehicle was gone, followed by the fire engines and the patrol cars. The crowd began to disperse and Adam drifted to the edge of the pavement.

Future Man, the missing figure from the time-travel diorama, lay in the gutter. The Englishman must have taken it before going to the roof. Retrieving the figurine, the junior executive got blood on his hands. He wrapped it in his handkerchief and slipped it into his pocket. All he could think about was the Minotaur had won.

He glanced at the building behind him. Tito Ladrón leant against the wall, smoking laconically and eyeing him like he was a goat platter. The Cuban had undone his tie and Adam could see something silver on a chain around his neck. A religious medal?

'¿Que bolá?' Tito said.

Miss Lamb moped at her desk in lonely silence. Instead of typing, she squeezed and unsqueezed several balled-up tissues. There weren't many people the executive secretary tolerated. Her mother, of course, and Penny. Perhaps a few of the other residents in their block of flats. And Del Dillard.

She was fond of the Englishman because he made her laugh, which was a rare gift. Knowing the derision he suffered from other members of the department, she wished she had done more for him. She could have been his friend.

Adam saw her, but deciding not to offer comfort, continued to his office, where he found a sealed white envelope addressed to him lying in the middle of his desk. He recognised Del's handwriting. Outside, people stood in small groups, nattering about the odd Englishman who they never understood. Random comments such as *'He's better off'* and *'It must've been the drinking'* wafted in.

He slammed his door shut. Sinking into his chair, he picked up his letter opener.

My Dearest Adam,

I know what a shock this must be for you. And for that, I am sorry. You're a good lad with lots of promise. As I've already stated, Bland don't deserve you.

When we first met, I assumed you were another of those vapid sycophants who feed off the system like Guinea worms in service of their tedious ambition. I didn't realise you had a kind and generous heart.

I myself had given up long ago. Beaten down by unscrupulous miscreants who never had an original thought. What can I say? It got to me. But you with your enthusiasm and gentle manner – you saved me.

As you know, I had one great success in my career. I thought if I could be of some assistance, you too might achieve a victory. But more than that, you might enjoy a successful life, something I was incapable of attaining in spite of my education.

Believe me when I say I had real hope for us, which is not easy for a man without faith. After quitting the drinking, my head became clear. I began to believe Bland might not be the seat of evil I had imagined. Our campaign was tangible proof that one could rise above and, therefore, be content in one's work. But all of it changed in a heartbeat.

This morning whilst in the washroom, I overheard a conversation. It was between Bruce Donovan and some Latin fellow I've never met. What they said shocked me to my very core.

Donovan never planned to use our campaign. It was all an elaborate ruse designed to show you up as a failure. His intention was for the interloper to take your place. What is worse, the advertising agency were in on it.

Of course, what Donovan hadn't counted on was my abilities. I'm sure he thought I was all washed up, which is why he assigned me to help you.

My dear boy, don't do what I did and squander your future. Their lot are finished and it's a new day. Leave this place of sorrow and find something worthy of your talents. I remain yours very truly,

It's not clear what happened next. Adam opened his eyes and discovered he was flat on his back in the conference room. The jagged, broken broom handle from the cleaning woman's trolley was in his hand. Bruce Donovan's face loomed over him. It sounded like he said, 'Fug ya dinka doin'?'

The junior executive sat up and came face to face with a security guard with beard stubble that suggested he'd reached puberty at the age of six. Everywhere, the photos, models and dioramas lay in pieces. Tito picked up Irenka's left eye and quirked his eyebrows at the VP, who stood by the door with his arms folded.

'You!' Adam said, pointing a trembling finger. 'You murdered him!'

'What are you talking about?'

'Del Dillard. It's all your fault. He was getting better and you fed him to the Minotaur.'

'The what?'

'I'm getting out of here.'

He stood and brushed off his suit. Two burly porters, who wore white and could've just come from a wrestling match, marched towards him.

'These nice men are going to help you,' Bruce said.

Adam attempted to get away. They grabbed him and, ignoring his violent kicking, dragged him out of the conference room past the horrified executive secretary and to the lift bank. A gaggle of reporters had assembled outside after receiving an anonymous tip. Flashbulbs exploded like fireworks, blinding the young man. Before he knew it, he was sitting in a padded van, wearing a straitjacket.

Exhausted from fighting his restraints, his eyes pleaded with the unconcerned porter, who was trying to score a home run on a mini pinball game. The driver swerved to avoid a pothole at East Forty-Eighth Street and Fifth Avenue and the men knocked heads. Furious, the porter flung the toy at the doors, where it shattered. The little steel ball rolled towards them and landed at the patient's feet.

'I tried to win,' Adam said, observing it. 'But I wasn't strong enough.'

CHAPTER 19

They Say It's Wonderful

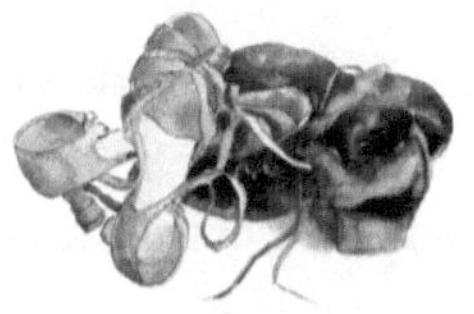

The sound of a door opening woke Adam but he had no idea where he was. For all he knew, he was lost in the labyrinth at Knossos and the Minotaur had come round to kill him. But unlike Theseus, he no longer had the strength to fight. Perhaps it was for the best.

'Hello, there,' a voice said a little too loudly. 'My name is Dr Jackle. I'm the chief psychiatrist, which means I'm in charge. What is your name?'

Fluorescent light fittings hung from chains in the claustrophobic padded room. They gave off a sickly, irregular light, intensifying the vertigo Adam already felt. He made a monumental effort to lift his head, which must have weighed more than Theseus's sword.

The Thorazine they compelled him to take made his mouth dry. For the past several hours, he'd drifted in a state bordering between light-headedness and nausea. On the positive side, any inhibitions he may have had were gone like yesterday's scandal sheets.

'What?' he said.

'I say, I'm Dr Jackle.'

'Yeah, got it. Obviously, you know who I am. What is this place?'

'Bellevue Hospital.'

'Why am I here? I'm not crazy.'

'You had a violent episode in the Bland offices today. Don't you remember?'

'Sure. It was because they murdered my friend.'

'Is that so?'

The chief psychiatrist wore an unattractive three-piece brown woollen suit, the likes of which hadn't been in fashion since the late forties. He was short and bald and wore rimless glasses that glinted whenever he moved his head. He smelt faintly of spearmint, and Adam detested him.

'It all happened because of Bruce Donovan,' he said.

Dr Jackle referred to the patient's intake form. 'Mm. Says here that's who arranged to have you brought in.'

'Wow, seems like that doctor title is really paying off.'

The chief psychiatrist bristled. 'Tell me about Mr Donovan.'

'He's a sonofabitch. Also, I'm dating his daughter.'

'Never mind that. Let's address the events that brought you here. I suspect things were not going well at Bland?'

'On the contrary. Bruce put me in charge of a big marketing campaign. I thought I was going places.'

'Go on.'

'It was all a charade. He set me up. Wanted to replace me with a Cuban.'

'Are you referring to a cigar or a person from Cuba?'

Adam smirked. 'Congratulations. You went from being the smartest man in the room to a moron. I'm talking about Tito Ladrón. He's the one who Bruce wanted, not me.'

'I'd like you to calm down. Why didn't they hire Mr Ladrón in the first place?'

'Excellent question, my dear doctor. You get a gold star. Because there weren't any other openings in the department, see? The Old Man felt sorry for me because my parents died on his watch. So, he hired me without telling the VP of Marketing. Get it?'

'I don't appreciate your tone. There was an old man, you say?'

'The CEO. He likes Cubans too – the cigars, that is.'

Dr Jackle capped his fountain pen and glanced at the door. 'This is all very interesting. I have a wonderful idea. Would you mind if I brought in a few colleagues?'

'Whatever tickles your fancy, Doc. I'm not going anywhere.'

Excited, the chief psychiatrist fled the cell. In three minutes, an assemblage of doctors, nurses, porters and a Puerto Rican delivery boy who happened to be passing returned to listen to Adam's tale of woe. Appreciative of his expanded audience, the former junior executive made himself comfortable and thought about the first time he met Del Dillard. With luck, he might make them understand the Englishman had been a talented showman and...

'The future is Bland,' he said.

Dr Jackle chuckled in the direction of his impromptu Greek chorus. 'Well, that's just not true. The future is exciting. Need I remind you of the pacemaker? Oh, and superglue.'

'You're not listening. Bland is the name of the corporation I work for, remember? Well, worked for. There are scientists in Cambridge who are, as we speak, investigating time travel—'

'Let's stay grounded in the present, shall we?'

'The point, Jackie-boy, is the future was the crux of my campaign. Bland owns the future. What they say matters. But Bruce wasn't interested in my ideas. He set me up so he could replace me with that damned Cuban. And if you mention cigars again, I'll rip out your lungs.'

Used to these kinds of outbursts, the chief psychiatrist gave the others a knowing look. He had seen Adam's type before and knew how to handle the situation. After all, he wasn't the chief headshrinker for nothing.

A pretty nurse who liked reading mystery magazines found herself attracted to the patient's raw, animal magnetism. For some reason, she pictured him holding a sword in one hand and a ball of red thread in the other. She wasn't up on her mythology, though, and guessed her brain might have suggested the mental image based on the Italian film *Hercules* with Steve Reeves.

'I think I understand now,' Dr Jackle said. 'Your company, the Bland Corporation, plans to invent time travel, the most sought-after, elusive scientific pursuit in the history of mankind. Yet you work for a card-carrying member of the Flat Earth Society, correct?'

The Greek chorus emitted a collective sigh, their eyes shiny with the promise of returning to an earlier time so they could fix every stupid mess they'd ever made since birth. Except for the sly delivery boy, whose thoughts were laser-focused on the horses.

Without warning, Adam vomited on the Puerto Rican's shoes.

'Sorry, it's the medication.'

'Tell me about the girl,' Dr Jackle said.

'Her name is Jenny. And a more beautiful soul you'll never meet. So you can see why I can't tell her about all the great sex I had with the Polish woman.'

'Polish...'

'She's older – and a sexpot.'

'Goodness.'

'It happened in a hotel room in Boston – not my idea.'

Slavering, the chief psychiatrist pulled at his trousers and leant in. 'Was it, um, all you imagined?'

'And more, Doctor. So much more. We did it all kinds of ways. Standing up, lying down, from every angle... You get the picture.'

'I'm beginning to.'

The nurse fanned herself with her starched white cap and imagined riding the patient all the way to Yonkers where her aged parents lived.

Coming to his senses, Dr Jackle signalled everyone to leave, including the frustrated young woman. The delivery boy wanted to hear more about the Polish prostitute. When he started to complain, the chief psychiatrist cuffed him on the ear and made a disparaging remark about his immigrant parents.

'Wait, where is everyone going?' Adam said. 'I haven't gotten to the part where Bruce murdered Del.'

Dr Jackle sniffed. 'I think we've heard quite enough, young man. It's obvious you're suffering from a persecution complex brought on by an abusive father and a mother too afraid to stand up to him. Tell me, did you ever play with dolls?'

The sycophants applauded the excellent spot-on diagnosis and left the room, inspired to begin reading books. The patient watched them go, drool leaking from his lower lip. He gaped at the chief psychiatrist.

'Are you insane?'

Dr Jackle snapped shut his manila folder. 'I should be

asking *you* that. Based on everything I've heard, it's clear you'll need years of therapy and lots more drugs.'

'Then I'll be cured?'

'Not in a million years.'

Struggling with the straitjacket, Adam managed to get to his feet. 'But I need to get out of here!'

'That's not going to happen,' the chief psychiatrist said.

CHAPTER 20

Pent-Up House

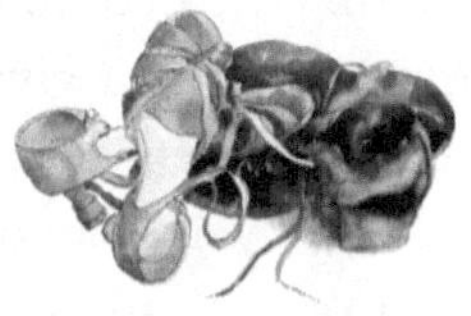

In the morning, Adam stood in queue across from the day room, waiting for his medication. The nurse handed him two paper cups, one containing Tofranil and the other tap water. A porter supervised to ensure he took the tablets. He popped them into his mouth and drank some water.

Strolling into the day room, he spat the tablets into a pot containing a tall rubber plant. Another magic trick.

'I saw that,' a voice said behind him.

He turned to find Leonard Yevstigneyev. Similarly dressed in a patient gown, flimsy bathrobe and slippers, he looked like he belonged there.

'Leonard? What are you—'

'I found out where you were and got myself admitted.'

'But how?'

'Oh, it was easy.'

Ignoring a hollow-eyed woman who was attempting to catch butterflies with her tongue, they found seats on a battered blue fabric couch near the wire mesh windows.

'I punched that Cuban in the nose,' the ex-accountant

said. 'When they found out I didn't work there, they tried throwing me out. So I threatened to set Mr Donovan's tie on fire.' Feeling the effects of the meprobamate, he guffawed. 'They bought it and sent me right over.'

'Okay, but why—'

'I didn't like how they treated you. You seem like an honest guy and I appreciated you giving me a chance to help with your presentation. Also, I figured you could use the company. Too bad about your friend.'

'I don't know what to say. Thank you?'

'Not necessary.'

'By the way, why did they fire you?'

'I set my manager's tie on fire.'

Adam glanced around the room, hoping to attract a porter's attention. 'I see…'

'He had it coming, though.'

'I'll bet.'

'Maybe after we get out of here, we can go for a drink. But it would have to be early.'

'Uh-huh. Leonard, I—'

'I live with my mother and she doesn't like me seeing other women. Says they're all tramps. But if I'm home by eight, she'll naturally assume I was with a guy friend. Tramps are known to stay out late, I guess.'

'I need to use the toilet,' Adam said and scurried away.

Adam decided to check on Leonard against his better judgement. When a porter approached them, he assumed they were there for the ex-accountant. But the humourless hospital worker pointed at him. A second porter, who was just as glum, joined his mate.

Great. Another session with Dr Persecution Complex.

They escorted him to a reception room with peeling paint where his solicitor was waiting. He hadn't seen Engel since graduation. The lawyer nodded to the porters and they left the room without locking the door.

'How did you find me?' Adam said.

The solicitor pulled a newspaper from his well-worn briefcase and unfolded it on the chipped Formica-topped table. 'You made the front page.'

Adam studied the black-and-white photo of himself, wild-eyed. In the background, the crowd waved at the camera like they were at a Mets game.

'I'm never getting out of here, am I?'

'On the contrary.' Engel set out several pages of double-spaced legal mumbo jumbo. 'That's a court order. You are to be released into the custody of your uncle.'

'My uncle?'

'Who, I assume, you've never met. Nathan West is actually your great-uncle.'

'I don't understand. Does this mean I'm not going to be charged with anything?'

'Why would you be? You were distraught over the death of the Englishman. Anyone would've done the same in your shoes.'

'I suppose.'

'I'm taking you to Dr West's home in the Hudson Valley. I brought you a change of clothes.'

'Thank you. I mean that.'

'By the way, there's someone here who wants to see you.'

The door opened and Jenny walked in wearing a yellow summer dress and matching shoes. There were little yellow bows in her hair. At the sight of her boyfriend, her lower lip quivered and she began to bawl.

'Jenny? What are you doing here?' he said, cinching his robe ties.

'Oh, Adam!'

She fell into his arms and wept on his shoulder. A million thoughts flooded his mind, dredging up a seething hatred for her father – and her. But this wasn't her fault, was it? Helpless to know what to do, he patted her back whilst shooting his solicitor a desperate look.

'I have to speak to Dr Jackle,' Engel said and left.

Adam helped his girlfriend to a chair and grabbing the other one, sat beside her. She was the picture of loveliness and more than anything, he wanted to believe she had nothing to do with his confinement. He thought of his night in Boston with Irenka and guilt washed over him like a river overrunning its banks. His cheeks flushing, he struggled to get the words out.

'Jenny, I've done something I'm not proud of.'

'Shh. None of this is your fault.'

'But—'

'It was Daddy, wasn't it? I hate him.'

'You were right about Tito. Del found out the truth and killed himself. I was never in charge of the campaign – it was all a conspiracy.'

Though she wanted to believe him, she was confused. What he was suggesting was unlike the man she knew. Sure, her father was uncompromising in business. But to her knowledge, he never acted unfairly.

He'd changed in the last few years, starting around the time he first visited the Miami offices. Come to think of it, that was when her mother began drinking. What on earth was going on?

'Mr Engel told me you're getting out,' she said.

'I'm moving in with my uncle. We're leaving in a few minutes.'

'When will I see you?'

'I don't know. After I'm settled, I could call you.'

'Will you, though? You won't forget about me?'

Her words broke his heart. It was all he could do not to add his tears to hers. Her seeing him this way had ruined everything. If what he felt for her was love, how could they be married now? He was damaged goods. Then another thought nagged at him. He couldn't help feeling that somehow she *was* responsible for his predicament. After all, she admitted it was she who had sought him out, knowing he worked for her father.

The solicitor returned, carrying a brown leather holdall. 'You can change in here,' he said. Then to Jenny, 'I'm afraid you must go now.'

She kissed her boyfriend and left without another word, her dress a yellow blur. His head swimming, Adam didn't know what he felt.

Instead of leaving straight away, the young man returned to the day room with Engel. Leonard was on the couch, gazing at a courtyard through the windows. Adam didn't know what demons the ex-accountant suffered from but sympathised. He sat beside the patient.

'I'm leaving,' he said. 'Will you be all right?'

'Oh, sure. I kind of like it in here. Are you coming back?'

'I don't think so.'

'Good. This isn't the place for you.' Then he whispered, 'Too many crazy people.'

Adam shook Leonard's hand and walked away. He and his lawyer followed a long white corridor leading to a locked gate. There was a guard sitting on the other side. He pressed a red button and the men continued through to the sound of a shrill buzzer. Outside on the pavement, the solicitor removed something from his jacket pocket and handed it to his client.

'I believe this belongs to you.'

Recognising his monogrammed handkerchief, the young man unwrapped it and found Future Man covered in Del Dillard's blood. He recalled the Englishman's words. *Don't tell the girl. It'll only make her cry.*

Engel laid a hand on his shoulder, his glasses reflecting the late afternoon sun. 'That beautiful young woman loves you. Whatever you do, don't let her go.'

'Don't be ridiculous,' Adam said with a bitterness he didn't know he was capable of. 'She's the reason I ended up in there.'

CHAPTER 21

Trav'lin' Light

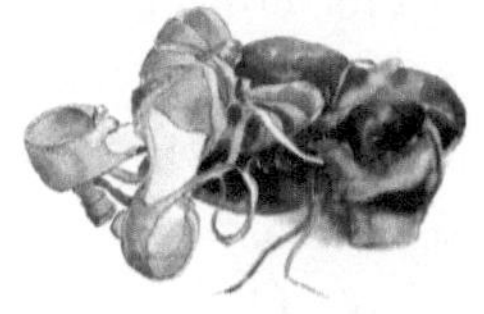

They travelled by train in the evening, departing from Penn Station. Engel wasn't much of a talker except when it came to the law, so for much of the journey, Adam mulled over his harrowing adventure at Bellevue, along with the bits and pieces of the prosaic story of his ignominious departure from Bland. In a gesture of goodwill, the Old Man had declined to press charges, provided the ex-junior executive never set foot in any Bland office again.

Adam wished he'd never accepted the job in the first place. Del would have compared the sentence to Napoleon being exiled to Elba, absent the six hundred guards. He asked how the solicitor had got everything in motion so quickly.

'I went to see a judge,' Engel said.

He was good friends with a sympathetic Manhattan Mental Health Court judge called Myron J. Liebowitz, who was well acquainted with the shady Dr Jackle. Outraged that Engel's client had been publicly humiliated and carted off to a madhouse, he didn't hesitate to make a phone call.

The chief psychiatrist listened, gnawing at his lip like a squirrel with an acorn. He had tangled with Liebowitz before.

The last time had concerned a young woman who Dr Jackle diagnosed as suffering from an overactive libido. She had hyperthyroidism. Her lawyer brought charges when it was discovered she was having sex with several of the porters. The presiding judge was Liebowitz. That was in the autumn of 1959. There were other incidents dating back to the end of the war. One notable case involved a pet mynah bird called Sir Talksalot.

This time, the chief psychiatrist felt he was on solid ground. Respectfully, he told Judge Liebowitz he performed the required evaluation and under the Mental Hygiene Law, was well within his rights to hold the patient for up to fifteen days. The judge countered with a writ of habeas corpus. Dr Jackle laughed hollowly. The old adversaries parried for another minute, and at last, Liebowitz had had enough. When he brought up Flossie, things took a dark turn. The chief psychiatrist emptied his bladder in his antique leather chair.

Flossie was Dr Jackle's pet dog, a beautiful long-haired terrier his mother had given him for his sixth birthday. One night, his dock-worker father came home drunk and slipping on a puddle of the dog's urine in the kitchen, flew into a rage. Grabbing a knife, he slit Flossie's throat in front of the boy. Then he sent his son out to buy milk whilst dragging his wife into the bedroom so he could abuse her.

Trembling with indignation, the chief psychiatrist thanked the judge. He ordered his staff to release Engel's client and wandered out of the hospital onto First Avenue, where he continued north for nearly thirty blocks. The police found him hours later in Central Park, hiding in a lilac bush as he extracted his eyelashes one at a time whilst making a wish on each.

After a hot meal and several cups of strong black coffee in the dining car, Adam felt depressed and wished he'd saved his medication. With a profound sorrow over his English friend's death, he stared out the window as names and places in upstate New York whizzed by.

The train followed the path of the Hudson River. As they passed Tarrytown, he wept. All he'd wanted was to make a contribution. He didn't believe in an afterlife, but if he had, he wondered what his parents must think of him. *No job, no girl and no friends. Our son is a loser.*

By Peekskill, he had cobbled together a plan. The last stop was Poughkeepsie. From there, they would take the bus to Hyde Park, where his uncle lived. Adam would make some excuse and ditch his travelling companion. Later, he'd throw himself in front of an oncoming train. He didn't have a will but was confident the solicitor would do something good with his inheritance. As for Jenny, well...

'Come on,' Engel said. 'I'll buy you a drink.'

It was dark outside. They sat in the uncrowded bar carriage, the lawyer with a glass of sherry and Adam nursing a gimlet in honour of his late friend. Engel had been the family's solicitor for who knew how long. From what the young man could gather, he was honest, respectful and dependable.

'Can I ask you something?' Adam said. 'How did you happen to work for my family?'

'Ah, now there's a story. It was because of Nathan Weisberger. That's your family's original name. It means *of the white mountain.*'

'My uncle is Jewish?'

'And so are you.'

'But my mother...'

'You'll recall her maiden name was Hoffman.'

'That explains the pickles, I guess. Why wasn't I raised in the Jewish faith?'

'When Nathan came to this country, antisemitism was rampant in Europe. Still is. Fearing the same would be true here, he changed his name to West and convinced his older brother Aaron – your grandfather – to do the same. Like his sibling, Nathan was handsome with blond hair and blue eyes. Strangers thought the brothers were Gentiles – a misconception they encouraged.

'My father helped your uncle get his first job. He was well-liked by our family. At the start of the First World War, the brothers sought their fortunes in America. I was in Hanover, practising law and looking after my parents and sister. In the years following the war's end, we watched the rise of the Sturmabteilung – the Brownshirts. Their violent ways were terrifying. Then came the Nazi Party. In 1922, they formed the Jugendbund – Hitler Youth. That's when I knew we had to get out.'

'And Uncle Nathan helped you?'

'He brought us over – my father, mother and sister, Letty. As soon as we were settled in New York, I became an American citizen, took the bar exam and married a girl. From that day on, I vowed to serve your family for the rest of my life.'

'I don't remember my grandfather.'

'He died of a brain haemorrhage in 1940. You were two.'

'And my uncle? There were stories. Are you sure it's all right, me staying with him?'

'He's eccentric, to be sure. But it was his idea that you

go to Hyde Park. Given your situation, I think it's a good plan.'

'What about my apartment?'

'I'll look after it until you return to the city. And don't worry about your estate – it's safe.'

'Thank you, Mr Engel. You've thought of everything.'

The solicitor put his hand on his client's. 'Always remember, you have a friend in me.'

After returning to their seats, Adam fell asleep. When he awoke, Engel was no longer sitting across from him. Instead, it was Jenny's apparition. She wore the same yellow summer dress from before. Her expression was at once curious and disapproving.

'*You're going to kill yourself? Whatever for?*'

'Because I have no one.'

'*You have me.*'

'Well, that's a relief.'

'*Are you angry with me?*'

'Forget it. Besides, I'm supposed to stay with a relative I've never met.'

'*It's only temporary. Soon, you'll be on your feet and you can come for me.*'

'What about your dad?'

'*What about him?*'

'I have to tell you something. I'm Jewish.'

'*Jew or Gentile, I love you, mister.*'

Engel returned from the gents and sat on Jenny, which gave her no choice but to melt into the seat like a vapour. The last thing Adam caught was her hand as it waved goodbye from behind the upholstery.

'We're almost in Poughkeepsie,' the solicitor said. 'A bus will drop us at the shopping centre. From there, we can take a taxi to your uncle's house.'

'Why didn't we drive?'

'I find trains more relaxing. Don't you?'

Adam realised he loved Engel. And by the time they reached the station, his original plan had flown off with the last train whistle. Now, he looked forward to meeting his mysterious relative. He thought about what the ghostly visitor said and hoped for his own sake it was true.

It's only temporary.

CHAPTER 22

Solitude

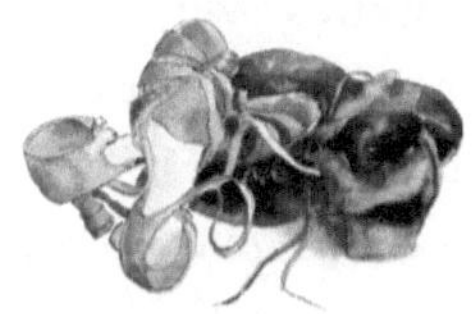

The taxi pulled up to the gates of the West estate, which lay in a forest of oak, maple and elm. It was after nine. There were two stone columns and mounted on each, a carriage lamp. The gates were locked for the night. The men waited for the driver to remove their luggage from the boot, then Engel paid him.

At length, Adam spotted a bobbing light moving towards them from out of the darkness. As it grew closer, he could make out a man wearing workmen's clothes. In his mid-sixties, he was large and wore a scowl. He unlocked the gates and let them pass.

'Hallo, Günter,' the solicitor said. 'Schön, dich wiederzusehen. Ich möchte dir gerne Adam vorstellen.'[1] Then to his client, 'This is Günter. He and his sister look after your uncle.'

The caretaker considered the Junge as if he were a bug and, grunting a terse 'Ja,' locked the gates again. Handing Adam the torch, Günter took charge of the bags. Adam walked ahead, unsure of where he was going. Halfway there, he noticed a barn in the distance. A dirt path connected it to the gravel driveway that led to an impressive Colonial Revival. The rest of the house's exterior was dark except for a light on the covered porch.

As Günter reached for the knob, the door swung open, revealing an equally severe-looking woman. She wore a long-sleeved dark grey dress with a white collar and cuffs. Her silver hair was arranged in a bun.

'Ah, Elsa,' the solicitor said.

'Herr Rechtsanwalt Engel.' Her expression softening, she squeezed his arms and kissed his cheeks. After exchanging greetings in German, she took Adam's hand.

'Ich bin so froh, dass du gekommen bist.'[2]

'I don't speak German,' Adam said.

Glancing at the lawyer, she pulled a face. 'Perhaps you'll have time to learn vhile you're here, ja? Kommen Sie.' Then to her brother, 'Worauf wartest du noch? Zeig ihnen ihre Zimmer.'[3]

'She likes ordering him around,' Engel said. 'They're fraternal twins.'

'How long have they worked for my uncle?'

'They came over in 1918.'

'They must've been pretty young.'

'Around your age.'

On the way to the grand staircase, Adam spotted a cherrywood occasional table piled high with unopened letters and unread newspapers. The *New York Times* lay on top. On the front page, there was a photograph of Karl Hiller with two prison guards escorting him to the electric chair. His lawyer had run out of delaying tactics. The only silver lining was the serial killer had completed his novel. As a last request, he asked the warden to critique it.

Whilst incarcerated, the other families had begged the condemned for the locations of their loved ones. He apologised, saying they should let sleeping dogs lie. Thinking he had shared some occult code, local police in New Rochelle organised search parties concentrated around area dog pounds. But they never found anything.

The newspaper headline read KILLER GETS HIS WISH. As they secured him to Old Sparky, his last words were, 'We'll be together again.' None of the guests in the witness room appreciated the humour.

Adam and Engel ascended the staircase on the right. Framed black-and-white photographs of graveyards taken on misty winter mornings adorned the wall. The last one at the top of the stairs featured a gleaming mausoleum in Germany. The name *Weisberger* was carved on the lintel in a Roman font. Now that the young man knew the truth about his family history, he wondered how many relatives lived in Hanover.

'Your uncle seems to have an obsession with death,' the solicitor said.

Günter entered the first bedroom and placed the lawyer's holdall on the leather-covered mahogany bench that stood in front of the four-poster. Elsa squeezed past and turned down the bed. Thanking her, Engel laid a hand on his client's shoulder.

'This is me – my usual room,' he said. 'I'll join you for breakfast. I must catch an early train to the city.'

'When can I see my uncle?'

'That's up to him. Perhaps in the morning.'

Elsa slipped out as quickly as she had come in. The caretaker closed the solicitor's door and led Adam across the hall to another bedroom. Alone now, the young man stood by the fireplace and admired the decor. The room was airy with high ceilings and large windows. The hardwood floor reflected the light from the chandelier. Like Engel's room, there was a four-poster bed with a canopy and a nightstand on either side. Pleased, he undid his tie.

After removing his jacket, he felt something in one of the pockets – Future Man. He sank onto the bench and turned the stained figure in his hands. There was a knock. The housekeeper walked in with a tray containing a roast-beef-and-cheddar-cheese sandwich, a pot of mustard and two bottles of beer. To his delight, the meal was accompanied by a large Sauergurken. When she saw the bloody monogrammed handkerchief, she pulled a face and set the tray on the writing desk.

'Danke,' he said. 'Especially for the pickle.'

'They are your uncle's favorite. I hope you are happy here, Herr West.'

'Call me Adam. And I intend to be. Goodnight, Elsa.'

'Schlafen sie gut.'[4]

He followed her to the door and handed her the figure. She examined the dried blood and scraped off a chip with her fingernail.

'I wonder if you could clean that.'

'Give me a few minutes,' she said.

Adam ate his late supper at a mahogany writing desk. Clean and polished, Future Man stood before a row of books on history, customs and language, including *German Made Simple* by Eugene Jackson and Adolph Geiger. He had picked up a few words here and there whilst travelling through Austria but was by no means fluent.

Biting into his pickle, he thumbed through the lessons and imagined himself speaking and writing like a native. The fantasy followed him into sleep as he dreamt of Jenny in her yellow dress, murmuring to him in flawless German. He realised he was no longer cross with her.

'Ich liebe dich so sehr,' she said. 'So sehr.'[5]

---

1. 'So nice to see you again. I'd like to introduce you to Adam.'
2. 'I'm so glad you came.'
3. 'What are you waiting for? Show them to their rooms.'
4. 'Sleep well.'
5. 'I love you so much. So much.'

CHAPTER 23

Something I Dreamed Last Night

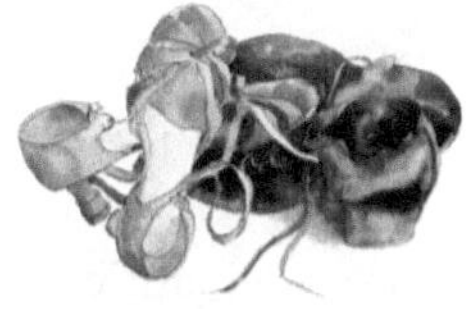

What sounded like an explosion awakened Adam. In his dream, he lit the fuse on a dynamite bundle and gleefully tossed it into Bruce Donovan's office as the VP puffed on an enormous Cuban cigar with his good friend Tito sitting on his lap. The effect was comical, resulting in the two dazed men lying amongst the wreckage with singed hair, blackened faces and torn clothes. Opening his eyes, Adam heard it again – a car backfiring.

Throwing aside the covers, he crossed to the windows and peered out. Moonlight shone blue-white, allowing him to see the entire barn. An outdoor light cast a yellowish glow over the front, illuminating the red paint and white trim. A 1940s Ford pickup with whitewall tyres sat idling. Günter closed the barn door and climbed in behind the wheel. As he manoeuvred towards the gates, the truck backfired again. *Where could the German be going at this hour?*

Scratching his head, Adam returned to bed and looked at his watch. It was a little after midnight. He closed his eyes and, in a minute or two, drifted into sleep. This time, he found himself in the physics laboratory in Cambridge. Irenka stood naked inside a full-scale version of the time-travel diorama. Laughing, she urged Del Dillard to enter the time machine. The Englishman didn't want to go, but she pushed him.

Dr Gibbon waved to him from the door and cackling, disappeared inside. Wearing Dr Jackle's brown suit, Del followed him, as if going to his eternal reward. As soon as he got in, the chamber door slammed shut and the chief scientist metamorphosed into a gigantic Minotaur. Adam had tried alerting his friend but to no avail. Exasperated, the mythical creature turned to him, its hands on its woolly hips.

'Ve are professionals, are ve not?'

Around four, another noise woke him from a dream he'd been having ever since his parents died. He is ten and standing alone on the eastern shore of Lake Como in Varenna. A rust-coloured skiff carries his mother and father westward. Jon has on a dark suit and Miriam wears a bright summer dress. They are dancing to 'Siboney' when a fire erupts. The boat continues drifting and its occupants become smaller and smaller. Ignoring the danger, his dad twirls his breathless mother as the flames engulf them...

There are words painted in faded white lettering on the side of the boat. This time, he was able to read them – Il Vecchio Charone.

Adam looked out the windows and saw the pickup returning and heading for the barn, the engine roaring. Something lay in the bed wrapped in black canvas. Judging by its length and shape, it could have been a human body. Günter parked in front of the barn.

A girl wearing a laboratory coat and work boots met

him. They spoke in German. She ordered the caretaker into the building whilst she lingered beside the truck. Soon, he returned pushing a wheelbarrow. The two struggled to unload the cargo. He wheeled it into the barn with the girl following.

Returning to bed, Adam tried guessing who she might be. Elsa would tell him. Yawning, he tried sleeping again. *Il Vecchio Charone.* When he was a boy, he and his friends used to go trick-or-treating in their neighbourhood. He remembered one particular house where a retired college professor lived. Every Halloween, he'd set up a skiff on his front lawn. In it was a tall, faceless wraith clutching an oar. The boat was called Il Vecchio Charone. Old Charon, the ferryman of Hades. Were his parents in hell?

It was around five. Giving up on sleep, he decided to shower. After getting dressed, he sat at his writing desk and laid out paper and pencils. He picked up *German Made Simple* and began with Chapter 1, 'Meet the German Language.' He would work for an hour, then join Engel for breakfast. Perhaps he would get to meet his uncle.

After a few minutes, he heard clumping footsteps, followed by a door opening and closing. Whoever it was, entered the room next to his. They must have sat on the bed because he could hear the springs squeaking through the grille in the floor. Ignoring the distraction, he resumed working.

Adam had lost track of the time, and it was half six when he entered the dining room. A vase bursting with marigolds stood in the centre of the mahogany table. There were two place settings across from each other. He sat, hoping the other was for Engel. The housekeeper came out of the kitchen carrying a white porcelain coffee pot with hand-painted blue flowers and filled his cup.

'Guten Morgen, Herr— Adam.'

'Good morning, Elsa. Werden— Wait, that's not right. Wird Herr Engel bald unten sein?'

His attempt pleased her. 'Nein. Er hat einen früheren Zug erwischt.'

'Okay, I didn't get that.'

'Herr Rechtsanwalt Engel caught an earlier train.'

Before he could ask any more questions, she hurried into the kitchen and returned with a plate that matched the coffee pot.

'Pancakes?' he said.

'Apfelpfannkuchen.'

He rubbed the back of his neck. 'I can't begin to pronounce that.'

'Ap-felp-fann-ku-chen.'

He repeated the word. The smell of apples reminded him of a Vienna café he'd visited the previous summer. He realised Elsa was waiting for him to try them and took a bite.

'Delicious. I saw a girl this morning out by the barn.'

'She is Herr Doktor West's protégée.'

'Oh? What's her name?'

Elsa looked past him and pursing her lips, returned to the kitchen without another word. He turned round.

The blonde girl he saw earlier was in the doorway and he got to his feet. In her mid-twenties, she was dressed in a cream-coloured long-sleeve shirt, dark woollen trousers and brown Chippewa work boots laced halfway up. She wore her blonde hair in a playful ponytail and her red lipstick reminded him of Irenka. Adam couldn't help feeling attracted to her.

She looked nothing like the female science students he used to know at Cornell. As she extended her hand, he noticed the fresh red nail polish and detected perfume.

'I'm Halsey Dean,' she said. 'It's a pleasure to meet you, Adam.'

CHAPTER 24

Too Close For Comfort

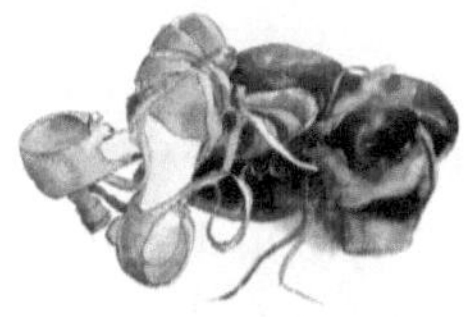

Halsey took her place at the table and unfolded her serviette. Elsa returned to pour her coffee and left the pot. After the housekeeper had gone, the girl leant over the table.

'Elsa must like you. She never makes apple pancakes unless it's someone's birthday.'

Determined not to let her distract him, Adam continued eating and assumed she was doing the same. Looking up, he found her observing him over her coffee cup, a sly smile crossing her lips.

'What is it?' he said.

'You're dying to know what I'm doing here.'

'I assumed research.'

'That's right. I'm helping your uncle.'

'I haven't met him yet.'

'He likes keeping to himself.'

'Is he unwell?'

'I don't think so. He's shy. You remind me of him, but cuter. Awfully formal, though. Try relaxing – I hear yoga is good. You have something on your face.'

143

Blushing, he wiped his mouth with his serviette. 'Are you a physicist?'

'I have a degree in biology from Columbia with a minor in chemistry. But my real passion is molecular biology.'

'That's not a major.'

'It should be. I was going to pursue a doctorate but it wasn't for me. Most of what I've worked on over the past two years isn't recognised in traditional academic circles, anyway. And for a woman to be doing serious research at all, well...' She took a quick bite. 'Kind of a boys' club – no offence.' Laying down her serviette, she stood. 'Come on, I'll show you around.'

'But I haven't...'

She grabbed his arm and led him through the French doors that opened onto a rambling garden in full bloom. It was surrounded by a drystone wall. He identified violas, hydrangeas and petunias amidst flowering dogwood shrubs. They walked under the magnolia trees.

'How did you and my uncle meet?' he said.

'Pure serendipity. One of my professors ran into him at a conference in the early fifties. Nathan presented a paper on the effects of electrical stimulation on supposedly dead cells. I say "supposedly" because no one knows the exact moment of death. The paper was called "The Scientist as Resurrectionist: From Limbo to Life".'

'Sounds a little fanciful.'

'Does it? I managed to get a copy. After reading it for, like, the twentieth time, it occurred to me. If you could prepare the cells before applying an electrical charge, you'd have a better chance of true regeneration.

'So I worked on developing a protein-rich culture media. Then I wrote a paper and showed it to my old professor. He sent it to your uncle without telling me and I got the most exciting call of my life.

'Nathan invited me here to talk about my work. Can you believe it? He told me over dinner he'd tried everything he could think of but could never keep the cells alive for more than a few hours. That's why he was so interested in what I'd dreamt up. I thought all he wanted was to pick my brain.'

'What do you mean?' Adam said.

'You know, find out more about what I was thinking. But I was wrong. We finished three hours later and when he offered me his lab and a place to stay, I was over the moon.'

Adam was intrigued. According to his father, Nathan West wasn't eccentric – he was barmy. No other details were given. The real story was more enlightening. He and his brother Aaron were hired by Bland shortly after they arrived in the US. Both men were considered brilliant and the science division flourished.

In the spring of 1916, Nathan met a Mexican woman ten years his junior who worked in a restaurant in Boston. He was thirty-five. They began an affair at once. She convinced him to accompany her on a pilgrimage to Nuevo León, where she was from. The country was embroiled in the violence of the Mexican Border War but they managed to make it through without incident.

There, amongst the Coahuiltecan people, he took part in a ceremony beginning with a public confession where the participants were urged to recount every sin they ever committed. His recital took a while. The sins were tied into knots on palm branches and tossed into a fire.

Everyone consumed a paste made from the peyote cactus, and the foreigner's eyes were forever opened. He saw a vision both terrifying and prescient. A glass skull materialised in space, fully conscious, soaring over mountains and rivers. When it opened its mouth to speak, its voice was like burning paper.

'We'll be together again,' it said.

Nathan returned to Bland a changed man. He began spending all his time on personal projects built on the work of Luigi Galvani and his discovery of animal electricity. He taught himself biology and chemistry. It was rumoured he'd set up a private laboratory outside Cambridge, where he conducted experiments on dead animals.

Meanwhile, Aaron was promoted to chief scientist at the end of WWI. He used the occasion to sack his unstable brother, who continued using the peyote his Mexican paramour provided. From then on, no family member was permitted to communicate with the drug-addicted outcast.

Still loyal to his friend and benefactor, Shlomo Engel stayed in touch over the years. Which was why Nathan West knew about his great-nephew's recent plight.

'Why do you think my uncle offered you a position?' Adam said. 'He could've read your paper and continued on his own.'

'I seduced him.' She waited for a response. 'Why aren't you shocked?'

'I'm not a child.'

'My gosh, I was joking. I don't know. Obviously, I'm not in the same league as him. I suppose we hit it off – kindred spirits and all that.'

'I was hoping to meet him this morning.'

'Don't take it personally. I barely see him myself these days. And anyway, I spend all my time in the lab. Hey, would you like to see it?' Then pointing, 'I'm in the barn.'

'I would love to.'

She took his hand, but before they could get any further, the housekeeper called to him from the house.

'What is it, Elsa?' he said.

'Herr Doktor West vants to see you.'

'Okay. Ich komme sofort.'

He turned to Halsey, who covered a giggle with her hand and left him there.

'Say hello to Dr West for me,' she said at the gate. 'Your accent needs work, by the way.'

Trouble In Mind

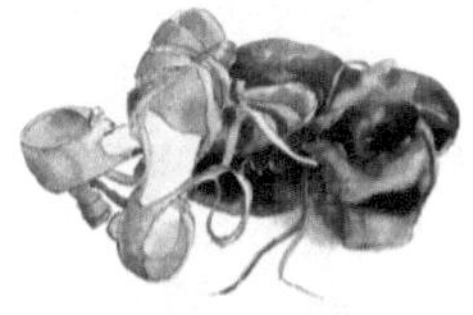

Elsa brought Adam to a set of six-panel mahogany double doors leading to a separate wing. Inside, the off-white walls were lined with black-and-white photographs of the indigenous people of Mexico – old, wrinkled men with no teeth, women carrying huge baskets of flowers on their heads and children running through fields of maize. Halfway down, there was a lift. There were no windows and the only illumination came from two rows of downlights.

Continuing to the first closed door, he thought about Halsey Dean. She was bright and funny. And her enthusiasm for working with his uncle seemed genuine. Something else occurred to him as he recalled the scent of her perfume. Was she flirting? He could never tell with women and dismissed the notion as the housekeeper stopped at a door and knocked.

A moment later, the door opened and a short, full-figured woman with silver hair and bright blue eyes greeted them. She wore a long, dark skirt, support stockings and sturdy shoes. Under her cardigan, there was a stiff white shirt.

'This is Liv Adler,' Elsa said. 'Herr Doktor West's nurse.'

He extended his hand. 'I'm Adam.'

'Nu?' she said. 'Don't stand there like a shlemiel. Come inside.'

Rolling her eyes, the housekeeper closed the door behind Adam. He was in a library. There was a tall window with a view of the property. The barn was visible in the distance and he noticed the pickup parked nearby. A coffee set had been brought in. She filled a cup and, bringing it over with a plate of freshly baked macaroons, found him poring over books on art, science and photography.

'Does Elsa dislike you?' he said.

'We're friends but she thinks I'm a kibitzer.' She handed him the cup and indicated two armchairs facing each other. 'You're a smart one like Nathan, I can tell.'

Taking a seat, he craned his neck. 'Is my uncle coming?'

'Young people are in such a hurry. Me, I have all the time in the world. So, tell me about yourself. Is there a girl? Because I have a niece around your age. Attractive—not beautiful. Good complexion. And she cooks.'

He tried a macaroon. 'Her name is Jenny.'

'A Gentile?' She clucked her tongue. 'Do you still see her?'

'No. We, um—'

'Ha! No wonder it didn't last.'

'Look, I only found out I'm Jewish last night.'

She cupped his chin and gave his cheek a pinch. 'Bubeleh, you've always known. Like Paul Newman, you look. Taller, maybe.' She took his hand and placed it on his heart. 'It's what's in here. This is where you find the emes.'

'Did my uncle hire you through an agency?'

'We met at Mount Sinai Hospital. He was there for gall-bladder surgery. I was his nurse.'

'And you've been with him all these years?'

'Such a comedian. I had a husband and children to look after. Not that I wasn't tempted by his sheyner punim. He flirted with all the nurses. A regular Tab Hunter.

'He gave me his card. Said I should look him up if my situation changed. That was in 1937. I raised two children – a son and a daughter. They each got married and moved to New Rochelle. And then...'

She paused as if remembering something unpleasant and sipped her coffee. 'In 1948, my husband got very sick. On his deathbed, Morris tells me to call Dr West. He knew I kept the card in my jewellery box. Such a worrywart but a real mensch.

'I waited a whole year. On the anniversary, I lit a yahrzeit candle, and the day after, I picked up the telephone. I was sure Nathan would have forgotten about me. I was wrong. He begged me to come right away. And here I am.'

'That's quite a story,' Adam said. 'Does he treat you well?'

'What a question! Yes, Mr Detective, he treats me well, but we're not intimate. My heart belongs to Morris.'

'I didn't mean—'

'Every week, I give your uncle his Vitamin B12 injections. Also, I prepare his meals, which is another reason Elsa has it in for me. He's diabetic.'

'And Halsey Dean?'

'The shiksa? What about her? I know you a little and here's some advice. Don't get mixed up with that one.'

'I wasn't planning—'

'She's clever. Convinced your uncle to let her into his fancy-shmancy laboratory. And for what? So she can make experiments like Dr Frankenstein. You know this character? It's all mishegoss if you ask me. The dead should stay dead.'

'She told me she was interested in molecular biology.'

'Feh! What she's interested in is his money, the gonif. I've seen it before. Flashes those big eyes at him and he gives her whatever she wants.' She leant over. 'Between you and me, there's something fishy going on in that barn. If I were you, I would stay away.'

He recalled Günter and his wheelbarrow. 'You're very protective of my uncle.'

'You bet. He told me about you when he was in the hospital. You had just been born.'

'But I thought he wasn't in touch with the family.'

'His brother Aaron came for a visit. Another looker. If I wasn't married at the time... I remember Nathan was so happy. They hadn't seen each other in years. Mishpoche – family. There's nothing more important.'

Liv looked at her wristwatch and got to her feet. 'Oy vey, look at the time!'

Glancing at his watch, he realised an hour had gone by. She took his arm to see him out.

'What about my uncle?'

'He's waiting for you in the garden.'

'Then why...'

She took his hands, her eyes shiny with pride as if he were her own son. 'It's my job to protect him, remember?'

'Oh, boy. This was an interview.'

'A little nosh, some shmoozing...' She wiped a crumb from his lip with her thumb. 'Now go, boychik. Mustn't keep Dr West waiting. You'll see me again.'

She closed the door before he could say goodbye.

Briskly, he made his way to the double doors, through the dining room and into the garden. There, surrounded by a spray of zinnias, he found an elderly man sitting in an electric wheelchair and facing the gate. Though it was summer, he had on a greatcoat.

'Uncle Nathan?'

The scientist wheeled himself around with spindly arms. He was frail, with a full head of white hair and liver spots on his hands. His eyes were hidden behind futuristic glasses that resembled something out of *Flash Gordon*. Instead of normal lenses, there were two telescoping tubes made of dull metal. As he focused on his nephew, miniature motors whirred, extending the tubes independently.

Adam approached him, then paused at the sight of his uncle's trouser legs. There was nothing below the knees but air.

'Hello, Adam,' Nathan West said in a voice like John Carradine. 'I've waited a long time for this day.'

CHAPTER 26

All My Tomorrows

WINTER 2000

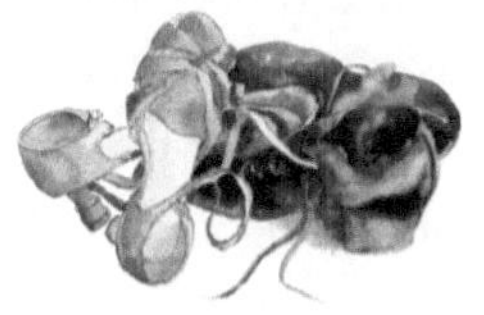

Dr Irenka Lewandowska made her way to the physics lab with the help of a cane. It was past seven. Though everyone else had gone home, she knew Claire would be there working on her confounded time travel experiment.

At eighty-two, the chief scientist was no longer vibrant. Still, her mind was as sharp as ever. Like her late mother, she suffered from arthritis and had difficulty seeing at night, even with the strong prescription glasses. On her doctor's advice, she gave up smoking and drank wine instead of the vodka she loved. Not wanting to end up alone, she married in her fifties but ended up a widow anyway, having lost her businessman husband to a heart attack when he was seventy.

The door to the lab was ajar and she could hear her favourite scientist talking to herself. Claire had always been a quiet girl. But after coming on full time, she turned into a regular chatterbox. When another physicist complained, Irenka advised him to write down everything she said word for word, as it was infinitely more intelligent than his last paper, which she had found lacking.

As the chief scientist entered, Claire looked up from the table, her black-framed glasses sliding halfway down her nose. The esteemed women had been colleagues for forty years. And though the younger scientist was fifty-seven, Irenka could still see the precocious seventeen-year-old in the starched white shirt, pleated blue plaid skirt and plain black shoes.

'Claire, there's something I vanted to discuss,' the chief scientist said.

'I was hoping you'd still be here. Come take a look.'

'Honestly, I don't know vhy you've spent so much time on this project.'

'Is that a pun?'

Irenka pulled up a stool opposite her. 'As I've often told you, vhat's important is the new exotic matter you seem to have stumbled upon.'

'I didn't stumble upon it. And anyway, I'm not interested in that.'

'Not interested? Because of your patent, Bland stands to earn a projected ten billion over the next five years. I've got eight other teams vorking on practical applications that vill—'

'You need to see this, though.'

Two twelve-inch metal arches stood opposite each other on the table, three feet apart. Wires attached to them led to a black anodised box the size of a book. On it were dials, switches and a miniature monochrome display. A shielded cable was also connected to the box and ran down and across the floor to another room, which housed Claire's exotic matter machinery she liked referring to as her 'factory.'

Nearby on a computer monitor, a curious-looking 3D blue wave pattern floated as if in space. In the upper-right corner, a dizzying progression of numbers whizzed past, like a stock market ticker but designed by the Mad Hatter.

The younger scientist reached for a plastic action figure – a German shepherd wearing a Batman mask and cape.

'His name is Ace,' she said. 'I chose him because he reminds me of Adam.'

'Adam West? You still think about him?'

'Every time I pass his parents' plaque.' Absently, Claire counted on her fingers again.

Smiling, the chief scientist patted her hand. 'I think of him, too, sometimes. It's a shame about... Vhat do you vant to show me?'

The younger scientist positioned the little dog under the right arch, equidistant from the two sides. She was about to pick up the black box when Irenka raised her hand.

'Are you sure this is safe?' the chief scientist said.

'My, you've become suspicious in your old age. Now, be quiet and watch. This happens fast, so you'll need to look at the right arch, then the left.'

Irenka stuck her tongue out at Claire as she checked the dials on the box and flipped three switches in sequence. Each triggered a different-coloured LED. A loud humming came out of the factory room and the lab table began to vibrate. As the noise increased, the chief scientist's heart beat faster.

Claire pressed a red button, generating a soft, high-pitched keening that seemed to come from somewhere between the two arches. A red pattern appeared on the monitor, overlaying the first. Soon, the waves moved in perfect synchronisation.

The action figure, solid only a moment ago, became

transparent. The air around it seemed to ripple and with a faint pop, the dog vanished. A strange luminescence seemingly materialised out of nothing inside the left arch. The air rippled as the light faded and Irenka could see the dog's outline. The humming ceased and the action figure was sitting under the left arch as sound as before.

Stunned, the chief scientist examined the object. It didn't feel warm, though she noticed part of it was deformed.

'Vas his paw alvays like this?' Irenka said.

'I need to work on my calibrations. I have another five hundred and ninety-nine of those things in the closet.'

'This is extraordinary. But I'm not sure it vould ever be safe for humans. Have you tested it on a living creature?'

Claire pretended to be shocked. 'We're a ways off from that.'

The chief scientist's phone vibrated and she glanced at the number. 'My car is here. Come vith me downstairs.'

The younger scientist took her friend's arm and walked her to the lift. In a few minutes, they were outside. It was a clear night and the stars were brilliant. A cold March wind wafted through the trees, chilling the women. Claire helped Irenka down the steps to the waiting town car and opened the rear passenger door.

'Still want me to give up and work on more practical ideas?' the younger scientist said.

'That's up to you now. Gratulacje, moja droga.'

'Why are you congratulating me?'

'As you know, my health isn't good. I've decided to retire.'

Claire's eyes glistened. 'But I don't want you to leave. I don't have many friends and—'

'It is time to make some. I met vith the board last veek

and recommended they promote you to chief scientist. The vote vas unanimous.'

'I don't know what to say. What will you do?'

'Vell, I'm in the process of selling my house. I plan to return to Warsaw and spend vhatever time I have left vith family.'

Claire embraced her friend. 'I'm going to miss you. And I'll never forget what you did for me.'

'The truth is I did very little. Your accomplishments are all yours. Your parents vould be so proud.'

'I'll perfect the device, however long it takes.'

'Glad to hear it. One of my last official acts vas to create a separate budget for your project, using some of the profits from all your incredible inventions.' She kissed the younger scientist's cheek. 'Goodbye, Claire.'

'Goodbye, Irenka. Kocham cię całym sercem.'

Her friend touched her face. 'And I love you. This may sound trite but I've alvays thought of you as my daughter. And I'm honoured to have vorked vith you. Now, you'd better let me go or I'll turn into a popsicle.'

Claire waved to her friend as the car drove away. Walking back to the building, she stopped at the plaque honouring Jon and Miriam West. Fresh flowers lay at the foot of the plinth.

Chief Scientist Claire de La Lune. It wasn't a title she coveted. In spite of her achievements, she was convinced there were others more qualified. Still, she was grateful.

She had wanted so much to tell Irenka the real reason she decided to devote her life to making time travel a reality. But in the end, she couldn't bring herself to do it. Her friend would have seen her reasoning as sentimental and not at all in keeping with pure science.

That no longer mattered because she was in charge now

and had a herculean task ahead of her. Something awful happened in late summer, 1960 – an event Claire had never got over. And it set her on her current path. Indeed, it had become her life's work.

'I *will* fix this, Adam,' she said, retreating from the March cold. 'I promise.'

CHAPTER 27

Mack The Knife

SUMMER 1960

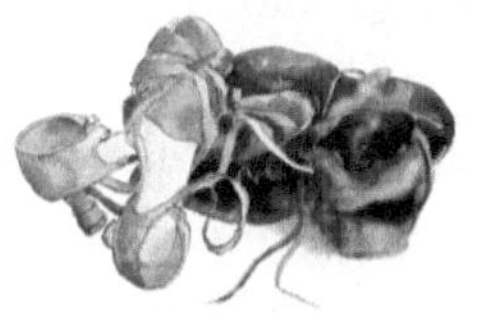

Detective Pat Quinn walked into the Carlyle at around ten in the morning, suffering the effects of the dirty-water hot dog with the works he'd consumed at East Forty-Eighth Street and Fifth Avenue. He considered himself lucky, though, having avoided a pothole two feet across as he made his way from Times Square, where he had been investigating a tourist stabbing.

There were 397 potholes in Manhattan, all scheduled for repair, provided the road builders didn't go on strike again. He'd seen the danger at the last moment and swerved, clipping a food trolley at the edge of the pavement. Cursing the city he loved, he stopped to ensure no one was hurt and to soothe the exasperated vendor, purchased the comestible that would lead to his present heartburn.

The Carlyle was considered one of the poshest hotels in Manhattan's Upper East Side. Quinn had been there only once when he took his wife to dinner on their twenty-fifth wedding anniversary. Getting off the lift on the thirtieth floor, he noticed an officer stationed outside the room. The man seemed dull and lacked motivation. The door was propped open and as the detective approached, he greeted the cop and flashed his badge.

The officer had cleared the floor of nosy reporters and busybody hotel guests. All that remained were a police photographer and a crime scene investigator wearing latex gloves. As flashbulbs fired, Quinn shielded his eyes, then moved closer to have a gander at the body.

The deceased looked familiar but he couldn't place him. Caucasian male. Late forties to early fifties. Unshaven with bulging eyes and an angry erection. The victim had been strangled with a nylon stocking, which was wound tight around his neck. To the detective, it appeared to be a crime of passion.

Behind him, a passing chambermaid glanced at the body and, spotting the priapism, gasped. Unable to keep a straight face, the officer at the door shooed her away.

'Somebody throw a towel over that,' Quinn said. Then to no one in particular, 'Thought we'd sealed off the floor.'

The investigator, whose name he couldn't recall, approached him, carrying a brown paper bag. Inside, there was a wallet and keys. The detective circled the bed whilst his colleague undid the stocking, folded it and placed it in a separate bag.

Kneeling, Quinn peered under the bed and squinted at the floor. His knees ached from arthritis, another reminder he should have taken early retirement as his wife suggested. His father had suffered from the same condition, he remembered. Getting to his feet, he pointed at the investigator.

'There's something there on your side.'

With a grunt, the other man got down on all fours and reached for the object. The detective stood next to him, looking at a small sterling silver elephant on a broken chain. Quinn snapped his fingers at the photographer, who documented the evidence. Shaking his head, the investigator dropped the jewellery into a fresh bag.

'What is it?' the detective said.

'Hell if I know. Some kind of charm? I hear elephants are lucky.'

'Not for this Joe. What else?'

'So far, we've got two sets of prints on glasses, a whisky bottle and some pubic hair around the toilet.'

'Female?'

'Can't tell. Wouldn't think so.'

'You think a man strangles another man with a nylon stocking?'

'Maybe, if he's queer.'

'I dunno.' Quinn walked over to the officer. 'Who discovered the body?'

'Hotel maid. They're sending for her.'

The detective lit a cigarette and waited. He'd been in homicide going on thirty-five years. In his experience, this sort of thing didn't happen in nice hotels like the Carlyle. Usually, you had to go to the South Bronx. What was the world coming to? He thought of the popular song he heard whilst stationed in Suffolk, England, during the war – 'We'll Be Together Again.' The music was better in those days. Now there was rock and roll and murders in posh hotels.

The lift chimed and he extinguished the cigarette butt in a wall-mounted ashtray. Two people approached – a man of around fifty in an impeccable blue suit with a rug on his head that reminded Quinn of a bird's nest. The other was a nervous Latin woman in her twenties wearing a maid's uniform.

'Detective Quinn? I'm Oliver Oberman, the hotel manager.' He neglected to introduce the woman. 'I understand you wanted to interview my staff?'

'That's right.'

'I'll leave you to it, then. If you need me, I'll be downstairs in my office.'

Quinn watched the ponce turn on his heels and walk off. Then to the maid, 'Nice guy.'

Appreciating her discomfort, he spoke to her as tactfully as he could in the hallway out of view of the body. He asked whether she saw anyone other than the deceased enter or leave and she told him no. She said her shift started at 6 AM and that perhaps he should speak to Lulamae Birdie, who worked nights.

He added Lulamae to the list of hotel employees he planned to interview. After taking down this woman's name, address and telephone number, he informed her he might need to talk to her again. Groaning at the news, she returned to work, trembling worse than before.

A service lift chimed and two ambulance attendants appeared carrying a stretcher and a canvas body bag. One of them – a smart-arse – saluted the detective as they entered the room. Presently, the crime scene investigator came out. He set down his heavy wooden equipment case and lit a cigarette. Quinn joined him.

'I still think a man did it,' the investigator said. 'Takes raw strength to strangle someone.'

'Unless they're upset.'

'We'll see what the ME says.' He put out the cigarette and, lifting the case with a grunt, started off.

The detective waved to him. 'Hey, I forgot to ask. What's the victim's name?'

'Bruce Donovan,' the investigator said and pressed the button for the lift.

CHAPTER 28

Mambocito Mio

Tito Ladrón walked in at half nine, expecting to find the VP of Marketing in his office. The door was open but there was no one inside. Against his better judgement, he gathered himself together and approached the overbearing Miss Lamb. She ignored him and kept typing. Tap, tap, tap. He cleared his throat. Tap, tap, tap. Her fingers flew across the keyboard like grouse driven by motivated beaters.

'I don't know how things are done in Miami, young man. But here, we begin work at nine AM sharp.' Tap, tap, tap.

Other than his mother, the only woman who had ever addressed him in that manner was his abuela. Both were in Havana, dishing it out to his younger sister. He was about to say something to the cabrona when she stopped and looked up. There was a coldness in her eyes and he felt the temperature drop. The bitch was diabolical. His palms sweating, he managed to squeak out a question.

'Is he sick today?'

Her interest flagging, she returned to her typing. 'He hasn't called in.' Tap, tap, zwing.

He waited for more, but there wasn't any. Like a fool, he stood there for a full minute, then slinked to the office he'd taken over from Adam West. He closed the door and sitting at his desk, lit a cigarette and brooded.

Last night was wonderful. He always suspected Bruce was attracted to him much the way older men were drawn to him at home – especially married politicians. If it hadn't been for the postmaster's jealous wife, he might still be living in his native city, collecting generous honorariums por la izquierda for services rendered. Instead, he made it out before they could arrest him. After the revolution in 1959, he told himself there was no going back.

Like many Cubans, Tito settled in Miami and found work as a dishwasher, then a waiter. He talked his way into a job at an insurance company catering to Spanish-speaking customers. It was located in the same building as Bland Corporation. He hated insurance, and one day took a lift to the top floor to enquire about a position.

He was in luck, they told him. Bland were looking to expand their footprint in Latin America and needed someone in the marketing department who spoke Spanish. He'd learnt English as a child and was fluent in both languages. He also knew a little French, which seemed to impress them. After interviewing the next day, he was offered the job.

A few weeks later, the VP flew down and took everyone in the department to dinner. He and the Cuban hit it off and ended up at the bar where they talked about cars, women and baseball until closing. Other than sports, Tito was on shaky ground and did his best to keep up.

Bruce struck him as a man of action and he found he

was attracted to him, though he didn't do anything to let on. They saw each other whenever the VP was in town but always in public and always in a group. In those early days, the Cuban thought his boss was a regular guy – a family man who liked taking an interest in his employees.

On his last visit, Bruce promised he would find a way to get Tito transferred to Bland's headquarters, further proof the VP wanted his people to succeed. Bruce had heard it on good authority the Old Man planned to open up a position in the marketing department in New York and without delay, he promised it to his Cuban protégé.

Final preparations were underway and the VP submitted the necessary paperwork to Personnel. All that remained was for the CEO to sign off. Then a bombshell dropped when Bruce learnt the position had been filled.

Outraged, he returned to Miami to deliver the bad news in person. Tito was crushed. He always wanted to live in New York and considered what he would do next since he didn't fancy being a copywriter all his life.

To soften the blow, the VP bought him dinner at Embers in South Beach. Later, they visited a few clubs to hear live music. By midnight, the Cuban was plastered and couldn't remember how he got home. Vaguely, he recalled a taxi ride and Bruce saying goodnight to him at his door.

Then, last night happened, starting with an elegant dinner in the restaurant at the Carlyle, followed by drinks in the hotel room. More and more, Tito suspected something had happened during the VP's previous trip. But he couldn't be sure and was reluctant to make the first move. Instead, he drank his whisky.

Bruce removed his suit jacket and loosening his tie, topped up his guest's glass. Before the Cuban knew what was happening, his boss kissed him on the lips. The feeling was incredible and Tito was profoundly moved.

Afterwards, he gave his new lover his most cherished possession, a silver elephant representing his favourite baseball team, Elefantes de Cienfuegos. He recalled their excellent slogan – *El paso del elefante es lento pero aplastante.*

But now in the light of day, he felt anxious. Maybe Bruce regretted what they did. He was married, after all, with a grown daughter. What would his family think if they found out? Was it possible the VP had decided to eliminate the Cuban as he did Adam?

He could feel his childhood asthma returning and struggled for air. Gasping, he closed his eyes and forced himself to breathe through his nose, praying there was another, more reasonable explanation for Bruce's absence – something along the lines of a minor car accident.

'Es chiflado,' he said. 'He's got a hangover.'

Lighting another cigarette, he got to work. He would check in with Miss Lamb after lunch. And this time, he would answer her impudence with a phrase that would put the cow in her place once and for all – something that always struck fear in the hearts of enemies of Cienfuegos.

The step of the elephant is slow but crushing.

CHAPTER 29

Stormy Weather

Quinn arrived at the Donovan home in Great Neck before noon. His mind boggled at the fact that he'd met the murder victim days earlier when the Englishman leapt to his death from the roof of the Bland building. What was the suicide's name? *Del Dillard.*

The detective spent all morning reviewing witness statements and writing his report. Whoever was in the room with Bruce Donovan managed to enter without anyone seeing them. Chances were, it was someone the victim knew, which would explain the intimate manner of death. He wondered whether the deaths were connected since Donovan was Dillard's boss. In any event, it was time to notify the family.

The houses in this neighbourhood were impressive, requiring staff to maintain them. They were a far cry from the three-bedroom bungalow Quinn shared with his wife in Brooklyn. As he pulled into the driveway, he spotted a gardener. He lingered, watching the man trim a hydrangea shrub. Perhaps on some level, he envied him.

After all these years, it wasn't working criminal cases that bothered the detective but rather delivering bad news. He'd done it enough and knew how to employ the correct facial expressions – seeming to care without being simpering. Nevertheless, it pained him.

He rang the doorbell expecting a maid to answer. But he was greeted by an attractive girl wearing a cashmere sweater and capri pants.

'Hello. I'm Detective Quinn from the New York City Police Department.' He showed her his badge. 'Is your mother at home?'

'I think so. What's this about?'

'I'd prefer to speak to her.'

'All right, come inside. I'm Jenny. Excuse me a minute.'

It was a warm day. Fanning himself with his hat, he gazed around the foyer. A maple side table stood opposite him and on it, a flower arrangement in a large, colourful vase. It saddened him he couldn't afford to give his wife the kind of home she deserved, not that she ever complained. From where he stood, he could see all the way to the sitting room, which was filled with expensive furniture.

There was a clacking on the tile and soon two women walked towards him. The older one wore her hair up and was attractive like her daughter. Poised, she had on a tailored silk dress and low-heeled shoes. Her jewellery was expensive but tasteful.

'Detective?' she said, extending her hand.

'Nice to meet you, Mrs Donovan. Is there somewhere we can talk?'

'Let's go into the living room.'

His stomach churned as she led the way. She had no idea Bruce Donovan was dead. As she showed him where to sit, he wondered why she wasn't more upset her husband hadn't come home the previous night. He sat on a floral brocade sofa and she chose an accent chair opposite him. The girl remained standing beside her mother. Setting aside a brown envelope, he took out his notepad and pen and glanced at a family photo on the mantelpiece.

'That was taken a few summers ago in Kennebunkport,' Mrs D said.

'When did you last see your husband?'

'Yesterday morning.' She looked at her daughter. 'We had breakfast together.'

'And then he went to work?'

'I assume so. Is he in some kind of trouble?'

'Did your husband come home last night?'

'No. He called to say he had a dinner meeting and would be very late. I suggested he stay in the city to get a good night's sleep.'

'Does he do that often? Stay in the city, I mean.'

'It depends.'

'Do you know who he was meeting?'

'Bruce never discusses business with me.'

'Okay. Which hotel does he stay at normally?'

'The Sheraton. I don't remember which one. Detective, I'm sure you could've gotten all this information from his secretary, Miss Lamb.'

He wrote down the name and closed the notepad. This was it – time to drop the bombshell. He looked at the girl. Her eyes were huge, as if she sensed something was coming. On the other hand, the mother seemed ignorant of any irregularity.

'There's something I have to tell you, Mrs Donovan,' he said, measuring his words. 'Your husband is dead.'

Someone said, 'Oh, my God' – it might have been the girl. He waited for the fireworks, but they didn't come. A mantelpiece clock ticked loudly. Outside, the gardener started up a power lawnmower.

Mrs D's eyes accused him. 'What did you say?'

It was always the same – disbelief as if you'd announced the landing of a spaceship in Central Park. The women waited for more. No choice but to go on.

'He was found this morning in his hotel room at the Carlyle. We've gathered all the evidence and are treating this as a homicide.'

'Wait, someone *killed* him?' Jenny said.

'He was strangled.'

The girl's mother paced, wringing her hands like Barbara Stanwyck in a Hollywood film noir. Her daughter eased her into the chair. He prepared himself for the denial phase. Mrs D didn't disappoint him.

'You've made a mistake,' she said. 'It's not my husband – it can't be.'

'We'd appreciate it if you could come into the city to make an identification.'

She hadn't heard a word and blinked stupidly. 'What?'

Her daughter took her mother's hands. 'I'll go with you.'

'No, I... All right.' Then to Quinn, 'When?'

'Sooner would be best. I'll give you the address. I noticed a gardener outside. I'd like to interview him before I leave. Are there any other employees?'

'Our housekeeper, Mary Malloy. But she's off today. I'll show you out.'

In the foyer, he stopped at the front door and removing a photograph from the envelope, showed it to the widow. It was a close-up of the silver elephant.

'We found this in the hotel room. I'm wondering if it belonged to your husband.'

'He would never wear anything so vulgar.' She looked closer. 'But I've seen this before. Let me think.'

'Take your time.'

'Bruce invited an employee for dinner a few weeks ago. I'm sure he was wearing one just like it.'

The detective couldn't believe his luck. 'Do you happen to remember the man's name?'

'I... He was Latin – Cuban, I think.'

She called to her daughter, who was in the sitting room. Wiping away her tears, she joined them. Mrs D showed her the photo.

'What was that Cuban man's name? The one who was here for dinner?'

The girl's lips became a thin line as she pictured Adam locked up in a lunatic asylum. She stared at the photo a moment longer, an intense feeling of contempt welling inside her like bubbling lava. Maybe her dad hadn't arranged for her boyfriend to be humiliated. What if it was the slimy Cuban all along? She'd heard stories about those people using black magic to control others. Was the elephant some kind of evil charm designed to manipulate her father?

Her mind raced as she pictured the Cuban luring his victim to an unfamiliar hotel and strangling him. Her dad was strong and would have put up a struggle, perhaps ripping the chain in the process. Sure, the murderer got away. But in his haste to leave the scene, he made a fatal mistake. He forgot to remove the damning evidence.

'His name is Tito Ladrón,' Jenny said, trembling with rage. 'I'm sure he's the one who killed my father.'

CHAPTER 30

Fever

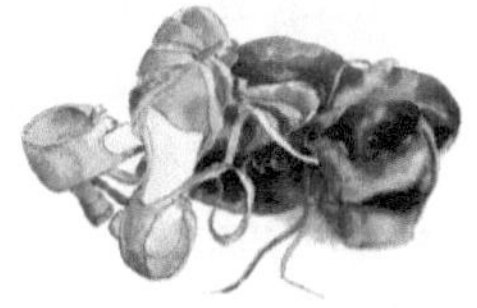

Calvin Lipinsky's back ached after moving the dead body. He was sixty-two and had no business exerting himself like that. As the owner of Bavarian Motorsport, an auto-repair garage in Great Neck, he'd never worked on a race car in his life and didn't plan on starting. But his wife liked the name and he always strove to please her. When the pain from her cancer became unbearable, he granted her final wish by smothering her with a pillow in the bed they had shared for close to forty years. It was the hardest thing he'd ever done.

Arriving at the garage in the late afternoon, he found the Puerto Rican he'd hired recently replacing the brake pads on the Mercedes-Benz Landaulet. He told the diligent young man to take the rest of the day off – with pay, of course. After putting away his tools, the employee, who was saving up for a car, thanked him and got on his bicycle.

Calvin hung the Closed sign and retreated into his office in the rear. He shut the blinds and opened a side drawer in his ancient tanker desk. There, he found a bottle of Glenfiddich and a juice glass. He was accustomed to Old

Crow. Pouring himself three fingers, he finished the drink in two quick gulps. Then, he wiped his mouth and wept.

It wasn't difficult killing Mrs D's husband, because the man was already half-drunk. Besides, Calvin was used to death, having served in the infantry in Korea where he defended freedom. Getting rid of an abusive spouse was about justice – and money, which he desperately needed. The business hadn't been doing well for a long time. After his wife's death, he was hit with a stack of medical bills. On top of the funeral expenses, it was all too much. He owed on the house and his savings had long since been depleted.

He'd known the Donovans for years and watched their beautiful daughter Jenny grow up. Sometimes, seeing her made him long for children. Pouring another drink, he went back to the beginning.

It was Bruce who always brought the car in for service. But he was in Miami on this occasion, on business, and his wife drove it over. Before she arrived, he was on the phone with a bill collector from the hospital. He made the mistake of complaining to Mrs D. He even joked about going to Atlantic City to win some money. Realising his mistake, he apologised. She was a classy lady and took it in stride. It would be their little secret, she told him. He thought that was the end of it.

Two weeks later, Mrs D returned, complaining about a funny noise whenever she accelerated. He checked out the vehicle and found nothing wrong. She insisted on paying him anyway and gave him a present – the bottle of Glenfid-dich he now enjoyed. It had got towards evening by then and the Puerto Rican was gone for the day. He found a second glass and they shared a drink.

Calvin was close to most of his customers and didn't consider the situation odd. Laying her hand on his, Mrs D said she was thinking about his predicament and wanted to help. She had set aside some cash and was interested in investing it in a business. Why not his? Her offer was like an answer to his prayers and he was eager to hear more.

They had known each other a long time and considered each other friends. After another drink, she let it slip she was having problems at home with her husband. He thought she might be a little tipsy and offered to make her some coffee. Sobbing, she told him Bruce was seeing someone else and hinted that he'd mistreated her for years.

He asked about Jenny, but she assured him the violence was always directed at herself. He recalled his younger sister, who married a sailor. One time, her husband beat her so severely, she was left disabled. Distraught, Calvin admitted to Mrs D that if the monster hadn't gone to prison, he would have killed him. He asked her what he could do to help. She promised to be in touch.

A week had gone by and Calvin hadn't heard from the woman. When she did ring at last, they agreed to meet at a diner in Kings Point. She showed him her bruised arm and told him she couldn't take it any more. Also, she was worried her daughter might be next.

'I have no right asking you this, Calvin,' she said.

Mrs D knew all about Tito Ladrón. And thanks to Miss Lamb, she learnt her husband would be staying at the Carlyle on Tuesday. Never mentioning murder, she instructed the mechanic to go there and do what needed to be done. She handed him an envelope containing five thousand dollars and promised another five after it was over.

When he didn't object, she offered to let him take the day to think it over and reached across the table for his hand. Seeing the bruise again, he decided he didn't need any more time.

On Tuesday night, he entered the hotel wearing a suit and sat on the far side of the lobby behind a potted palm. After an hour, Bruce Donovan appeared with another younger man, who was swarthy and well-dressed. Mrs D had briefed Calvin, so he knew this was Tito Ladrón. Donovan took a lift upstairs whilst his companion lingered in the lobby, at one point making eye contact with the stranger.

Fifteen minutes later, the Cuban entered a different lift and the mechanic joined him. Arriving on the thirtieth floor, Tito headed for the suite whilst Calvin pretended to go in the other direction. After noting the room number, the mechanic waited in the emergency exit stairwell.

Two hours had passed. Calvin was concerned the Cuban might stay the night. Though the thought of two men having sex sickened him, he didn't like the idea of murdering both. Besides, he needed Tito alive. The Cuban left at around one. The mechanic waited another few minutes, then approached the door. After slipping on gloves, he pulled a nylon stocking from his pocket and knocked.

Donovan must have thought it was his sex partner and opened the door wide, wearing only a robe and the elephant charm. He recognised his mechanic. But before he could say anything, the other man rabbit-punched him in the throat, sending him backward. Calvin closed the door and pushed Mrs D's husband to the floor as he grabbed his attacker's hat. Getting behind his victim, the mechanic wound the stocking around his throat and choked the life out of him.

It took less than five minutes for Bruce Donovan to die.

The mechanic removed the robe and tossed it aside. He dragged the naked body to the bed and placed it in the middle. Tearing off the chain, he threw it and the charm under the bed. He removed the victim's pinkie ring and pocketed it. Doing a quick check of the room, he found the whisky bottle and glasses. Those would have the two men's fingerprints. Satisfied, he checked the hallway through the peephole and remembering his hat, left undetected. Later, he found a payphone and rang Mrs D. She answered on the first ring.

The next morning, Calvin waited outside the patsy's block of flats. Spotting the Cuban on his way to work, he entered his flat and hid incriminating evidence in the bedroom. Tomorrow, he would ring the police station anonymously to report a man matching Tito Ladrón's description leaving the hotel suite in the early hours.

Shaken by the experience, the mechanic drove around aimlessly, trying to blot out the image of Donovan's bulging eyes and protruding tongue. He convinced himself he did the right thing by ending an abusive husband's reign of terror. After a greasy hamburger lunch in a bar near Locust Point, he returned to Great Neck.

Calvin looked forward to seeing Mrs D again and getting the rest of his money.

CHAPTER 31

Portrait Of Jenny

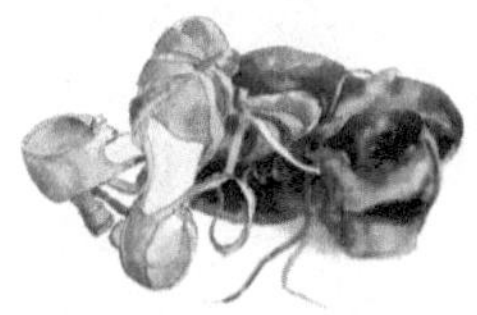

Jenny opened the housekeeper's sewing kit and removed a heavy duty needle and extra-strong thread. She picked up the glass eye Hannah, the little Delancey Street girl, had gifted her. Though Jenny was sad, the memory of those curly blonde locks gave her a warm feeling. She thought of the child often.

After threading the needle, she passed it through the loop and positioning the eye so it was symmetrical with the other one, jabbed the needle through her teddy's head until it came out the back at the seam. Expertly, she tugged on the thread until the eye was secure and tied it off with a knot.

'Good as new,' she said as her tears fell.

A month had gone by since the funeral and she felt lost. She'd attended Tito Ladrón's trial daily, praying he would be convicted. The evidence, she felt, was overwhelming. The police found his fingerprints and hair in the hotel room, as well as the elephant charm he admitted belonged to him.

Witnesses testified they saw the Cuban having dinner with Jenny's father. Then there was the anonymous tip describing how he had been observed leaving the crime scene during the probable time of death. The final nail in the accused's coffin was what the police found in his flat – a nylon stocking still in its package, identical to the one used to commit the murder, and her dad's pinkie ring.

The prosecutor called a witness, a night maid named Lulamae Birdie. She testified she saw the defendant leaving the hotel room around one o'clock in the morning. The lawyer gave the jury a knowing look and declined to ask her any further questions. Now it was the defence attorney's turn. The effusive maid stated that later she was in the supply closet and upon emerging, noticed another man getting into the lift. He was old, she remembered, and he moved as if in pain. Thinking nothing of it, she loaded her trolley with fresh towels. The prosecutor asked whether she knew the direction he came from. Alas, she did not.

The district attorney was a family friend and vowed to do everything in his power to see to it the accused received the death penalty. He had assigned his top prosecutor who, in his closing argument, painted the defendant as a violent, jealous lover who couldn't stand the thought of sharing the deceased with a woman. By the time he was done, no reasonable person in a pantheon of reasonable people could conclude anything other than Tito Ladrón had murdered Bruce Donovan in cold blood.

After all the evidence was presented and the closing arguments made, the jury took only three hours to reach their verdict. They found the defendant guilty of first-degree murder and conspiracy to commit murder.

Tears of relief sprang from Jenny's eyes and she wanted to jump up and cheer. Instead, she focused her attention on the Cuban as he stood trembling before the judge, his lawyer's hand on his shoulder. Something troubled her.

Why was the murderer surprised by the verdict when it was clear he had planned the whole thing?

Two weeks later, Tito Ladrón was sentenced to death by electrocution and transported to Sing Sing to await his punishment. His lawyer vowed to appeal the decision but the Cuban had given up all hope by then. Since discovering his sexuality at eleven, he always knew one day he would have to pay the price for what he was.

Before being led away, he turned round to face the widow and her daughter, who were seated in the front row. He said although he was sorry Bruce Donovan was dead, he was innocent. They'd had a loving relationship. It was inconceivable that he would harm the man. Furthermore, he regretted leaving Cuba. His one wish, in case God was listening, was to go home.

Instead of offering sympathy, Mrs D called him a filthy pig and told him he could go to hell. Her daughter said nothing.

Detective Quinn was also in the courtroom and took note of the interaction. Though the evidence was incontrovertible, he felt the unknown man in the lift was a loose thread. Moreover, there was something about the widow that didn't sit well with him – he could never get his arms around it. Indeed, it had kept him up at nights.

At the start of the investigation, he interviewed the housekeeper, Mary Malloy, who was reluctant to say anything critical of her employer. He persisted and she admitted the woman had been under great strain and was abusing alcohol and pills. Yet when he met the widow that first time, she was sober. The shock of her husband's death might have straightened her out. Then again, she couldn't have known about the murder. Weary of it all, he let it lie.

Tito Ladrón got what he deserved, at least according to the jury.

Outside on the courthouse steps, Mrs D thanked the prosecutor. He asked how she was holding up and she told him she planned to concentrate on her daughter's well-being.

Returning to Great Neck, Jenny thought about what she said. Things were different now – her mother was different. She no longer drank or took prescription medication. She seemed to enjoy life in the same way her daughter remembered as a little girl. It was as if a cloud had lifted, a dripping darkness containing the ghost of her father.

So much had gone wrong, but she missed her dad. She thought seeing the Cuban sent to prison would make her happy. It didn't. Inside, she was as hollow as a carved pumpkin, its leering face a mask. And she longed for Adam. Why hadn't he rung? She hadn't heard from him since that awful day at Bellevue Hospital, and she had no way of contacting him.

Getting through the funeral and the trial would have been so much easier with him at her side, supporting her and her mother. Instead, it was Roger Davies who stepped in. After learning what happened, he forgave Mrs D and promised to help in any way he could. If it hadn't been for Roger...

Jenny's birthday was coming up in August and she had hoped to spend it with Adam. As a consolation, her mother offered to take her to Europe. But what if her boyfriend tried contacting her whilst she was out of the country? She needed to reach him, if only to hear his voice over the telephone.

'I have to find a way,' she said to her beloved bear with the wondrous eye.

CHAPTER 32

I'm A Fool To Want You

It wasn't yet morning when Adam opened his eyes. In his dream, a woman screamed. It was Jenny standing over the body of her father. Like the cover of a pulp novel, her eyes were wild as she held a bloody knife, which cast a long shadow. He'd read about the murder and subsequent trial in the *New York Times*. It surprised him Tito Ladrón was the killer. Though he detested the Cuban, he couldn't picture him strangling anyone.

Since leaving New York, Adam had come to the realisation that Jenny was blameless. Everything lay at the feet of the late Bruce Donovan. Still, it didn't change anything. Though Adam wanted to ring his girlfriend, he was ashamed. He could still see her expression, confronting a doped-up lunatic in a patient gown, surrounded by other crazies on medication. You didn't come back from that. What they had together was brief and beautiful. But it was over.

Uncle Nathan encouraged him to help Halsey, insisting his nephew needed something to keep him busy and to get over Jenny. Reluctantly, Adam agreed. It was time to move on.

In the beginning, the elder West had done his best to oversee his protégée's work, but being confined to a wheelchair made that difficult. Thanks to Liv, he was managing his diabetes. But losing his legs due to poor circulation prevented him from being of any practical use in the laboratory. Also, there was the macular-degeneration problem, which forced him to wear the strange glasses he'd invented. Without them, he was, for all intents and purposes, blind.

Nathan had granted his research assistant access to the notes from all his experiments and she was making good progress. Two weeks earlier, after adjusting the ingredients of the culture media and tweaking the voltage of the electrodes, she succeeded in reanimating a Syrian hamster's head. More excitingly, she managed to keep it alive for a week.

At the time, Adam was working in the lab and witnessed the animal regaining consciousness. At first, he was thrilled and imagined reviving accident victims. But something disturbing happened on the last day of the experiment. The poor creature looked at Halsey with its tiny black eyes and shrieking in terror, gave up the ghost a second time. She tried saving the head, but it was no use. Undaunted, she started over with a new test subject.

Was it possible she would make the leap to humans eventually? He assumed with his contacts in the science community, Uncle Nathan could easily acquire a corpse for Halsey to experiment on. Though gruesome, he thought of all the good she could accomplish, restoring the dead to their grieving families, for example. But somewhere, Liv's voice hammered at him. *The dead should stay dead.*

Adam squinted at his watch. Two-thirty. His windows

were open and a cool breeze moved the white voiles like restless spirits. Yawning, he wandered over and peered out. It was a moonless night, and the only light came from outside the barn. He knew the girl was in there working. She was a night owl who liked taking long naps in the afternoon. After dinner, she would return to the lab, where she would remain until early morning.

Feeling undervalued, Adam cleaned animal cages, kept a detailed supply inventory and typed up the girl's illegible handwritten notes. In the evenings, he would visit his uncle or the nurse. Other times, he practised his German or read the books he'd borrowed from the library.

The barn door opened and Halsey staggered out in her laboratory coat. Though she was far away, he could see her bent over with her hands on her thighs, breathing hard. He dressed and, cutting through the garden, ran to the barn. As he approached, she threw her arms around his neck and held on.

'What happened?' he said.

Pulling away, she looked at him, her eyes glistening. Grabbing his face, she kissed him and taking his hand, brought him inside.

Though the building's exterior resembled the kind of barn you could find anywhere in upstate New York, the interior was a modern laboratory. Bright incandescent pendant lamps hung from the high ceiling. The floor was polyurethane-coated concrete. There were long white tables containing microscopes, centrifuges and other electronic equipment. In the centre, there was a six-foot Plexiglas cylinder that, up until now, had been empty. Now there was a high table inside with wires and tubes running down. On its surface was a man's head in an open titanium enclosure, its eyes open.

It was *alive.*

Adam's knees began to buckle as Halsey led him closer. He thought he might still be dreaming. She must have known what he was thinking and squeezed his hand.

'This isn't a dream,' she said.

'But how...'

The head looked him over and, giving the girl a cunning smirk, spoke into the slender microphone in front of him. 'Hello, Adam,' he said.

The voice was thin and hypnotic over the speakers that hung from the ceiling, even though it sounded as if it were inside his own head.

As Adam teetered back, Halsey caught him and linked her arm through his. Delirious, he turned to the abomination and said, 'Excuse us,' then marched her out of the building.

Outside, he took a laboured breath and gaped at her. 'Are you out of your mind?'

She played with his earlobe. 'You're cute when you're mad.'

'What were you thinking? Hey, stop that.'

Contrite, she withdrew her hand. 'I thought you'd be proud of me.'

'I am proud. But this... This is way beyond what I—'

'What did you think we were doing here? This is what your uncle and I have been working toward. I know it's a shock. To be honest, I didn't expect it to work after what happened with the lab animals. But it did. I brought a dead man to life!'

'It wasn't a dream — it was you who screamed earlier.'

'I was scared. He opened his eyes and when he looked at me, I guess I wigged out.'

He could see how sincere she was. 'How did you acquire a body?'

'Nathan arranged it.'

Whilst she continued her story, he thought about his first night seeing the German pushing something corpse-like into the barn.

'I severed the head and kept it on ice,' she said. 'Not literally. I've got a cryogenic refrigerator. Earlier, I bathed the specimen in my solution for an hour, then I hooked up the electrodes to kick-start brain activity.'

'Who's the test subject?'

Her eyes wide, she closed the barn door as if her creation might be listening. 'You have to swear never to say his name. I mean it – promise me.'

'Okay, I won't.'

'Karl Hiller.'

'Whoa, the serial killer? *That* Karl Hiller?'

'Lower your voice. Your uncle paid the warden at Sing Sing a lot of money to ensure the body would be turned over to Günter after the execution.'

'What did you do with the rest of him?'

'Burned it in the cremator.'

'This is hard for me. Why would Uncle Nathan think a murderer would make a good test subject?'

'Because he has an IQ of 190. And in case you haven't noticed, there aren't a lot of other dead geniuses lying around.'

'I need a drink,' he said.

They had to be quiet so as not to wake the house. In the kitchen, Adam opened all the cupboards until he found a green liqueur bottle with a red label that read JÄGERMEISTER. He took down two shot glasses and was about to pour when Halsey stopped him. She opened the refrigerator and grabbed two bottles of Bitburger Simonbräu Pilsner, whose slogan was *Bitte ein Bit!* After filling two beer mugs, she poured a shot of the digestif into each and handed him one.

'Prost,' she said.

He thought he detected notes of liquorice, a flavour he was not fond of. But somehow, combined with the pilsner, the overall effect was pleasing and he finished his drink.

She smacked her lips. 'I was going to say it's an acquired taste, but it looks like you've mastered it.'

'Let's have another one.'

'Hey, I'm curious. What's the wildest scientific concept you've ever heard?'

He narrowed his eyes. 'You mean besides a talking head? Parallel universes.'

'You don't think they exist?'

'I once attended a fascinating presentation on time travel. The idea was that you cannot go backwards in your present reality.'

'You're talking about the grandfather principle.'

'But you know, I wish I could. I'd like very much to see my parents again – my real parents and not some copy.'

'I know what you mean. I wouldn't mind going back a few months...'

After their third drink, Halsey was in the mood to play. Her eyes pools of unscientific desire, she ran her finger down Adam's nose. This time, he didn't try to stop her. Then she kissed him.

'I've wanted you since that first day,' she said.

Aroused, he returned the kiss. 'Um...'

'Let's go upstairs... Unless you'd like to try it in the barn. Maybe our test subject could watch.'

He grabbed her hands. 'You can't be—'

'I was kidding.' She stroked his face. 'Buck up, soldier. Time to report for duty.'

They bounded upstairs to her bedroom, which was lighter and more feminine than his. In no time, they were in bed.

'Wait. I don't have a...' He was very drunk. 'A...you know.'

Rolling over, she opened the nightstand drawer and pulled out a small cardboard box. Opening it, she removed something wrapped in cellophane.

'Put this on,' she said. 'I have lots more.'

CHAPTER 33

Ain't Misbehavin'

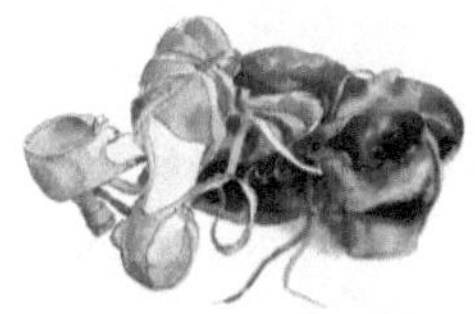

Adam awoke in Halsey's bed with a splitting headache and a parched mouth. *Shit. I did it again.* What was the difference, anyway? Jenny would never marry him. He and the blonde girl had gone at it most of the night, and the last thing he remembered was falling asleep near dawn. *What a louse.*

He reached for his watch, but it was in his bedroom. Sitting up, he looked around. The sun was bright through the curtains. Halsey must have gone downstairs for breakfast.

Throwing on his clothes, he cracked the door. Judging it safe, he slipped out and sneaked into his room, where he found Elsa tidying his bed. Sheepishly, he waited for her to finish. She crossed to the door and walked past without looking at him.

'Das hat nicht lange gedauert,'[1] she said.

After his shower, he trotted downstairs, hoping there was coffee. Voices drifted from the dining room. He found Halsey conversing with a man he didn't recognise.

The stranger had slick dark hair and a pencil moustache. His cardigan was brown with plain sleeves and a chequered front and back. A straw snap-brim hat hung from the back of his chair. Liv sat alone at the end of the table, drinking coffee and reading the Yiddish weekly *Di Tzeitung*, which Adam remembered seeing on the newsstands.

'Oh, hi,' the girl said.

Instead of her usual work clothes, she wore a yellow and blue summer dress. Her hair was tied with a matching blue ribbon. The transformation was astonishing.

'Adam, I'd like you to meet my boyfriend.'

The stranger stood and extended his hand. 'Fox Hickenlooper. Halsey's told me all about you.'

Adam blinked at him and looked at the girl, who gave him a demure smile. He worried this bloke would find out he'd shagged his girlfriend. Under that tasteless cardigan, he could tell the boyfriend was in good shape and prayed he didn't have a temper.

'Nice to meet you,' he said. 'Halsey never mentioned you before.'

'I'm not surprised. She tends to get caught up in her work. Sometimes, she forgets I exist, ha ha.' Then to the girl, 'Isn't that right, Schmoopie?'

He said the word like an accusation. Adam could feel the tension. He wondered how long Fox would be around and hoped he was only passing through. Then, a disturbing thought. What if she introduced him to Karl Hiller?

This guy didn't strike Adam as the scientific sort. He might spread the news about the experiment all over town. Liv poured a cup of coffee and handing it to him, left the room. He thought he heard her say, 'This is what comes from shtupping where you shouldn't.' Oddly, Fox didn't react.

Adam drained his cup. 'I have to check on the lab animals.'

A nervous minute passed and Halsey got up. 'One of the cages has a dodgy door. I should warn him.'

The boyfriend stood. He was short. 'Do you want me to go with you?'

'No! I mean, that's okay. Besides, Nathan, Adam and I are the only ones allowed in the laboratory.'

'Right. Uncle Nathan.' He picked up the Yiddish paper and perused it. 'Guess I'll hang out here, then.'

She bolted through the French doors, across the garden and out the gate. At the barn, she found Adam loitering outside like a lost child.

'I'm scared to go in there,' he said.

'It's fine. I gave him a sedative earlier. He'll sleep for hours.'

'Are you sure?'

She swung open the door and they entered. Looking at the Plexiglas cylinder, he found the test subject asleep and wondered if a severed head dreamt. Relieved, he took her hands in his.

'I know what you're thinking,' she said. 'There's no way I'm letting Fox meet Karl Hiller.'

'That's not what I was thinking. Why did you and I have all that amazing sex—'

'You thought it was amazing?' She walked her fingers up his arm.

'And the whole time you had a boyfriend.'

'Because I found you attractive. Anyways, it's not like he and I are exclusive. I'm sure he sees lots of other girls. Why wouldn't he?'

'And you're okay with that?'

'He is a man and I work all the time.'

He scratched his ear. 'I suppose it makes sense.'

She grabbed a stool and, patting the one next to her, sat at a laboratory table. 'If this is going to be a problem, maybe we should...'

'You mean he's staying?'

'Not here. He found a room in town.'

'What does he do, anyway?'

'He sells encyclopaedias.'

'Which is how he meets all those women.'

'Horny housewives, most likely. It's a living.'

'Are you planning to marry him?'

'Why? Are you jealous?' She got the giggles and holding up one hand, took a moment to compose herself.

'I don't see how that's funny,' he said.

'Look, just because a girl likes having sex doesn't mean she wants to get hitched. Can you imagine me married? To a travelling salesman no less?'

'I guess not. So, this is like a, a...'

'It's temporary – in the moment.' She sighed. 'We get along for the most part. He hasn't hit me yet, and he isn't bad in bed.' Seeing him blush, she stroked his arm and kissed him. 'Aw. If there was a contest, you'd win hands-down.'

'Thanks, I guess.'

'Oh, Adam, don't be like that. Wait, you didn't think you and I would ever—'

'What? No. It's just that I'm not used to, um...'

She arched her eyebrows. 'Fast girls? Things are changing. We're in a new decade. Women are taking charge. And guess what? We like it.'

He thought of Irenka. 'You're right, I'm a square.'

'You're a *man*.' She kissed him again and grabbed her laboratory coat. 'What do you say we get to work?'

'Okay. Thanks for putting up with my naivete.'

She gave his bottom a squeeze. 'Thanks for showing me a great time.'

He glanced at the head and, finding Karl Hiller eyeing them, tugged on her sleeve.

'Someone's awake,' he said.

Outside, Fox spied on the couple through a crack. They were talking in front of a tall, transparent cylinder. What-ever was inside must be what Halsey didn't want him to see. He felt a tickling in his brain but ignored it. Then, a noise startled him.

The German caretaker plucked something from a nearby tree – a red squirrel. The encyclopaedia salesman thought perhaps the animal was unwell. He heard it squeal as it struggled to get away. Without any visible emotion, Günter broke its neck and went off, swinging the body by the tail.

'Okay, that was weird,' Fox said.

---

1. 'That didn't take long.'

CHAPTER 34

My Little Brown Book

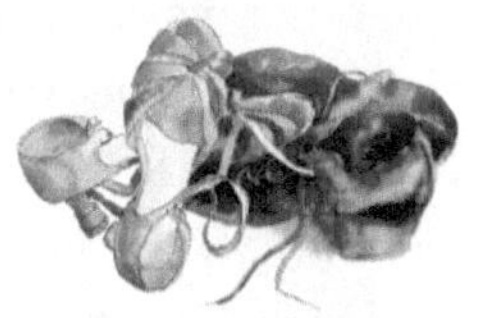

The whining of the electric motor signalled Dr Nathan West's arrival. Though in pain, he couldn't put this off any longer. Who knew how long the test subject would survive? Initially, he was excited when Halsey gave him the news but he was also afraid. As he propelled himself into the barn, she shut the door and followed.

He continued towards the Eye of Sauron, the research assistant's pet name for the severed head. A fan of The Lord of the Rings trilogy, she thought the moniker appropriate since the test subject refused to sleep for very long despite the pentobarbital she injected into the IV set. Standing beside Adam, she squeezed his fingers. The severed head eyed the scientist as he parked in front of the cylinder.

'Hello, Dr West,' Karl Hiller said. 'Say, I like your glasses.'

Nathan leant forward, his mechanical spectacles whirring. He turned to his research assistant. 'How long after attaining consciousness did he speak?'

'Almost immediately. Then he tried singing.'

The mass murderer blinked. 'I do likes me a good tune. And stop treating me as if I'm not in the room, or I'll be forced to—'

'Silence!' The scientist faced him, his glasses telescoping. 'You don't have a body, remember?'

'True. But there are other ways. Wait and see.'

There was a crash behind them. Turning round, Halsey noticed a microscope lying on the floor on its side.

Nathan addressed her. 'Does he—' Then to the test subject, 'My apologies. Do you know who you are?'

'I know who I used to be. Karl Emil Hiller. Born October 31, 1920, in Shelbyville, Indiana. I turn forty this year and am looking forward to my spiritual crisis. How about a nice game of chess?'

'Later, perhaps. Do you have any questions for me?'

'Such as...'

'How you came to be here.'

'I assume I arrived in a car. I'm curious, though. If the police had stopped you, how would you explain a dead body? By the way, are you aware Halsey and your nephew are having sex? I don't blame him. With a little persuasion, I could make her my type.'

Adam blanched. How could he know that? Unless... Had the girl told him? He glanced at her and saw her perplexed expression.

'I know how to put two and two together,' Karl Hiller said.

The scientist gave his nephew a sidelong glance. 'I am aware you have a sharp mind.'

'I prefer the word *intuitive*. It's an ability I've honed over the years. In fact, it's what helped me select my victims. I always seemed to know what they were thinking. Not that they were intelligent or anything. With their pencil skirts and permed hair and loutish boyfriends or husbands. They were all members of the same club but never got around to attending the meetings.

'Thoreau was wrong. It's not men who lead lives of quiet desperation. We're too thick-headed. Cook us a good meal and throw in a little grab-ass once in a while and we're jake. No, it's the women, frustrated and unsatisfied and unable to tell anyone.

'All of them had a burning desire to get out of that perfect little town, with its good schools and churches and holiday parades. I became their saviour, in a way. Intuition is a gift, Doctor. Perhaps if Oedipus had been a little more on the ball, he wouldn't have shacked up with his mother.'

'You seem upset,' Nathan said.

'I fried in the electric chair. Fun fact – they use sea sponges containing a nine per cent saline solution. There's a brass screen on the inside of the headpiece secured by a nut, which is attached to a high voltage wire. Somehow the nut came loose and Old Sparky couldn't do its job. Talk about your cliffhangers.

'Eventually, they corrected the problem and it was showtime. Twenty-two hundred volts for eight seconds. Followed by one thousand volts for twenty-two seconds. Then another twenty-two hundred volts for eight seconds. I must say, I like the symmetry. The experience was electrifying – *of course, I'm upset!*'

Unperturbed, the scientist continued. 'Tell me, do you experience phantom limb pain?'

'Pain? No. But I do feel as if my body is out there somewhere doing God's work.'

'Let's talk about when it began.'

'Happy to. I was twelve. There was this girl, Tammy Zink. She was a year older and lived down the street. I hadn't mastered my intuition yet, but I wanted to' – he leered at Halsey, making her blush – 'fool around with her because I'd heard she'd necked with other boys in certain back alleys and rest stops. I figured why not me?

'We'd spoken one or two times at school. She didn't like me much. You see, my mother left when I was two and, I guess, boys raised by a father on disability were a little suspect. Still, I had hopes and made a plan.

'She liked hanging out in Morrison Park after school with her girlfriends. I followed them several times and memorised their routine. They would gather near the band shell and smoke. Around five, the others would leave.

'Tammy always stayed behind so she could enjoy one more ciggy. Poor girl, I think she was addicted. On the day in question, I waited until she was alone and asked if I could have one. We talked awhile and I made a rather clumsy move. She didn't like it and slapped me. Then she called me a weirdo and tried to leave. So I hit her.

'I would've killed the bitch, but her older brother showed up. Something happened at home and he came to get her. I hadn't counted on him. When he saw his sister on the ground bawling and me standing over her, he beat me until I couldn't walk. Then I lost consciousness.

'They put me in the hospital. A week later, they sent me to a reform school in Plainfield. I spent two years there nursing my wounds. After I got out, I no longer cared about Tammy Zink.

'My plan was ill-conceived. So, instead of trying again, I focused on perfecting my craft. I dropped out of school, got a job on a farm and supported my dad until the day he died. And I read everything. Later, after the Japs bombed Pearl Harbour, I enlisted in the army. Best decision I ever made. The opportunities for killing were endless.

'My favourite weapon wasn't a rifle or a grenade – it was my bayonet because I could get close to my enemy. There was nothing to do after I got out and I needed a distraction. So I got my GED, enrolled in college on the GI Bill and earned a degree in psychology. I particularly enjoyed the *criminal* psychology classes.'

'Is that what led you to murder people?' Nathan said.

'Don't blame our great institutions, Doctor. Killing's in my blood.'

'Isn't it true you wrote a novel as told through the eyes of a dead housewife?'

'Someone's done their research. It's set in Terre Haute – Sin City. It's where I was living at the time. The real victim was a prostitute who went by the moniker Miss Jones. She thought it would make her sound classy. But a hooker doesn't make for a sympathetic character, so I changed her to a sweet, doting housewife. Miss Jones was my first kill since the war. Put up quite a fight too.'

The scientist didn't react. 'Later, you settled in Yonkers but committed all those other murders in New Rochelle. Why?'

'They almost caught me in Terre Haute and I learned a valuable lesson. You don't get your meat where you buy your bread.'

'Are you surprised we revived you?'

'Not really. I've always considered myself to be lucky.'

Nathan addressed his assistants. 'I'd like to speak to him alone.'

Taking Halsey's arm, Adam walked her out. Halfway to the door, Karl Hiller began singing 'We'll Be Together Again' in a reedy voice. They ignored him. Outside, the girl closed the barn door. Neither said anything.

Then, Adam vomited in the boxwoods.

CHAPTER 35

You Do Something To Me

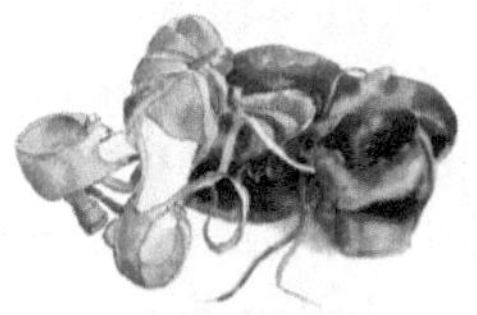

It was quiet inside. The housekeeper, who Fox suspected disliked him, had gone to the shops. He knew Halsey was napping and neither Adam nor the crippled uncle were around. In the kitchen, he opened one cupboard after the next until he found a large keyring hanging on a hook.

He used the back door to cut through the garden. The air smelt good out here and he thought he heard a meadowlark. He stopped and listened and, remembering what he saw earlier, tried to work out what kind of person would kill an innocent squirrel.

Hoping he wouldn't run into the deranged caretaker, Fox continued past the parked pickup to the barn. There, he tried each key. Cursing, he kept at it. He inserted the penultimate key and turned it. To his surprise, the heavy padlock clicked open. Checking all round, he went inside and closed the door.

The lights were off and the vast interior was in shadow. Ahead, he saw the mysterious cylinder's outline. He waited for his eyes to adjust and walked forward. The lights came on, startling him. He turned round, expecting to see his girlfriend, but he was alone. Or so he thought. He faced the cylinder again and discovered a human head watching him.

'What in the hell?'

His eyes darted from side to side and he had an irresistible urge to run. He was about to leg it when the test subject addressed him.

'My eyes aren't what they used to be,' Karl Hiller said. 'Why don't you come a little closer?'

His legs like rubber, the encyclopaedia salesman couldn't resist and found himself moving inexorably forwards until he was next to the enclosure. The severed head looked as if it might bow to him in greeting.

'What are you?' the intruder said.

'I might ask you the same thing.'

'I'm Halsey's boyfriend, Fox.' Why had he told the monster the truth?

'Yes, of course. How does it feel? Indossare le corna?'

'What did you say?'

'You're wearing the horns. I can't say I blame the girl. She's a real looker, if you get my drift. And Adam is handsome – and tall. Tell me, whatever possessed you to grow a moustache? You remind me of a carny I used to know.'

'You better shut your mouth.'

'Wish I could remember his name. It'll come to me.'

'I'm warning you!'

'Mm, sensitive too. Why are you here? Did you think you'd find the lovers screwing under a lab table? Hoping to get in on the action? You look like the type.'

'I said cut it out.'

Fox couldn't believe he was having this conversation. Nevertheless, he felt compelled to defend himself. His interrogator didn't look like he cared either way and began whistling a wartime tune.

'Halsey refused to let me in here,' the encyclopaedia salesman said. 'I wanted to see what she's working on.'

'Why, she's working on me.'

A glass beaker flew off the table, hurtling itself at the visitor's skull. He ducked in time and watched it shatter against a wall.

'Jesus!'

'He has nothing to do with it, I'm afraid. There's more where that came from. I think you'd better leave.'

'Not until I know what's going on.'

'What's going on, my unwashed friend, is I'm coming into my own. I was worried I wouldn't be able to do anything without a body. Turns out there are advantages. For example, there's no ass that needs wiping. But as I told the charming Dr West, Nature has provided other ways for me to be effective.

'It's not so bad in here, either. They give me all the glucose-rich blood I want and getting ready in the morning is a breeze. Your girlfriend doesn't brush my teeth, though. I've been meaning to speak to her. Think you could put in a word?'

Though Fox's knees wobbled with fright, he had to know more. 'Does she know you have these powers?'

'Not sure. It's possible she suspects. But then, she's focused on the big picture – helping mankind. To what end I couldn't say.'

'And, um, what are *you* focused on?'

With hooded eyes, Karl Hiller gave him a threatening look. 'That's for me to know and you to find out. Go away now, you bore me.'

Tucking his hands behind him, Fox circled the cylinder,

attempting to uncover the trick. He once saw a magician perform a 'Talking Head' illusion. His assistant's noggin sat on a table, having a pleasant conversation with her master. Below, her body was nowhere to be seen. They accomplished it using mirrors.

There was no such set-up here. All he found were lots of metal drums containing ethanol, acetone, hexane and other dangerous chemicals. Satisfied the cylinder wasn't rigged, he returned to face the test subject.

'I don't like you,' Fox said. 'And I don't believe Halsey is safe.'

'Safe? That's a good one. The only time anyone is safe is six feet under being devoured by worms. No one can harm you. Perhaps some might even envy you. Think of it. No need for a house or food or intimacy. You just lie there. They don't say "rest in peace" for nothing.'

'What do you know about it?'

'Oh, I know plenty. So do those twenty-two women I murdered. They're all resting in peace now – pieces, if we're being technical.'

'Wait. You're not—'

'Karl Hiller at your service.'

'Oh, God!'

'Again, no. Just good ol' Karl.'

Panicked, Fox turned to leave. 'I need to warn people.'

'That's not a good idea.'

'Shut up!'

'Temper...'

Fox saw the exit in front of him but couldn't move somehow. Against his will, he turned round and was again staring at the severed head.

'Tell you what,' Karl Hiller said. 'Here's a little trick I learned last night.'

The encyclopaedia salesman felt strange, as if a spider monkey's hand had somehow got inside his brain and now attempted to claw its way out. As the pain came, he fell to his knees, blood leaking from his nostrils.

'Stop it!'

'I can't have you blabbing all over town like a fishwife.'

'You're insane!' The simian's hand began ripping out hunks of grey matter.

'Still going to tell someone?'

'No, I swear! I, I won't say anything! For the love of God, *stop*!'

'All right then. Remember. You made a sacred promise.'

Exhausted, Fox gripped the corner of a table. Pulling himself up, he staggered towards the door. Before he could get out, Halsey walked in and grabbed him by the shoulders.

'What have you done?' she said.

CHAPTER 36

Alone Together

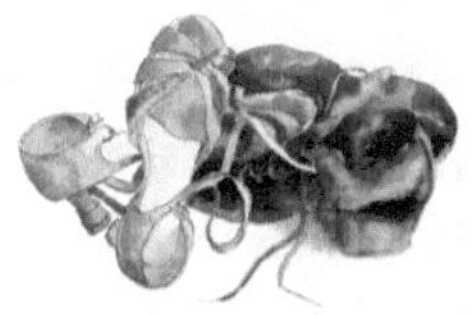

Adam gazed into Liv Adler's warm eyes, attempting to recover from the creeping nightmare that was Karl Hiller. One of the books he'd borrowed was Nietzsche's *Jenseits von Gut und Böse*[1] because he was eager to read German. Using a dictionary, he laboriously worked his way through and came across what was arguably the work's most renowned passage.

'Wer mit Ungeheuern kämpft, mag zusehn, dass er nicht dabei zum Ungeheuer wird. Und wenn du lange in einen Abgrund blickst, blickt der Abgrund auch in dich hinein.'[2]

He was familiar with the English translation but had never grasped what it meant until now. Gazing at Karl Hiller was like staring into the mouth of hell. He wanted to grab the nearest spade, beat the fiendish head to a pulp and burn the remains. Regrettably, it wasn't his property to destroy.

'I need to get out of here,' he said.

She refilled his coffee cup. 'Your uncle told me. A talking head. What will they think of next?'

'It's not funny.'

'So who's laughing? Nathan thought having you here would be good for your health. But seeing what the monster has done to you... He's concerned, bubbe. It's time to leave. How about you go see that girl of yours, Jenny?'

'That's finished. The last time we were together, she—'

'What's the big deal? So she found you in the crazy house. Adam...' She pinched his cheek. '*I* know you're not meshugge. *You* know you're not meshugge. And I'll bet she does too.'

'I think I might be, though. Sometimes, I see—'

'Feh! Such words. You're a nervous wreck and why not? That blonde shiksa did something she shouldn't.' Liv lowered her voice. 'And your uncle, who should know better, encouraged her.'

'He's a murderer.'

'Nathan?'

'The test subject.'

She slapped her forehead. 'Oy gevalt! Good thing it doesn't have any hands. Tell me, does it talk? Or is this some kind of ventriloquist shtik?'

'He talks. Do you think my uncle would be hurt if I left?'

'Your health comes first. You can always hang yourself later.'

'I'm worried about Halsey. What happens if the test subject becomes too much for her?'

'She'll be fine. She has her boyfriend to protect her.'

'Fox? I don't trust him.'

'Ha, me neither. Fox in the henhouse. He looks like a car salesman. With his skinny moustache and those beady eyes. A real mamzer. But that's her problem.'

He finished his coffee and stood. 'I'm glad I spoke to you, Liv.'

'Me too. Ad me'ah ve'esrim shanah.'

'What does it mean?'

'You should live to be a hundred and twenty,' she said. 'Relax, it's not a curse.'

There was a telephone on a side table near the dining room. Adam rang Engel to get his opinion. The solicitor's secretary answered, and after he gave her his name, she put him through straight away.

'It's nice to hear your voice, Adam. How are things in Hyde Park?'

'Not good.'

He glanced around to ensure no one was listening and noticed Halsey in the garden with Fox. They were in the midst of a row. He grabbed her by the wrists and pulled her towards him. When she protested, he let her go but continued shouting. The git was apoplectic.

'Hello?' Engel said.

'Sorry, I was distracted. I want to go home.'

'Has something happened?'

'I miss the city.'

'Jenny Donovan called me.'

'What? When?'

'A few days ago. She wants to pay you a visit up there.'

'That's a bad idea. She can't come here, understand?' He felt a sharp pain in his chest. 'How is she doing?'

'We met for lunch. She seems blue. I suppose losing her father has a lot to do with it. You heard they caught the guy?'

'I read about it in the paper.'

Halsey's voice carried across the garden. Adam turned round and found her marching towards the dining room. The gate was open and her boyfriend was nowhere to be seen.

'I advised you before about Jenny,' the solicitor said. 'And I still believe—'

'I have to call you back.'

The girl came in just as Adam rang off. She'd been crying. There was an awkward silence and as he walked towards her, she slipped into his arms and wept.

'He's a pig,' she said.

A cool afternoon breeze billowed the voiles. Somewhere, a whippoorwill called. They lay in her bed, her head on his chest rising and falling. He hadn't planned on having sex with her. Intending to leave her at her door, he helped her upstairs. But when he opened it for her, she pulled him inside.

It was as if she'd planned it. But why go to all that trouble? She could have admitted what she wanted. He thought of Millicent Taylor and her trickster dream. She'd told him he would never understand women, and she was right. Halsey was proof. It was a good job he'd left Jenny behind. He was a pathetic weakling who didn't deserve her.

'Why were you two fighting?' he said.

'I can't tell you.'

'I wish you would. Maybe I can help.'

'You're sweet.'

She kissed him and made herself small next to him. He felt her warm breasts and stomach against his side and hated himself for becoming aroused. Taking notice, she slid her hand down under the sheet and gave him a gentle squeeze. A moment later, she straddled him and they made love again, this time to the distant thunder signalling a summer storm. Afterwards, she rolled off and lay on her back.

Staring at the white canopy, she pointed at something. 'I think I see a house spider.'

'Let's not kill it.'

'Why would I? I'm not a monster.'

He brushed her cheek. 'What are you thinking about?'

She turned on her side and snuggled him, finding the little pocket she'd occupied earlier. He stroked her hair and kissed her fingertips.

'I wish I'd met you first,' she said. 'Things might be different.'

————————————————

1. *Beyond Good and Evil*
2. 'He who fights with monsters should be careful not to become a monster. And if you gaze long enough into an abyss, the abyss will also gaze into you.'

Why Was I Born?

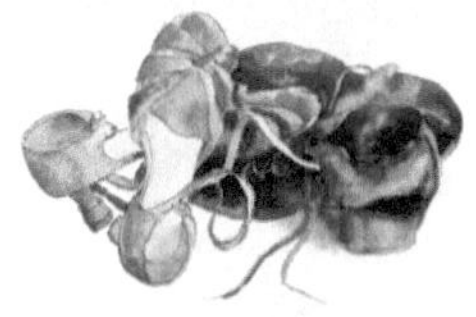

Fox Hickenlooper didn't consider himself lucky, unlike the garrulous mass murderer Karl Hiller. With the exception of his current position, he'd been sacked from every job he ever had because of his quick temper. Now he travelled door to door around the Tri-state area, hawking complete sets of *Encyclopaedia Britannica*.

Most people could only afford the modest clothbound edition, even though his firm offered an instalment plan. Sometimes, he might sell leather-bound sets and the odd deluxe or premium edition in wealthier enclaves, such as Scarsdale and Greenwich.

The work suited him because he could be alone instead of trapped in a sweltering building amidst tedious, gap-toothed office clerks with button-down collars and pen pockets. They were insufferable, with their inane nattering and endless invitations to disreputable bars. He liked being on the road. Driving long distances allowed him to daydream about exotic, faraway places like Key West.

Fox never knew his father, which might have contributed to the constant undercurrent of rage he bore, like a cross made of granite. A psychiatrist once told him he suffered from abandonment-related anxiety. But what good was that? Nothing he could do would change the past. The only way was forward.

Troubled by what happened in the barn, he lit a cigarette and looked out the window of his modest room. It was pouring rain. Across the street, a bar stood on the corner and next to it, a drugstore with a soda fountain. Beyond that, there was a dress shop with svelte mannequins in bright colours. He didn't mind boarding houses except for the communal meals. Often, he would go out to dinner rather than put up with uninteresting people prattling on about baseball or film stars he'd never heard of.

According to his mother, Vicky Larue, Fox was the illegitimate son of her and Jon West. She was born Effie Hickenlooper in Flatbush and had made her living as a burlesque dancer in the late twenties and early thirties. His father met her at his friend's stag party in Long Island, where she performed a cunningly effective striptease number. That was in 1932. They had an affair, and the following year, she gave birth to a boy, a moment she would always treasure.

She claimed Jon told his new wife the truth, and she forgave him. But after their son Adam – Fox's half-brother – was born, Miriam had a change of heart, insisting her husband cut off all contact with the woman and her illegitimate child, who was two.

Instead of supporting them, Jon gave Vicky a one-time cash payment and a residence in SoHo, which was purchased in her name. Should she die before him, however, he would regain ownership. True to his word, Jon never saw the former entertainer or her son again.

Fox never forgot the day his mother succumbed to

cervical cancer. It was in the summer of 1945 before V-J Day. The boy was eleven. She hated hospitals and insisted on spending her final days at home. On her deathbed, she gave her son a letter written by Jon West in November 1933 after her baby was born. In it, he promised to look after mother and son but stopped short of acknowledging the boy as his biological child.

Vicky also gave her son a photograph of the three of them at Coney Island. And she shared a name and made him memorise it – Shlomo Engel. As the West family's solicitor, he knew everything, she said. After the funeral, the boy was sent to an orphanage, where for years he remained bitter over his father's refusal to acknowledge him.

Possession of the SoHo residence – Fox's childhood home – had reverted to Jon West after Vicky's death. So at eighteen, the young man began living on his own in the first of many boarding houses. After attending community college for two years, he built up the courage to confront his father and demand his inheritance. But his timing was awful, and the scientist was killed in the explosion at Bland before they could meet.

As a result, Fox ran riot in the accounting office he worked at and was sent to Bellevue Hospital for observation. There, he met Dr Eldon Jackle. The chief psychiatrist listened to his story and without delay, made a surprisingly accurate diagnosis. The patient suffered from anaclitic depression. After seventy-two hours, Dr Jackle released him, advising the young man to take up a hobby – bowling, perhaps.

Fox never forgot the name his mother had given him and visited Shlomo Engel at his offices. The solicitor knew all about the situation and had a feeling Vicky Larue's son would show up one day. In case he was thinking about a paternity suit, Engel informed him there was no actual proof Jon West was his flesh and blood. But in a gesture of goodwill, the wily lawyer offered to write him a cheque for ten thousand dollars provided he signed a settlement agreement that stated in exchange for the money, he would make no further claim on the estate. The young man told Engel he could rot in hell.

In the 1950s, jobs were plentiful and Fox drifted from one company to the next. Each time, something trivial would set him off and he'd get the sack. One morning, he wandered Manhattan, contemplating his next move. He found himself outside a bar called Shanty's. With nothing else to do, he decided to get drunk on the cheap. There were few customers – one, a boorish Englishman telling some hapless rube about something or other that happened in 1934, the year of the Dust Bowl.

Irritated, he ordered a boilermaker and searched for a booth. A man in a seersucker suit sat alone, nursing a whisky. A large leather catalogue case stood on the floor next to him. On the side, stamped in gold lettering, were the words ENCYCLOPEDIA BRITANNICA. The stranger caught the young man eyeing his property and waved him over.

'Try lifting it,' he said.

Fox didn't know what to make of the loony and looked around for another booth.

'It won't bite, you know.'

Curious, he set down his drinks and picked up the case. Though heavy, he thought it manageable and waited for an explanation.

'Look at that,' the stranger said and slid over his business card. 'I'll bet you'd make a good salesman.'

A week later, Fox was hawking encyclopaedias door to door. He purchased a used car with the advance the company had given him. Then he bought some new clothes and grew a moustache. Months later, whilst passing through Millbrook, he met Halsey Dean, who was home from university. Soon after, they began an affair.

Meanwhile, he researched the West family extensively, looking for Adam, who no longer lived in Long Island. Fox wanted to show him the letter and demand the money he believed the West family owed him. But the opportunity never presented itself.

The next time he visited Millbrook, his girlfriend informed him she was moving to Hyde Park to work for Nathan West. He knew who the scientist was and decided to pay him a visit. Upon arriving at the estate, he was delighted to find the West heir there too.

Halsey reminded him their relationship was casual. She had no difficulty telling him she and Adam had had sex. Instead of acting jealous, he confirmed her understanding of their situation, which surprised her.

Fox had arrived in Hyde Park with a plan. After showing Dr West the letter and the photograph, he would appeal to the scientist's sense of decency. Though he'd told Engel to sod off, he later realised the solicitor was right. He could not claim an inheritance – legally.

Instead, he would ask Dr West, who was also his uncle, for one hundred thousand dollars. He was sure the scientist could afford it. In exchange, he would sign whatever papers were required. But that was before he discovered the secret in the barn. Now he devised a new, more lucrative plan – one that didn't require him to reveal his connection to the family, although his girlfriend knew the truth.

Fox was prepared to go to the newspapers. When he instructed Halsey to continue having sex with his half-brother to gain his trust, she refused to cooperate. He reminded her she could lose everything if the truth got out before she had a chance to publish her findings. Shattered, she agreed.

To emphasise the urgency, Fox wanted her to let it slip her boyfriend was violent and capable of harming her. Then Adam, seeing the girl and him in the garden earlier, fell into his scheme nicely. When the time was right, Fox would confront the Wests and demand five hundred thousand dollars or he would tell the world they were keeping a mass murderer's head alive in the barn. The devious encyclopaedia salesman was confident he would get his money.

The matron pounded on his door, informing him he had a phone call downstairs. Stubbing out the cigarette on the windowsill, he gazed at the photo of himself with Jon West and his mother.

'I'm gonna make you proud, Mommy,' he said.

CHAPTER 38

You'd Be So Nice To Come Home To

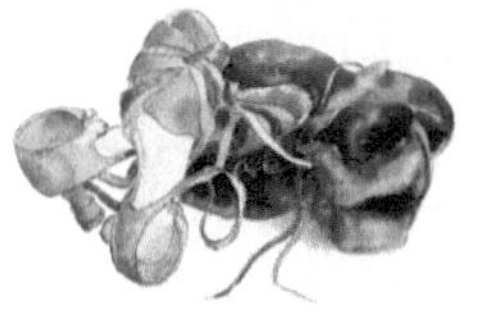

There was a time, in his third year of high school to be precise, when Roger Davies wanted to become a doctor. He came from a long line of lawyers, all quite successful. In the spring, he dated someone whose father was a well-respected orthopaedic surgeon. After meeting him, Roger imagined how refreshing it would be for a Davies to choose medicine over the law. But there was a complication.

Unlike his younger sister, who was fearless, ever since he injured his leg in a boating accident at thirteen, the very sight of blood made him feel unwell. After endless therapy sessions with prominent psychiatrists, which included hypnosis, he couldn't stave off the inevitable vasovagal syncope. Something as minor as a nosebleed would trigger it. So, his life path returned to the comfort of the law. He attended Harvard College for four years, then entered law school as his father and grandfather had done before him.

After passing the New York State bar exam, his dad set him up in his Manhattan law practice. Roger first met Jenny Donovan at a charity function whose cause he could not recall. Their mothers were volunteers and knew each other socially. He and the girl only spoke for a moment, but he found her enchanting. Though she was only seventeen, he considered seeing her again one day.

His social calendar was filled with endless lunches and dinners with eligible young women courtesy of his socialite mother. Before he knew it, months had gone by. Then one day, an invitation arrived in the post inviting him to Jenny's eighteenth birthday party. So far, none of the other women he met impressed him and he RSVP'd at once.

Roger's father liked spending Thursday afternoons at the Union Club on East Sixty-ninth Street. He'd been a member since the Great Depression and saw to it that his son was admitted as well. Though talking was allowed in the lounge, they kept to themselves, reading the papers and drinking whisky and soda.

Business acquaintances would stop by to chat about the stock market and such. Some had eligible daughters. At his wife's urging, the elder Davies used every opportunity to sing his son's praises, never forgetting to mention the young man was single. Later, Mrs Davies would follow up with a telephone call to the acquaintance's wife.

Thinking of the Donovan girl again, the young man put down his *Wall Street Journal*. At university, he'd had plenty of sex with other girls whose names escaped him. But lately, it was Jenny's face he would always see in the darkness of his rooms.

The incident at her birthday party nearly two years ago still plagued him. And though it had been humiliating, it wasn't the girl's fault. She had a lush for a mother. On his way home from Great Neck, he felt he had acted cowardly and considered ringing her the next day. But after telling his mother what happened, she gave him a stern warning not to get mixed up with the Donovans lest he risk his good name.

'In the end, your name is all you have,' she said. 'You come into the world with it and you leave with it. Remember, some stains don't wash out.'

When Roger read about Bruce Donovan's murder, he ignored his mother's fervent pleas and contacted Jenny to see if there was anything he could do. As expected, the girl was distraught and welcoming his offer, invited him to her house. Unwilling to risk another run-in with the crapulous Mrs D, he suggested they meet at a restaurant. The girl told him she was in no shape to be seen in public. And so, preparing himself with the idea he was doing this for Jenny, he agreed to stop by.

Her mother greeted him as if he were a stranger. Unlike the dreadful night she attacked him, she was sophisticated and charming. And more importantly, sober. He felt he was speaking to a different woman, one very much like his own mother. He ended up spending the entire afternoon with the Donovans. When it was time to leave, her daughter walked him to his car.

'I don't think your mom remembers me,' he said.

'Thanks for coming. This whole experience has been hard.'

When she squeezed his hand, he misconstrued the situation and tried kissing her. She backed away, and he was once again embarrassed. He was never at ease around women and other than sex, didn't understand what was expected of him. Like most men of his class, he was well groomed and always strove to be polite. Making a pass was wrong and he wondered what had got into him. To his great relief, she remained poised.

'I'm in love with someone,' she said.

'I figured. It's all right. Where is he, by the way?'

'Staying with a relative.'

'Well, I'd like to be your friend. You shouldn't have to go through this alone.'

'I'd love it if we could be friends. Thank you, Roger.'

She kissed his cheek and he drove off, confused about where he stood, relationship-wise. His mother had arranged for him to have dinner that evening with a banker's daughter at Tavern on the Green. Not being in the mood, he declined. She reminded him there was no guarantee things would improve with Jenny and insisted he keep his appointment. He agreed although he wasn't looking forward to another tedious dinner date with an ex-debutante.

'How's everything with the Donovan girl?' his dad asked at dinner one evening. 'It's a shame about her father.'

His parents knew Mrs D had stopped drinking alto-gether and didn't mind their son spending so much time in Long Island. Jenny's boyfriend, Adam, was still missing in action, and as the summer wore on, Roger hoped Jenny would realise she and her new friend had something genuine and would desire to act on it.

Once again, Mrs Davies advised her son, saying he should bide his time. The girl was only nineteen, after all — a diamond in the rough. She, like many women of her generation, could use some polishing. He told her his almost-girlfriend would be twenty soon. His father reminded his wife she was eighteen when they married.

She became defensive. 'Things were different then. Girls were much more sophisticated in our day.'

'Certainly, dear,' her husband said.

At the club, Roger sipped his drink and looked past his father at the others in the lounge. He knew his was a life of privilege. But unlike some of the other chaps he went to school with, he intended to take his responsibility seriously.

'Jenny and I are going to Birdland next week for her birthday,' he said.

'Isn't that where the police beat up that trumpet player last year?'

'Miles Davis. And it wasn't his fault. Because of his skin colour, they—'

'I'm not sure that's the sort of place for a young woman.'

'She'll be fine – and she likes jazz. Besides, it's all part of the master plan. I figure this guy Adam isn't serious about her. Otherwise, why would he stay away so long? She and I have been seeing a lot of each other. Once she understands how much I care, she'll give him the brush.'

'Interesting theory,' his father said. 'But you're assuming this Adam fellow doesn't care. What if he does but something else is preventing him from seeing her? A family commitment or a promise? You need to think about all the angles. Otherwise, you might end up making a fool of yourself. Don't forget what happened with the Babbage girl.'

Dorothy Babbage was Roger's one and only steady girlfriend at Harvard. She grew up in California and lived in San Marino, an affluent neighbourhood in Pasadena. Her father was also a lawyer. Dorothy read political science and was interested in politics. She smoked and drank like a man. Sometimes after a little too much vodka, she cursed like one too.

Women resented her and men adored her. She was free

and fun and Roger fell for her like a tonne of bricks. It was she who introduced him to sex but he mistook their mad, passionate nights for love.

In their junior year, against his mother's wishes, he asked her to marry him. Advising him to grow up, she ended the relationship. Devastated, he remained in bed for a week.

Now, Roger was ebullient. 'I have a good feeling about this.'

'You know best. Have you told your mother?'

The young lawyer finished his drink and signalled the steward for another one. His father returned to his paper whilst Roger opened a book he'd borrowed from the club's library, *Atlas Shrugged*.

'Thursday is the day I make Jenny mine,' he said, though his father wasn't listening.

CHAPTER 39
Twisted

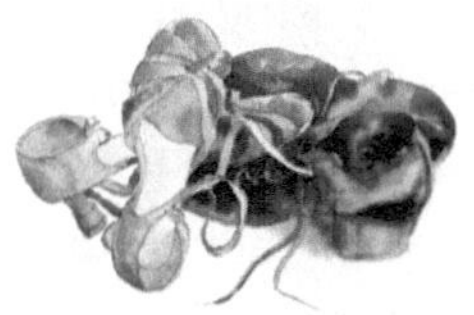

Mrs D never imagined colliding with a two-hundred-pound deer would cause so much destruction. As she came to, she managed to make out through the shattered windscreen the steam billowing from her battered Mercedes engine. One of the antlers had gone right through the glass, nearly spearing her in the process. The car had come to rest beyond the deer crossing.

Other vehicles drew up near a group of nattering bystanders. A bloke wearing workman's garb approached her driver's side door, enquiring whether he could be of any assistance. Scarcely hearing him, she shut her eyes.

She was awakened by two ambulance attendants lifting her from the wreckage. The bonnet was crumpled, the headlights were nothing but shards of glass and the bumper hung precariously from its frame. As they shifted her onto a stretcher, one remarked that the vehicle was most likely beyond repair. The grim sight of animal blood and fur coating the twisted grille pleased her as they hauled her into the waiting ambulance. Her eyes half closed, she managed a faint, chipped-tooth remark.

'I'm glad it's a total loss,' she said.

On the way to the hospital, Mrs D could only think of her daughter. She had taken a huge risk – thank heavens the accident wasn't fatal. Losing two parents in such quick succession would have crushed Jenny. There were Bruce's parents, of course, who also resided in Great Neck. Hers lived in Philadelphia and though they adored their grand-daughter, they rarely saw her.

The driver switched on the siren. As he sped along the highway, weaving between the other cars, the second atten-dant held the patient steady to avoid further injury to her spine. She was in acute pain and after she complained, he injected her with something that made her dreamy.

She never wanted to kill Calvin Lipinsky but the old chancer brought it on himself. Weeks had elapsed and she had got on with her life. Then out of the blue, he rang her. After settling with the hospital and the auto-parts suppliers and the bank, he was skint. Ten thousand dollars didn't stretch as far any more, he insisted. He demanded more money, claiming he was entitled to it for seeing to her abusive husband.

When she refused him, he tried another approach. This time, he attempted to use her love for her daughter against her. If he were to surrender to the authorities, they would see him in prison, where because of his dodgy heart, he would most likely die before they could execute him. She, on the other hand, was young and hale. With a murder conviction, she would live long enough to face the electric chair. What sort of life would Jenny have then?

Having considered the matter, Mrs D rang the mechanic and proposed they meet at Rocky Point in the middle of the state park. She told him she was prepared to pay him fifty thousand if he promised to never bother her again. He was delighted to accept. She cautioned him, however, about Detective Quinn. The policeman had decided to reopen the case, suspicious of the circumstances surrounding her husband's death. Afraid he would uncover the conspiracy, she gave Calvin strict instructions to park his car amongst the trees along Rocky Point Yaphank Road and wait for her by the roadside.

An imbecile of a man, the mechanic had no conception of the trouble awaiting him. All he could think about was the tax-free cash that would allow him to make a fresh start. And if that curtain twitcher of a detective was stirring the pot, he could always flee the country. So, he waited for Mrs D as instructed.

She stopped about a mile away to observe him. Occasionally, a vehicle or two would pass, making it impossible for her to proceed. At last, as the way cleared, she started up her engine and made a dash. The speedometer climbed ever higher as she raced towards her intended victim.

Frantically, he waved his hands to alert her to the danger but she didn't slow down. Glancing in both directions, he didn't have time to get out of harm's way. She caught him on his side, knocking him to the ground and shattering his right arm.

Applying her brakes, she stopped and checked her rear-view mirror. *Not dead yet!* After a swift U-turn, she accelerated again and flattened the life out of him. Then she continued out of the park, only easing up just before she reached a more populated area.

Mrs D pulled over and examined the car's bonnet, which was smeared with blood and gore. There was more traffic than she'd anticipated. What if she were stopped?

She needed to get rid of the evidence. Avoiding the main roads and their prowl cars, she sped eastward in search of a car wash. After a frustrating forty-five minutes, an unbelievable stroke of luck.

As she approached a deer crossing, an eight-point buck came into view, standing brazenly in the middle of the road. There were no other cars in the vicinity. Either the obstinate animal was half-asleep or blind. No time to think – she accelerated towards it. The impact was so great, she thought she'd hit a tree and was knocked unconscious.

The doctors told her she'd suffered a perforated liver from a broken rib and required immediate surgery. In addition, she had a concussion, a spine injury necessitating traction and a broken arm. Someone notified Jenny and when they wheeled the patient into the recovery room, her daughter was waiting for her. Roger Davies had offered to accompany the girl but she wanted to go by herself.

'I'm sorry,' Mrs D said, groggy from the anaesthesia.

Jenny took her mother's hand and kissed it. 'Why are you apologising?'

'I know how much you were looking forward to your date tonight.'

'It's not a date. Roger and I are friends, remember?'

'And now I've spoiled everything.'

'It doesn't matter. All I want is to look after you. You're the most important person in my life. Do you hear me, Mom? I need you to get better.'

Mrs D never loved her daughter more than at that moment.

CHAPTER 40

I've Got The World On A String

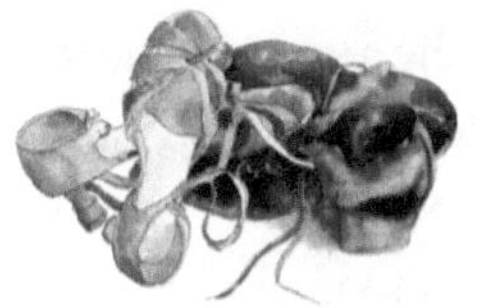

Fox was due in Chicago for a sales meeting. Getting the call had annoyed him initially. He wanted to see his new plan through and resented anything that stood in his way. Now there wasn't enough time. If he made his demands in haste, he might slip up. Still, better to get things in motion before proceeding with his travel arrangements.

Instead of taking the train, he planned to drive the two hours to Idlewild Airport. From there, he would take a plane to Chicago. The firm had arranged for everyone to stay at the Drake, a beautiful old hotel located on the Magnificent Mile. He'd never been there and looked forward to trying one of the city's famed hot dogs.

For the first time in his life, Fox was happy. Once he received the money, he would invite Halsey to come away with him. Truthfully, he didn't care either way. After all, he would be rich and could have any woman he wanted. He did, however, ponder the severed head's comment about his moustache. Perhaps Karl Hiller was right.

After packing and loading his car, he took his breakfast

in the boarding house dining room, where he found several other residents. As soon as he sat down, a homely girl brought him a plate of scrambled eggs and bacon. Thanking her, he took a sip of the weak coffee these places seemed to specialise in. A sixty-ish bald man sat at the head of the table, peering at the encyclopaedia salesman over his newspaper.

"'Death is now the Phoenix' nest, and the Turtle's loyal breast to eternity doth rest",' he said. 'That's Shakespeare, son.'

'Are you speaking to me?'

'Why, of course. Haven't seen you around much. Must be a busy man.' He consulted the others. 'Too busy to break bread with common folk, I guess.'

'Now see here...'

Fox was about to get up when a woman in a faded flowered dress and a permanent wave touched his arm. He observed her swollen knuckles with alarm.

'Don't mind him, dearie. You enjoy your breakfast.' Then to the other man, 'Leave 'im alone, Cy.'

The bald man stood and, carefully folding the newspaper, laid it on his chair. His eyes glistening, he addressed the nosy parker.

"'What freezings have I felt, what dark days seen!"'

When he was gone, Fox smirked at the others. 'What an odd duck.'

A skinny bloke wearing a vest put down his copy of *Confidential* and lit a cigarette. 'He's a gasbag. Don't take it personal.'

The woman clucked her tongue. 'You shouldn't be so hard on him.' Then to the young man, 'He lost his son in Korea. His wife passed last fall.'

'What's with all the fancy quotes?'

'Poor thing used to teach high-school English. I suppose those words are all he has now.'

The encyclopaedia salesman had lost his appetite and muttering goodbye, walked out to his car.

'All a bunch of weirdos,' he said.

As Fox drove past the entrance to the West estate, he saw Günter sawing dead branches off a tree. The young man didn't like the German and was glad his business was nearly concluded. He parked near the gate and walked in. Nathan West sat in the middle of the garden with his nurse.

Fox had an urge to confront the invalid. *No, stick to the plan.* He was under the impression he was a welcome guest and gave Liv a friendly wave. She looked up, and saying something in Yiddish, returned to her book. Holding his tongue, he continued towards the house. *Jew bitch.*

The French doors leading to the dining room were unlocked. Elsa was polishing the dining room table with lemon oil and ignored him. Giving her his best closer's smile, he wished her a good morning.

'Guten Morgen,' she said, but her heart wasn't in it.

What is it with everybody around here?

He searched the rooms downstairs looking for Adam, but he didn't find his half-brother and decided to try the barn. Fearing another bloody nose, he had no intention of entering the lab. He cut through the garden and made his way across the yard. There was a wooden stake in the ground fifty feet from the building. Tied around it was a red ribbon fluttering in the morning breeze. Halsey came out and seeing him, hurried over.

'Don't do this,' she said, taking his arm.

'What are you talking about? It's all fixed. Where's Adam?'

She glanced behind her. 'Inside. Why can't you just tell them who you are? I'm sure he and Nathan would—'

'Offer me ten thousand bucks? The way that shyster did? No, I have this coming and you better do as you're told.'

'I hate you.'

'Everyone hates an orphan, sweetheart. Look it up. Did you tell him about my—'

'Temper? He wondered why I was still seeing you. I had to think of something. So I said I invited you over to break it off.'

'That's pretty good. You're smarter than I thought. What did he say?'

'Well, he was relieved. He's really very sweet, you—'

'I don't care. You can screw him all you want after I leave.'

She slapped him, knocking off his hat. Instead of reacting with violence, he sneered.

'Just do your job and get him out here,' he said.

'All right.'

Before she could walk away, he grabbed her wrist. 'And don't mention our family.'

He dusted off his hat and lit a cigarette. His cheek stung but he didn't mind. Soon, he would be rich. Then he could purchase a beautiful home with a library. And he would order the premium edition of *Encyclopaedia Britannica*. Hell, he might even marry and have children. He could start a new dynasty that would dwarf the West family's. His one regret was his mother wouldn't be around to see it.

The barn door opened and he stubbed out his cigarette. Fox offered his hand as his half-brother approached.

'What's this all about?' Adam said.

'What did Halsey say?'

'Only that you wanted to see me.'

'Let's take a walk.'

They made their way through the sugar maple, black cherry and red oak trees towards the edge of the property. Fox explained everything as he had practised. He'd anticipated several possible reactions from Adam except one. When he stated how much money he wanted, his half-brother laughed in his face.

A feeling of burning shame – one he was intimately familiar with – overtook him. It was what he'd felt after arriving at the orphanage. A gang of older boys stripped him naked and painted his todger bright blue. Lugging him across the quad, they deposited him in front of the girls' dormitory. Instead of offering sympathy, the little pigtailed bitches jeered him.

Adam West hadn't taken him seriously at all. How was it possible? Didn't he know Fox was prepared to destroy the West name by revealing something so heinous the family would never recover? It boggled the mind. This rich upstart was acting as if he had the upper hand. For a moment, Fox didn't know what to say.

'I can see why Halsey wants to be rid of you,' Adam said. 'You're nothing but a bully and a thief. You want to harm an innocent girl and destroy my family's reputation? I'll tell you what – go ahead.

'No one in their right mind would ever believe you. Think about it. The head of a serial killer being kept alive in a barn in the middle of the Hudson Valley? They'll lock you up.'

'But I saw it!'

'You don't know what you saw.'

The encyclopaedia salesman heard a click and turned to find the caretaker pointing a double-barrelled shotgun at his head. Before he could stop himself, he wet his trousers.

'You should leave,' Adam said.

His mouth falling open, Fox clenched his fists. He blinked away hot tears and glowered at the West heir, whose superior expression hadn't changed.

'I'll be back in a few days,' he said. 'You better have my money.'

With as much dignity as he could muster, he marched to his car and drove off. At the gate, he bellowed, startling a murder of crows that took to the air like damned souls fleeing their earthly existence.

'You'll all be sorry,' Fox said, weeping.

Have You Met Miss Jones?

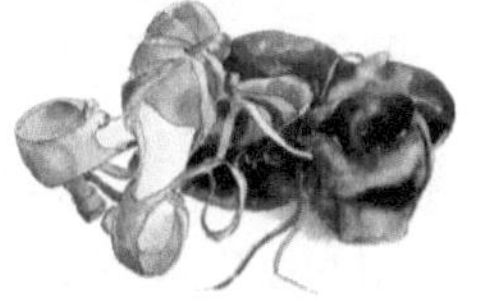

Elsa stood before the mahogany double doors and smoothed her dress. She'd been hesitant to come. But after speaking with Günter, she knew she had to say something. Taking a laboured breath, she went in. The library door was ajar. She knocked anyway, and Liv greeted her. The nurse had set out a tray of fresh rugelach. It was her specialty and also her late husband's favourite dessert.

The housekeeper could see the barn through the tall window and shuddered. Things were different back when she and her brother came to this country. More to the point, Herr Doktor West was different. Before he became ill, he would spend hours in his laboratory working on things Elsa didn't understand. But it wasn't her business to know and she concentrated all her efforts on her duties.

Liv arrived after the war and the housekeeper welcomed her. By then, the scientist's health had deteriorated and looking after him and the house was proving too much even with Günter's help. She recalled with fondness the nurse teaching her how to play gin rummy. To reciprocate, the German taught her friend to play Schnapsen but without the requisite drinking. They used to spend hours together. Then in 1959, everything changed.

The FBI arrested Karl Hiller for the brutal slaying of a prostitute in Terre Haute. They searched his home in Yonkers and not only discovered her clothing and jewellery but that of twenty-one other missing women. They also found a scuffed brown leather notebook containing a detailed outline for a roman-à-clef.

Amongst the evidence was a wallet belonging to a young married woman called Abbey Cohen, née Adler – Liv's daughter. When the nurse's son-in-law rang her with the dreadful news, she broke down. She told Herr Doktor West, and soon he became obsessed with recovering her daughter's body.

But Karl Hiller relished his role as an agent of mystery. Ignoring ardent pleas from the grieving families, he declined to reveal the whereabouts of the other victims' remains. Priests, rabbis and politicians made the pilgrimage to Ossining. None could convince him.

The FBI pored over his notes, hoping to uncover hidden clues. All they found were pairs of random numbers sprinkled throughout the margins of the ink-stained pages. Thinking it was a secret code, they turned the notebook over to colleagues specialising in cryptography. But none were able to crack it. Meanwhile, the mass murderer died in the electric chair along with his secrets.

Believing there was nothing else to be done, Elsa's friend rededicated herself to her job. Her scientist patient continued his obsession by acquiring the mass murderer's body and enlisting a bright young woman from Millbrook to help reanimate its head. The housekeeper hadn't known about any of it until her brother explained. Sitting here now,

Elsa still couldn't believe it. She told Liv the truth, leaving the nurse in shock.

'You must stop him,' Elsa said.

Her friend sighed. 'Of course. I want to bury my daughter – it's a mitzva – but not at this price.'

'Then, you'll speak to him?'

'I'll convince him to destroy it.'

'The monster is getting stronger. His powers are extending beyond the barn. Günter—'

'If he doesn't listen, I'll light the fire myself,' Liv said. 'Keyn eynhore.'[1]

Liv rode the lift to the second floor. Entering the suite, she found Nathan shivering and lit a fire. The still air was oppressive, trapped between the heavy curtains and dark walls. She dreaded going there to see him, which was why she spent her days in the library or her rooms. He lay in bed, his breathing wheezy. He had used all his strength to compel the test subject to reveal the location of Abbey's remains.

She used to give her patient Vitamin B_{12} injections every month. But she'd increased the frequency to once a week. She rolled up his sleeve and administered another one. Aware of the severed head's powers, she would never venture near the barn. Knowing the mother of one of Karl Hiller's victims was on the premises, there was no telling what the monster might do if she got too close.

After Elsa left the library, Adam came to see Liv. Even though she hadn't known what Nathan was up to, she felt responsible for what happened to his nephew. Burying her daughter wasn't worth the risk the scientist was taking. So what if she was denied the ability to perform the prescribed rituals? God would forgive her.

Her son-in-law had organised a memorial service the previous year. But he always hoped his wife's body would be recovered so the family could bury her properly in a Jewish cemetery. God would forgive him too.

'I know you're disappointed,' Nathan said in the flickering firelight. 'I've tried everything but he won't tell me.'

'This is not your responsibility.'

'I want to help.'

'It's killing you.'

'Karl Hiller has committed many crimes. But ruining my health isn't one of them.'

'And your mind?' she said.

'He can't control me. I think it's because of all the drugs I used to take. It pleases me how frustrated it makes him.'

'The shiksa hasn't been so lucky. She harmed your nephew today. Baruch Hashem, he's all right.'

'Blessed be God indeed. Thanks for letting me know, Liv. Tell her I said she's no longer permitted inside the lab. And another thing. Don't think ill of the girl. She did everything I asked her to do without knowing the real reason.'

'Okay. But everyone is frightened. Elsa is right – it's time to end the experiment.'

He folded his arms. 'I made a vow.'

'I don't care, Nathan. Abbey's soul is gone and I've accepted that. There is nothing more he can do to harm her.'

'Give me until the end of the week.'

'Then you'll destroy it?'

'I promise,' he said.

. . .

Günter stood beside the red-ribboned stake, staring at the barn in the fading light. It was September and the evenings were getting cooler. Soon, it would be autumn. Ever since the night he delivered Karl Hiller's body to the laboratory, he'd never again set foot inside except one time. The girl had sawn off the mass murderer's head by herself and asked him to dispose of the rest. Impressed with her fearlessness, he was happy to do whatever she asked.

When he was nineteen and living in Germany with his sister, he got into a heated confrontation at a Hofbräuhaus in Munich, where he was visiting a friend. The incident wasn't his fault – he was trying to break up a fight. One of the men was a member of the Freikorps, a paramilitary organisation with a long, violent history. Like his comrades, the Schweinehund hated Jews and communists and was always starting trouble after getting drunk.

He attacked Günter's friend and the young man from Hanover sprang into action. Günter was stronger than most men his age and savagely beat the mercenary, never stopping until he was dead. The police were well acquainted with the victim and not surprised he'd met a bad end.

After taking witness statements, they declined to arrest the young man and he returned to Hanover. But the image of the brute lying in a pool of his own blood haunted Günter for years. Looking back, he was sure if Halsey had been there, she wouldn't have batted an eye.

The monster in the barn knew the caretaker was outside. Sometimes, he could feel its presence behind his eyes, like a spider that could see what Günter saw. That must have been what happened the day he killed the squirrel. He never wanted to – he loved animals. But something compelled him to walk up to the tree and snatch the critter.

Günter pictured its small, frightened eyes as he broke its

neck. Now, he ventured no closer to the barn, knowing soon he would have to move the stake out another ten feet to avoid being mind-controlled. Before long, the demon's range would extend to the house.

On that day, there would be nowhere left to hide.

---

1. 'No evil eye.' A Yiddish expression.

CHAPTER 42

Isn't It Romantic?

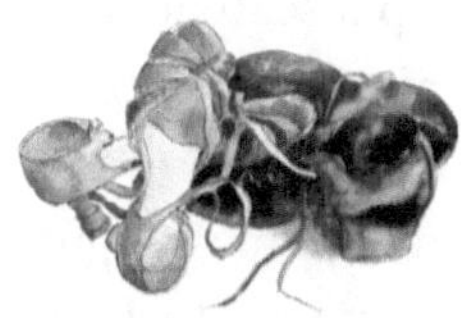

Adam lay in bed, desperate to ignore the voice coming through the grille in the floor. Earlier, he heard Halsey blowing her nose. Soon, she began talking to him from her side – more like pleading. Whatever. He was finished with her.

He tried covering his head with his pillow but could still hear her. Groaning, he sat up and examined his plastered hand, which throbbed from where she'd cut him. So much blood.

'It wasn't me,' she said, her voice cracking. 'I swear.'

Rolling his eyes, he climbed out of bed and kneeling on the floor, leant over. 'Then who was it?'

'Him.'

'Are you saying he made you do it? How?'

'I don't know. It's like he has this power – something unexplainable. I'm not lying – he can make people do things. When I asked Nathan about it, he dismissed the idea. Said the man was very good at manipulating everyone around him, especially women.'

'But you attacked me.'

'I know, and I'm sorry. He was bragging about having fooled the police for so long, referring to them as half-wits with badges. I made the mistake of saying without a body, he was harmless. And, well, that set him off. Then you walked in at just the right moment and the next thing I knew, I was picking up a scalpel. You have to believe me. I didn't want to – *he* wanted me to.'

'Why?' Adam said.

'To prove he wasn't harmless, I guess.'

What Halsey was saying was fantastic. For years, scientists tried proving extrasensory perception, or ESP, was real. He recalled reading about a botanist at Duke University who, in the 1930s, conducted experiments with student volunteers. J.B. Rhine's work led to establishing parapsychology as a legitimate branch of psychology. But those studies and others dealt with clairvoyance and telepathy, not mind control.

The scientists at Bland looked into the field and concluded it had no practical application. In other words, there was no way for them to make money. At the time, Adam's parents told him the CIA was developing a method of interrogation involving LSD and other psychoactive drugs.

Their techniques included hypnosis, electroshock and sensory deprivation. Still, these had nothing to do with one's ability to influence another person from afar. In Adam's view, the idea was pure science fiction. On the other hand, so was a talking head.

Halsey began crying again. Unable to stand it, he knocked on her door and found her in dungarees and a jumper. Her eyes were puffy. He brushed the hair from her face and held her. The urge to leave Hyde Park was never stronger but anyone could see she was in serious trouble. Who knew what would become of her if he didn't help?

He wasn't sure he believed her story about Karl Hiller. Nevertheless, something did happen and it was uncharacteristic. She wasn't a violent person. Come to think of it, it was she who had bandaged his hand with great care afterwards.

She clung to him as they sat on the bed. Her windows were open and he could hear a great horned owl. Adam thought of Jenny again and realised she had most likely moved on. Not that he blamed her. He'd been horrible to his girlfriend and would have to do his best to forget her. If only he could. He loathed the severed head and wished it would expire on its own. Then there was that lunatic Fox Hickenlooper.

'I've instructed Günter not to let your boyfriend onto the property,' Adam said. 'If he tries anything, I'll call the police.'

'It's not his fault. He's an orphan.'

'What does that have to do with anything?'

Halsey had promised Fox she wouldn't reveal his connection to the West family. But after the tense scene outside the barn, she believed Adam had a right to know. Besides, he and Nathan might be sympathetic and arrange some sort of cash payment to appease the unlucky encyclopaedia salesman. She braced herself.

'He's your half-brother,' she said.

'What did you say?'

'Don't be upset. Your father had an affair.'

'That can't be true. He would never have betrayed—'

'It was before he got married. Her name was Vicky Larue.'

'Shit.'

At the reading of the will, Engel had mentioned a particular property in SoHo, purchased in 1937 under that name. He declined to explain why it was part of the estate. As far as Adam knew, he wasn't related to anyone with the surname Larue. Now it all made sense.

Jon West must have given Fox's mother the flat so she would have a place to raise their son. Then she died, leaving the boy without a home. Why hadn't his dad done something to help Fox? Neither he nor Adam's mother ever mentioned another child. Had she even known about him?

'Why Hickenlooper, though?' he said.

'It was his mother's real name.'

'This is unbelievable – I have a brother. But I don't understand why he wants to blackmail us. Why not come out and ask for his inheritance?'

'Because your lawyer told him he didn't have a claim. He offered Fox ten grand to disappear.'

'Huh. I would've given him ten times the amount. My God, I have a brother!'

'This is too crazy,' she said. 'Fox was going to come clean and ask you for a hundred thousand. But I guess he got greedy.'

'Sure, after learning about Karl Hiller.'

'And now he plans to go to the newspapers, unless you give him what he wants.'

'That doesn't concern me. I already told him no one would believe him. Do you think he's a bad person?'

She gazed out the window. 'He's been hurt a lot. I feel sorry for him.'

'I'll speak to Uncle Nathan in the morning. I'm sure we can agree on two hundred thousand between us. But Fox must sign something saying he can't ask for more. I'll instruct Mr Engel to draw up a contract.'

She threw her arms around him and kissed his lips. 'You're an angel. It's a lot of money and you're willing to write a cheque? Just like that?'

'Thanks to my parents, I'm well off. Besides, Fox is family. It's like you said, it's not his fault. But I can't have him hanging around with that temper of his. I'd like him to take the money and beat it.'

'You're hot when you take charge.' She kissed him again. 'I think I might love you a little, Adam West.'

Grabbing the bottom of her jumper, she pulled it over her head and shook out her hair. She wasn't wearing a brassiere.

'Feel like showing this girl a good time?' she said.

But something had changed and he no longer wanted to have sex with Halsey. Unlike his parents' marriage, he couldn't picture a future with her. She was smart and funny but wasn't the type to play the role of wife and mother. Sooner or later, they would divorce and he would be alone again, still pining over Jenny. Handing her the jumper, he stood.

Confused, she pressed it to her chest. 'Where are you going?'

'I'm such a cluck.'

'You mean about us?'

'Her name is Jenny. I hurt her and, parallel universes or not, if I could go back and change things, I would.'

'Adam, time travel isn't real.'

'Then I'll have to do the next best thing,' he said and walked out.

I'm Old Fashioned

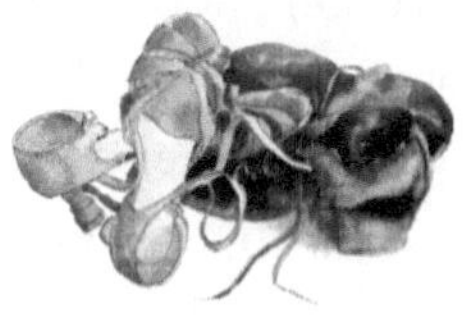

Mary Malloy finished putting up the decorations in the dining room and turned her attention to laying the table for dinner. She couldn't believe it was Thursday already and Mrs D's daughter was turning twenty. The housekeeper first came to work for the Donovans before the baby was born. She adored Jenny although, in Mary's opinion, the girl with the Audrey Hepburn bob had always been a bit spoiled. She recalled a particular incident when Jenny was ten.

She had come home from school in a foul mood. At snack time, she demanded another biscuit. She'd had three, and the housekeeper wasn't about to let her ruin her tea. So the little girl flung her plate on the floor and ran off. Mary said something unkind to her and immediately regretted it.

In the evening, she went to confession at her local church. The priest, who she knew well, was a kindly man who suffered from narcolepsy. Often whilst giving his homily, he would drift off. Then, moments later, snapping awake, he would continue with the Mass. The congregation didn't mind because he always left them wanting more.

Lately, Jenny was beginning to show new maturity. First, there was her father, killed by that awful Latin man. Then Mrs D's unfortunate encounter with the deer, which might have left her crippled had it not been for her guardian angel. Both incidents changed Jenny.

Unwilling to leave her mother after the accident, the sweet girl chose to forgo a night on the town to celebrate her birthday at home with her friend Roger Davies. Friend, indeed. He was a beau if there ever was one. The housekeeper liked him, though. He was always polite and treated her as if *she* were the mistress of the house.

Mary could smell dinner as she walked into the kitchen to get the cutlery. That was something else she loved about Jenny. The girl was used to dining at some of the finest restaurants in New York yet her tastes were simple. Irish stew was one of her favourites.

The housekeeper made it the way her mam taught her, with a generous portion of Guinness stout. Mrs D would not be joining the couple, preferring to take her meals upstairs in her bedroom due to her constant pain. This time, Mary made sure there was enough for her and her nurse.

Everything was ready by seven o'clock. Eager to take on more responsibility, Jenny insisted on serving dinner herself and told the housekeeper she could go home. Mary left the stew to warm in the oven and checked the refrigerator one last time to ensure the salad was visible at the front.

The girl walked into the kitchen and the housekeeper showed her the apple tarts she made earlier in the day in place of a birthday cake. Jenny hugged her.

'Thank you, Mary,' she said. 'I love you.'

· · ·

With his hands full, Roger struggled to ring the doorbell at seven-thirty. Jenny answered wearing a black Christian Dior cocktail dress and matching gloves. Her hair was arranged in a bouffant thanks to a hairpiece. She had on red lipstick. Her small diamond earrings were a present from her mother.

The young man was floored, having worn a modest Brooks Brothers suit. At least he'd had the good sense to choose black. Seeing her made him think he had an excellent chance to move their relationship beyond the friend stage. He gave her a chaste kiss on the cheek.

'My gosh,' he said. 'You look... like a dream.'

He handed her a gold floral box containing a dozen long-stem yellow roses and another small robin-egg-blue box tied with a white ribbon. Blushing, she accepted both.

He pointed at the smaller box. 'I hope you like it. I wasn't sure if—'

'It's Tiffany, silly. I'll love it.'

She escorted him into the sitting room, where there was a drinks trolley filled with bottles of soda water, ginger ale and other soft drinks. He sat on the two-seater, admiring the woman he hoped would someday love him and not the elusive Adam West.

'Can I fix you something?' she said. 'There's no alcohol because of my—'

'It's fine. What are you having?'

'Well, I'm a sucker for cherry Coke.'

Grabbing the bottle of grenadine, she prepared their drinks. She sat beside him, admiring his Hermès tie, which was grey silk with a white stirrup pattern. He encouraged her to open her gift and she was delighted to find a gold rope bracelet.

'Happy birthday, Jenny,' he said.

As he fastened it for her, his fingers lingered over her delicate wrist redolent with perfume. They were both hungry and didn't want to wait until eight. In the dining room, she showed him where to sit. She entered the kitchen and put on the apron Mary left for her. Rather than interrupting their conversation with multiple trips, she set out all the food at once.

Roger didn't regret staying in. On the contrary, he was thrilled to be alone with Jenny. Careful not to reveal his true feelings, he asked about her mother. They chatted about art, fashion and music. Though she didn't attend university, he thought she was one of the most cultured people he'd ever met. And she was beautiful. He considered Adam a fool for ignoring this precious creature. Then again, the situation was to the young lawyer's advantage and he congratulated himself on pursuing the relationship.

After coffee and dessert, they were full and walked out to the garden. They stood beside the fountain, the fairy lights twinkling all around them. She surprised him by taking his hand and before he knew what he was doing, he kissed her glove with tenderness and longing.

'Jenny, I—'

'Roger, I've been thinking. You've been so sweet these past few weeks, what with my dad and my mom's accident. And you never asked for anything. You've been a perfect gentleman, except for that one time when you tried kissing me. But I didn't hold it against you. I told you then that I loved Adam. And I think I still do, but not in the same way. You see, we've grown apart and I, um...'

Unable to wait any longer, he took her face in his hands and kissed her perfect lips. They were soft and warm and he thought he would burst. This time, she did not pull away.

'I love you, Jenny,' he said. 'I have for a long time.'

'Roger.' Her voice was breathy.

They held each other, kissing in the moonlight the way lovers have done since the world was young. She took his hand again and led him to the hidden alcove. Then she looked into his eyes. Unlike Adam, his were calm – even wise. Okay, so he was a terrible dancer, but she would learn to live with that. She recalled how she'd been such a petulant little girl in the past, always demanding sex. Now, with this new young man, she wanted to do things properly.

Sitting, she patted the place next to her. He touched her cheek and kissed her again, his hands exploring her bare shoulders. Then he kissed her ears and neck and the fragrant spot between her breasts as she moaned with pleasure. But he would go no further. Heeding his father's warning about Dorothy Babbage, he restrained himself. It wasn't easy. But she was his prize and there was nothing he would do to risk a future with her.

'You're mine, Jenny Donovan.'

'Yes, Roger, I am,' she said. 'But I have to tell Adam.'

CHAPTER 44

Don't Explain

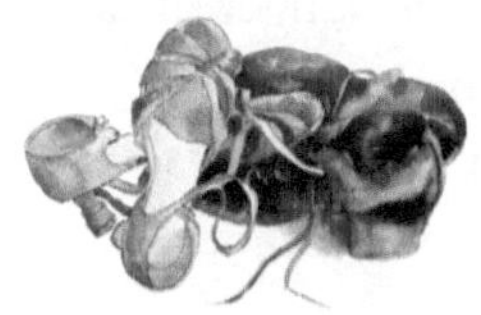

Halsey was desolate after Liv gave her the news over breakfast that the lab was off-limits. So far, it was only the two women. Adam hadn't shown up yet. Ignoring the incident with Karl Hiller, the girl felt there was so much work left to do. For starters, she wanted to refine the formula she administered to the test subject to ensure it would live years instead of months. But there was a problem.

The severed head was beginning to show signs of an antibiotic-resistant infection. Concerned, she was anxious to treat it with newly developed glycopeptides. When she objected to the ban on the grounds she needed her notes, the nurse handed her a box containing all her papers.

'Nathan is kvelling over the work you've done, bubbe,' Liv said. 'Such naches I've never seen. But he's also concerned for your safety and wants you to concentrate on writing your research paper.'

With her head bowed, the girl handed the nurse the key to the barn. 'I understand.'

'It's for the best.' She pinched Halsey's cheek. 'You're

going to be famous, like Madame Curie. Or Sophie Tucker, maybe?'

The research assistant squeezed Liv's hand. 'Thanks.'

Adam appeared in the doorway, wearing his suit and carrying his bags. He'd heard about his uncle's decision and felt the girl was out of danger at last. Now he could leave with a clear conscience.

'I'm going home,' he said.

Halsey reached for his hand. 'I wish you wouldn't.'

'It's time.'

As far as the nurse was concerned, those two had been in a cockamamy marriage of convenience. It was all she could do not to tell them to their faces on her way out. Still, she was proud of Adam for choosing well.

Taking Halsey's hand, he walked her into the garden. 'I think you're brilliant. And I'm glad I met you.'

'But you're not in love with me.'

'Remember when we first met? You said and I quote, "Just because a girl likes having sex doesn't mean she wants to get hitched."'

'*I* said that? Well, it was before I knew what a sexy, sweet hunk of a man you are.'

She tried undoing his tie, but he stopped her. Dropping her hands, she pouted.

'My mind is made up,' he said. 'Being in this place, I don't know – I lost myself. Now I've realised I *am* in love. It's like I said before, I messed up everything and I want to fix it.'

'Sounds serious.'

'It is.'

'Is she prettier than me?'

'It's not about that.'

'At least let me kiss you goodbye.'

She threw her arms around his neck and pressed her lips to his. His back was to the house and when the French doors opened, she looked up with an amused expression.

'Looks like you have a visitor,' she said.

The last person Adam expected to see was Jenny. As always, she was a vision, this time wearing a turquoise summer dress with little white polka dots. She had on an expensive gold bracelet he didn't recognise.

Beside her was a stranger. A little older than him, he wore a grey-check sports jacket, black knit shirt, cream-coloured chinos and loafers with no socks. They were holding hands.

'Adam?' Jenny said.

Glancing at Halsey, he approached the couple. 'What are you doing here?'

'I came to see you. There's something I need to tell you.' She looked past him at the blonde. 'But it looks like you've got your hands full.'

'No, this isn't... We were just saying goodbye. I'm leaving for Manhattan – I was going to call you as soon as I got to my apartment.'

She was still looking at the other woman and hadn't paid attention. 'This is Roger Davies. He and I—'

He tried taking her hand. 'No, please, Jenny. Don't say it.'

Like a bodyguard to the stars, the freshly minted boyfriend intervened. 'Let's not make this more awkward than it is, fella.'

'No one's talking to you, *fella*.'

Jenny got between them and gripped Adam's uninjured hand. 'You were gone and never called. I thought you didn't care about us any more.'

'So you take up with the first jerk who comes along?'

'Roger's not a jerk.'

'Believe me, anyone who wears shoes without socks is a jerk.'

'Stop it. He was there for me after my dad died. Then later, after I almost lost Mom...'

'What happened to her?'

'It doesn't matter. The point is, he's been there the whole time while you turned into a, a ghost.'

'I meant to call, I...'

The gate opened and Fox Hickenlooper walked in wearing his trademark sneer. He approached Halsey and took her arm. She shook him off.

'What's going on here?' he said. 'Who are they?'

'Not now. Can't you see we're in the middle of something?'

Ignoring Roger, Adam looked into Jenny's eyes, hoping to find a glint of the love he hoped she still felt for him.

'Can't we talk about this?' he said.

'I don't know...'

Adam faced the pretender. 'Be a sport and give us a minute, will you?'

Gaping, Roger looked at the girl he loved. When she nodded her assent, he marched across the garden past the other couple and exited through the gate, slamming it on his way out. Reading the situation correctly, Halsey took Fox's arm and urged him out of the garden.

Adam escorted Jenny into the dining room and pulled out a chair for her. 'Can I get you some coffee?'

'Sure. What happened to your hand?'

'It's nothing.'

He poured two cups and gave one to her. When Elsa showed up, he shooed her away. She returned to the kitchen, muttering in German.

'So much has happened,' he said. 'I don't know where to begin.'

'What's there to tell? You have a new girlfriend.'

'She's not my— We, um... Never mind. I only stayed here because, well. I can't tell you. But you have to believe me. Halsey was in physical danger.'

'You mean from the guy with the ridiculous moustache?'

'No, he's an idiot. And my half-brother, apparently.'

'You have a brother? But I thought—'

'It's a long story I'll tell you someday. Look, Jenny. I want you to know something. I never stopped caring about you. It's true. Even when I was mad at you because of your father, I couldn't help myself. When you came to the hospital that day, I was so ashamed. I believed you thought less of me and I couldn't face you again.'

'But I didn't think less of you. Oh, Adam.' She reached for his hand. 'Sure, I was upset seeing you there – anyone would be. But I never stopped loving you. You need to believe that.

'And then when you didn't call or write, I figured it was your way of telling me it was over – *we* were over. I've heard the stories. Men do this all the time – they just disappear like it never happened. And we're left to wonder...'

'Okay, I can see why you'd think that,' he said. 'This Roger, who is he?'

'He's someone I met before you. But we were never together. It wasn't until later that he started coming around.'

'I'll bet. As soon as he heard I was out of the picture.'

'Because he knew I was alone. He didn't have a clue I had a boyfriend until later. When I told him, he asked if we could still be friends. Recently, it grew into something more.'

He pointed at her bracelet. 'Birthday present?'

'What did you expect? He loves me.'

'Happy birthday, by the way. Are you in love with him?'

'I'm pretty sure he wants to marry me.'

'That's not what I asked.' He stroked her cheek. 'Are you in love with him?'

Kneading her fingers, she looked towards the garden. 'He's kind and responsible—and he's a lawyer. He says he wants children and...'

When she broke down, he embraced her and kissed her soft lips. Instead of pulling away, she melted in his arms and kissed his face all over.

'I missed you so much,' she said. 'And I can't help it – I love *you*. God, this is a mess! What am I going to do?'

He kissed her eyes. 'You're going to let me spend the rest of my life making it up to you. All I care about is your happiness. And if I ever get out of line again, you can call what's-his-name.'

'Does that mean you love me? If you don't say it right now, I'll go out of my mind.'

'First, I need to tell you something. I've developed a new theory on inertia, but it doesn't seem to be gaining momentum.' Then on her confused silence, 'Okay, how about this? I love you, Jenny Donovan. I'll always and forever love you. You're my heart. You—'

'Shut up.'

As they kissed, the French doors banged open. With her eyes like hot coals, Halsey could hardly catch her breath. Adam sprang to his feet.

'What is it?'

'He-he's dead. Fox, he... He killed him.'

'Who?'

'That man,' she said, staring at Jenny. 'Roger.'

CHAPTER 45

Let's Get Lost

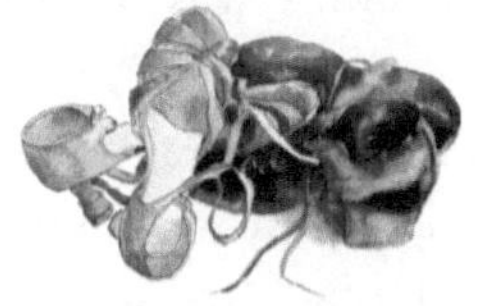

They ran through the garden and found Günter standing beside the wooden stake. He was holding his shotgun in the muzzle-down position. Roger's body lay face down in front of the barn. Shrieking, Jenny tried to go to him, but Adam and Halsey prevented her.

'If you get any closer, the monster vill take you,' Günter said.

Jenny looked at the others. 'I don't understand. What's he talking about?'

Adam sighed. 'He means Karl Hiller.'

'The serial killer?' She pointed. 'He's in there? But he's dead.'

'Most of him, anyway,' he said. Then to Halsey, 'How did it happen?'

'Fox and I were standing here talking. I told him what you said about the money and he was excited. He was glad you knew you were brothers and said he never wanted to hurt anyone.

'Roger must have been wandering the grounds. Before

we knew it, he was over by the barn, just kind of staring at it. Fox tried to warn him to get out of there.'

She pointed at the stake. 'But something happened after he crossed the line. He started moaning and holding his head. Instead of helping Roger, he, he strangled him. I wanted to stop him, but I was afraid Karl Hiller would control me too.'

Adam turned to the German. 'Where is Fox now?'

'I saw him heading for my tool shed.'

'We have to find him. Jenny, go inside and call the police. The rest of us will search the property.'

The girl folded her arms. 'I'm not leaving you.'

'This is no time to – do you know how dangerous this guy is?'

'I said I'm not leaving you.'

'All right. Take my hand and don't go anywhere near the barn.'

'I'll call the police,' Halsey said, trotting off.

Günter led them in a wide circle behind the structure, past the cremator. An old wooden shed stood amongst the trees. In front of it, they found several dead animals – a raccoon, three or four squirrels and a neighbour's dog who had wandered onto the property. All had their throats slit. After examining the bodies, which were still warm, the caretaker searched the shed. He came out wearing a grim expression.

'My hunting knife is missing.'

'That's the kind of weapon Karl Hiller used to murder all those women,' Jenny said.

Adam squeezed her hand. 'There's something I don't understand. How can he control someone this far away from the lab?'

Günter racked the shotgun with an unnerving clunk. 'He's unstoppable now.'

Adam looked towards the house. 'Dammit, where are the police?'

'They're not real quick out here. He could be anywhere. Ve should go.'

They returned to the front of the barn, where they found Nathan and Halsey waiting. Jenny recoiled at the sight of the scientist's weird glasses.

Nathan focused on his nephew. 'Elsa and Liv locked themselves in the basement. You don't know where this man is?'

'He could have left the estate by now.'

'We can't let that happen.' He propelled himself towards the barn.

Releasing Jenny's hand, Adam started after him. 'Uncle Nathan, where are you going?'

The scientist stopped and spun around. 'Don't come any closer! I'm going to talk to him.'

'It's too dangerous!' Halsey said, eyeing the stake. 'Let me go with you.'

'You're vulnerable – I am not. You must remain here. I want you to live to write your paper.' Then to Günter, 'Finde ihn. Und tu, was erforderlich ist.'[1]

Passing Roger's body, Nathan entered the barn. The lights flickered erratically, which made it hard for him to get his bearings. With determination, he wheeled himself forward.

Karl Hiller watched him, his expression like that of a clown in a demonic circus. There was a bluish glow around the severed head, as if it was being illuminated from inside the titanium box. Suddenly, the barn door slammed shut.

Ignoring the cheap theatrics, Nathan positioned himself

in front of the Plexiglas cylinder, the lenses of his glasses telescoping.

'Let the boy go,' he said.

'I'm just getting started. All this time, you and the girl thought *I* was the experiment.'

'That's not the case?'

'I've been conducting some tests of my own. First on the lab animals. Then on the caretaker and Halsey.'

'Not Adam?'

'I'll admit it puzzled me. Like you, he seems to be immune to my powers of persuasion. Must be a family trait. I gotta tell ya, I don't like it. It's not very scientific if you can't explain the outliers. Wouldn't you agree, Doctor?'

'I can see how that might frustrate you. And Fox?'

'Oh, he's my star pupil. His brain, it's so malleable – like Play-Doh. You want to know the best part? He's impressionable. I can imprint him with all my future instructions – it doesn't matter how far away he is. They'll stick. Now, I'm not an engineer, but I suspect computers work in a similar fashion.'

'You mean you can program him.'

'It's a good thing too. I'm sure your research assistant has told you about the chronic infection I can't seem to shake. That's the trouble with germs – they're everywhere.

'I'm thinking I don't have much longer. Oh, she'll try a new drug therapy, but my days are numbered, at least in my current form. Time to pack my bags and move into some new digs.'

'Where you can continue your killing spree,' the scientist said.

'I like to think of it as picaresque. There are a few adjustments I need to make first. Wouldn't want any screw-ups like getting caught by some half-wit with a badge. Soon, I'll take my show on the road. Wonderful, isn't it?

'None of this would be possible if you and Halsey hadn't revived me. And with Fox, I've got a whole new lease on life, killing-wise. No one would ever suspect an encyclopaedia salesman.'

'We'll see,' Nathan said. 'Now, about Abbey.'

'Oh, not that again. I told you. She's where she belongs, like all the others.'

'And that's final?'

'What do you think?'

The scientist headed to the rear of the cylinder. The unfamiliar noises he made began to worry the test subject.

'Hey, what are you doing back there?'

'Making a few adjustments of my own,' Nathan said.

Günter went off to find Fox as sirens wailed in the distance, whilst Adam led the women towards the garden.

'It's better if we go inside where it's safe,' he said.

He swung open the gate only to discover Roger's killer waiting for them. Wearing Karl Hiller's malevolent grin, he brandished the blood-stained hunting knife, his eyes darting from side to side like pinballs.

'Run!' Adam said.

Halsey grabbed Jenny's arm, but the girl fought her.

'I said I'm not leaving him!'

'There's nothing you can do. Now, come on!'

With no weapon, Adam tried rushing the maniac. Fox brought down the knife, just missing his half-brother. He was about to try again when he stopped, mesmerised by something in the distance.

Backing away, Adam turned to find the women staring

at a shimmering rift in space. As the light faded, the air began to ripple, distorting everything behind it. There was someone inside – an elderly black woman with close-cropped white hair and wearing clothes that were sleek and strange.

Stepping out of the rift, she beckoned to him. She looked so familiar, and he found himself drawn to her. Taking Jenny's hand, he started towards the stranger. But the girl was petrified and tried pulling away.

'It's time to go, Adam,' Claire de La Lune said, a little breathless.

She extended her wrinkled hands and he took them in his. There was something calming about her. He didn't know how or why she'd come here, only that he had to go. And more than anything in the world, he wanted Jenny to accompany him.

For no reason at all, he thought of the time travel diorama and Future Man. And his friend, Del Dillard. The greatest tribute you can pay a man is to remember him. And the greatest tragedy is to have gone before you can thank the rememberer.

'Do you trust me?' he said to Jenny.

She stared at the time traveller, her eyes wide. Then to the only man she ever truly loved, 'I trust you.'

As they stepped into the rift, the elderly scientist gazed around the estate. The police would be here any minute. She turned to leave.

'What about me?' Halsey said.

Smiling, Claire kissed her cheek. 'Oh, child. You're going to be just fine.'

After everyone was inside, the shimmering tear in space winked out like a fading firefly. Halsey turned round in time to see Fox coming at her with frenzied eyes, still clutching the bloody knife. She screamed.

But before he could harm her, a loud blast stopped him in his tracks. He dropped to his knees, his chest perforated with buckshot. Günter emerged from the shadows, both gun barrels smoking. The unlucky encyclopaedia salesman held himself.

'I didn't mean to do that,' he said and fell over dead.

A massive explosion rocked the estate, followed by another and another. Halsey watched as smoke and flames poured out of the laboratory.

'Nathan!'

She and the German ran towards the barn. The heat was so intense it was impossible to get inside to rescue the scientist. It took half an hour for the structure to burn to the ground. By the time the fire brigade arrived, there was nothing left but ashes and wrecked laboratory equipment.

'He's gone,' Halsey said.

The next day, Günter and Halsey, both wearing wellington boots and gloves, waded through the mud and debris, looking for anything salvageable. Uneasy, she approached what was left of the cylinder, which had melted. The titanium box lay in the centre. Inside was Karl Hiller's charred skull.

Staring at it, she no longer cared about her research and wanted only to return to Millbrook to see her parents. Having lived through a nightmare, she wanted nothing more to do with cell regeneration or resurrection or any of it. And there was something else – she didn't like who she had become.

Adam and Jenny vanishing in the bright light was a sign

and as if the idea had always been there, Halsey saw her future. She would attend medical school, become a GP and dedicate herself to delivering babies and treating chickenpox in the town of her birth. That was a life worth living.

The German called her over and showed her a fire-resistant safe. The combination lock was melted and he had to use a hammer and chisel to get the door open. There was a worn brown leather notebook inside. He handed it to her. As she opened it, a scrap of paper fell out. She recognised Nathan's handwriting, scribbled in haste.

The NUMbers are The Key, Halsey.

At first, she didn't understand the significance. All this time she thought the scientist was interested in the test subject's intellect. But flipping through the notebook, she realised what he cared about was the murders. Pairs of numbers were scattered across Karl Hiller's meticulous notes. But they weren't ordinary numbers.

In a flash of inspiration, she counted them and came up with twenty-two sets. That's when she guessed what her mentor was trying to tell her. These were longitudes and latitudes. What if each pair represented the location of a victim's body? Then she saw the name – Abbey Adler Cohen. *Adler.* When she showed Günter, he confirmed it was the nurse's daughter.

'I have to tell Liv,' she said and bolted towards the house.

---

1. 'Find him. And do what is necessary.'

Goodbye

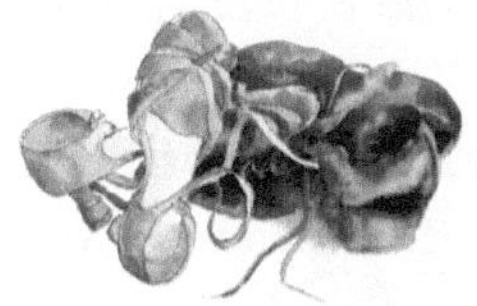

Mrs D opened her eyes only to discover she was in hospital again. Under the window, there was a large vase of yellow roses. And in front of that, Jenny's teddy. Mary was asleep in a chair by the window. Had the housekeeper been there all night?

It was almost Christmas – three months since Roger Davies's death and Jenny's disappearance. Mrs D remembered attending the young man's lavish funeral. So many people. But what could she do for her missing child? Each time she spoke to the police, they told her the same thing – she was last seen with Adam West. Her mind was foggy as she tried recalling the events that had led to her being here.

Returning from her solicitor's offices, she had taken East Forty-Eighth Street. She'd struck something – no, she had pitched forward. It was sudden and violent – a pothole! She'd failed to see it in time and her left tyre fell sharply into it. As she came out the other side, she hit her head on the roof. After that, everything went black.

Her head ached and she wished she had some aspirin. The left side of her body felt weak. She couldn't move her arm. Sharp waves of pain shot through the top of her skull as she tried reaching for a paper cup on the over-bed table.

The housekeeper opened her eyes, startled by a moan. Seeing the patient conscious, she poured some water and helped Mrs D to drink.

'Oh, thank God you're awake!' she said.

'I, I am a-wake.'

'Don't try to speak. I'll get the doctor.'

Alone now, Mrs D was left to wonder what was wrong with her. People didn't end up in hospital as a result of a pothole. Her left foot tingled and after having slept, she still felt tired. She wondered how hitting her head could cause all this bother.

In another few minutes, the housekeeper returned with a doctor Mrs D didn't recognise. He was young and pleasant-looking with dark, curly hair and good teeth.

'Hello again, Mrs Donovan. I'm Dr Saperstein, remember?'

He was Jewish. Where was her regular doctor? And why was this one so cheerful?

'Do you know where you are?'

She struggled to answer. 'Hos-pi-tal.'

'That's right. You're at Mount Sinai. If you don't mind, I'd like to examine you.'

Amongst other things, he tested her reflexes and sensory perception. Then he checked her eyes using a medical torch. Satisfied, he stepped away and glancing at Mary, addressed the patient.

'Do you remember what happened?'

'Stu-pid pot-hole.'

'Correct. You hit a pothole. A pretty nasty one too, from what I hear. I understand they repaired it the day after your accident. Can you believe it? Now, I've reviewed your medical history and saw you were involved in another auto-accident several months ago.'

'She hit a deer,' the housekeeper said.

'Boy, oh boy. At the time, you had a concussion. But there was some bleeding in your brain and a teeny-tiny clot formed in a blood vessel. It's what we call a thrombus. You were fine all this time. But when you hit the pothole, you banged your head.

'We can't be for sure if this was the cause. But we believe the subsequent jarring loosened the thrombus and caused an embolic stroke. The result is you've got some paralysis on your left side and you're also suffering from aphasia, which is why you're having trouble speaking. Are you with me so far?'

Mrs D had no idea what he'd said and turned to Mary for help. The housekeeper approached the bed and took her employer's hand.

'It was the pothole that gave you the stroke.'

'Guess I shouldn't have buried the lede,' Saperstein said. Then to Mrs D, 'We're going to keep you a few more days for observation. Provided you're stable, you can go home. How's that sound?'

The only word the patient recognised was *home*, which made her happy. Then, she realised there was nothing for her there and warm tears sprang from her eyes. Clearing his throat, the doctor excused himself and promised to check on her later.

Mary patted Mrs D's hand. 'Don't worry, I'll look after you. You'll be pleased to know I've put up the tree.'

Using a tissue, she gently wiped her employer's face and kissed her left cheek, which the patient could not feel.

'Need a fa-vour,' Mrs D said. 'Im-por-tant.'

· · ·

Detective Quinn was surprised to get the call. Walking into the hospital room, he found Mary Malloy feeding the patient. He removed his hat and approached the bed.

'You wanted to see me, Mrs Donovan?'

She patted the housekeeper's arm with her good hand. Mary wanted to stay but her employer insisted on a private conversation with the policeman. Pushing aside the tray, she picked up her handbag and left.

The detective assumed this was official business and took out his notepad and pen. Weakly, the patient indicated the chair. He pulled it up and made himself comfortable.

Since regaining consciousness, Mrs D had thought everything over. She didn't know what would happen to her – whether she was meant to live or die – but she wanted to put things right. In a way, the housekeeper had a lot to do with her decision.

Over the years, she observed how Mary conducted herself. Though not perfect, she was a woman of faith, which was what guided her in everything she did. Sometimes in the afternoons, whilst Bruce was at work and Jenny did her homework in her room, they would have long conversations in the kitchen about God and heaven and what we were meant to do in this life.

Over the past few years, Mrs D considered attending Mass with the housekeeper and the notion stuck with her. But then she learnt the truth about her husband and a creeping darkness poisoned her, shutting out any desire for goodness. It was then she decided to kill the perverted bastard. The only problem was an innocent man would die for her crime. And that she could no longer abide.

So she admitted to everything – hiring Calvin Lipinsky to murder Bruce and then killing the mechanic to shut him up. She claimed it was all for Jenny but that was a lie. She did those things for revenge.

It took her a long time to confess due to her aphasia. After finishing, she was exhausted and fell asleep. Quinn returned to the station to prepare a statement based on his notes. Later at the hospital, he read it aloud and asked the patient to sign it.

Mrs D passed away the next day.

Tito Ladrón was released from prison. He had a permanent limp and was blind in one eye after a severe beating by another inmate who found out he was a homosexual. But he was free. Instead of returning to Miami, he chartered a fishing boat to take him to Havana.

The political climate there had worsened but he didn't care. He was desperate to see his mother and sister again. Over the next few years, he worked odd jobs until he'd saved enough money to open a restaurant. The last anyone heard, he was doing quite well.

The Cuban shook Quinn's hand outside the courthouse where reporters were gathered, waiting for him to make a statement. He wasn't in the mood to talk to anyone but decided to give them something.

'I told you I was innocent,' he said.

Someone To Watch Over Me

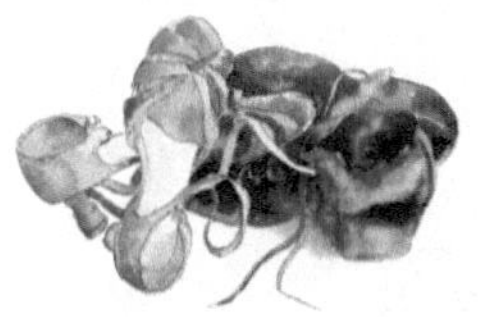

Dr Claire de La Lune was always talented. She had an astonishing IQ which a psychologist claimed was off the scale after testing the precocious eight-year-old. Whilst pursuing her studies in the 1960s, she would often think about Adam West and their adventurous dance in the Dome Room. She was sure she'd fallen in love with him then, but it wasn't meant to be. To begin with, there was the race question.

Though she was French Creole and light-skinned, people were not inclined to welcome a woman of colour into white society with open arms. Her father had warned her, advising his daughter to concentrate on her studies to become the smartest, most successful person she was capable of being. Knowledge was like a suit of armour, he told her. And she should wear it fearlessly.

She promised him she would and earned her PhD in physics from Harvard. Soon after, Dr Irenka Lewandowska, who adored the girl, invited her to join Bland's science division. Excited to be part of the celebrated team, Claire taught herself Polish. She was already fluent in French and Italian.

Despite Dr Gibbon's earlier ill-treatment, Claire wanted to learn everything there was to know about time travel from him. His initial reaction was to send her off with homework assignments, as if she were still at university. Each time, she returned with answers to questions he hadn't even begun to think of. He quickly learnt to appreciate her exceptional mind and took her under his wing. Ultimately, they became friends.

After he retired, they saw each other regularly. Over dinner, she would pick his brain about a new theory she'd come up with. He passed away at seventy-five from lung cancer. She attended his funeral and, in the following years, those of so many other colleagues she admired, including Dr Lewandowska, who died in Warsaw.

It was summer again in Cambridge, and Claire de La Lune was eighty-nine. The chief scientist was a Nobel Prize laureate and the holder of a whopping 3,900 US patents. Unimpressed with her achievements, she reported to the West building each weekday morning and sometimes on Saturdays. The heat was oppressive but she loved the season.

Walking across the Bland campus, she found the park bench she and Adam West had shared. She remembered it as if it were yesterday, even hearing snatches of their conversation in her head. A tabby like the one from all those years ago sidled up to her, purring and rubbing itself on her leg. She recalled asking Adam whether he'd ever owned a pet.

On the way into her building, she stopped to look at the plaque dedicated to his parents. The flowers at the base of the plinth were beginning to wilt from the unrelenting sun.

She made a mental note to have them replaced. Since she began working at Bland, she saw to it that a fresh bouquet was placed there every day, even in winter.

Emily Chen, an android whose mind contained everything that was known, greeted Claire as soon as she entered the basement lab containing the time-travel device. She informed Dr de La Lune that the machine was ready and reminded her that due to the device's limitations, Claire should stay no more than ten minutes. The woman who had invented time travel touched her assistant's childlike face as if she were human.

'You say that every time, dear.'

'Because I worry about you. We all do.'

'I've always said it's a blessing to have people around you who care.'

'Thank you for calling me a person.'

When she wasn't working on official projects, the chief scientist would spend nights and weekends researching the lives of Adam West, Jenny Donovan and everyone of significance who had ever come in contact with them. Never married, she devoted herself to her work. Hers was an arduous task and it took her years to compile the necessary data.

The new computers helped and, at length, she was able to create a time map of all the events of interest. From there, she built a 3D model in software, which allowed her to pinpoint any particular moment and display the connected threads. More importantly, she could retrieve an event's exact instant and geographical coordinates. It was at this point she made the most important decision of her life – to fix what had broken.

The device she and her team spent years working on

was by no means perfect. For example, there was no way to travel to the future as Dr Gibbon's diorama had suggested. Also, the time one could spend in the past was limited. This was because the energy required to power the machine was enormous. If a traveller stayed too long, there wouldn't be enough to get them home. Still, the technology worked well and thirty-two years after she showed Irenka her primitive experiment, Claire believed the device was ready for a human time traveller.

In the preceding months, they'd sent animals in cages to various points in the past along with a video camera to record what was visible outside the golden corona that seemingly appeared out of nothing. Later, her team analysed the footage to confirm the trip had been successful. In other words, whether they'd transported the test subject to the correct destination and time. They had. And to their delight, they found the animals unharmed upon their return to the present.

Fortunately, these test subjects could not comprehend what happened and didn't die from fright. However, the chief scientist noticed a minuscule deterioration in their health that increased with each trip. Ignoring the risk, she tested the machine herself by travelling to a railway station in Hanover, Germany, in the summer of 1922. Though people were alarmed by the miraculous appearance of a woman of colour, they left her alone to retrieve a gold locket that had fallen unnoticed onto the busy platform.

A few days later, she made another trip to visit Shlomo Engel. It was early September 1960 and he was distraught over the recent tragedy in Hyde Park. Adam West and his girlfriend, Jenny Donovan, had been butchered by a crazed half-brother out of his mind over some imagined inheritance. The client's great-uncle, Nathan West, perished in an unrelated barn fire.

Claire's sudden appearance threatened to give the poor man a fit as she calmly explained how she got there. Unwilling to believe her, he insisted she leave at once. When she showed him the locket, he collapsed into his chair. He opened it and immediately recognised the photo of his mother and father.

The keepsake had belonged to his sister. She lost it at the station in 1922 when she, her brother and their parents boarded a train bound for Munich. From there, they would catch a plane to Paris on their way to the United States. Convinced the time traveller was telling the truth, the solicitor followed her instructions to the letter.

The next trip would be perilous. Emily begged her not to go but Claire was adamant, even though her health was beginning to suffer from cell degeneration. Everything had led up to this moment and if the chief scientist didn't see it through, her life's work would have been in vain. Her assistant suggested someone else could go in her place.

Claire knew Adam would never agree to get into the time machine unless it was she who invited him. So in September 1960, she travelled to Nathan West's estate, knowing a killer was on the loose. Like the other trips, her timing was impeccable and she managed to rescue the young couple before Fox Hickenlooper could murder them. What she hadn't counted on was the effect seeing the handsome young man would have on her. Her heart leapt.

Upon arriving at the laboratory in the present, Adam and Jenny were taken to comfortable patient rooms. The next day, Dr de La Lune explained that it was now 2032 and promised that shortly they would be returned to their own time. Moreover, they would be together but not in New York.

When Jenny insisted on seeing her mother, the chief scientist assured her there was nothing to go back to. She'd never met the girl and found her to be a lovely person – one who would make her future husband happy. Adam was thrilled to see his friend again and begged her to let them explore this new world of tomorrow. But Claire refused, advising him that to know the future, he would have to live it.

He embraced her. 'When did you become so wise?'

'People can surprise you,' she said.

The scientists positioned the young time travellers inside a metal arch that was eight feet tall. They were to be transported to Hanover around Christmas 1960, arriving at the estate of one Adam Weisberger. Thanks to Engel, all of his client's wealth in America had been transferred to Weisberger. The solicitor was already waiting for them in Hanover. He had arranged all the necessary documents, including a deed to the estate.

As citizens, Adam and Jenny would marry and raise their children in Germany beginning with their firstborn, Hannah. Jenny would teach. Adam would devote the rest of his life to helping people who were less fortunate, especially those suffering from mental illness. They would live to see their great-grandchildren. And they would be remembered.

At the last moment, Adam stepped out and taking Claire's hands, asked her the question burning in his heart. *Why?*

She gazed into his eyes and imagined herself young and in love. Then, in the peace of a promise fulfilled, she looked past him and smiled.

'Jenny's waiting for you, dear,' she said.

. . .

Before making her final trip, Claire underwent a complete physical. The effects of time travel were evident in the slight trembling in her limbs. To ensure the machine's stability, they'd had to increase the power to 94 lunes. Nevertheless, she believed someday her team would overcome the adverse effects.

Giddy with anticipation, she changed into her pink petal dress, which still fit her, and hugged Emily. Then Claire took something from her pocket and handed her Future Man.

'Hold on to that for me,' the chief scientist said. 'I'd hate to lose it.'

'He looks like Adam West.'

'Really? I hadn't noticed.'

'Don't stay too long, okay?'

'I promise. Wait, what's this?' She removed a shiny fifty-cent piece from Emily's ear.

The android gave her a musical laugh. 'I didn't know you could do magic!'

'Adam taught me before he left.'

As Claire took her place under the arch, they activated the device using a holographic controller. In seconds, she would be transported to Tuesday, 22 March 1960, at precisely 7.58 PM. EST. According to Emily, that was the day Arthur L. Schawlow and Charles H. Townes of Bell Labs were granted a patent for the optical maser, or laser.

The chief scientist's destination was a spot outside the Dome Room of the Lenox Hotel in Boston. Upon arriving, Claire would observe herself at seventeen wearing her pink petal dress and dancing to 'Siboney.' After all these years, it was by far the best day of her long life – a day she treasured above all others.

She heard the soft hum of her exotic matter factory, now the size of a broom closet, and thought of Adam and Jenny Weisberger. She imagined them out there somewhere, happy and in love.

And as she winked into the past, she hoped with all her heart they were dancing.

I hope you enjoyed *Let's Get Lost*. These are the songs that inspired me as I wrote the novel. You can listen to them by visiting my Spotify profile **bystevenramirez** and selecting the Let's Get Lost Soundtrack.

"What Am I Here For?"
Clifford Brown, Max Roach Quintet (Clifford
Brown and Max Roach)
"Good Bait"
John Coltrane (Soultrane)
"It Could Happen To You"
Tony Bennett (Long Ago And Far Away)
"Close Your Eyes"
Ella Fitzgerald (Like Someone In Love)
"Well, You Needn't"
Miles Davis Quintet (Steamin' With The Miles
Davis Quintet)
"Little Girl Blue"
Nina Simone (Little Girl Blue)
"Just Friends"
Sonny Stitt Quartet (Saxophone Supremacy)
"Siboney"
Caterina Valente (Presenting Caterina Valente)
"Teach Me Tonight"
Dinah Washington (The Complete Dinah
Washington On Mercury, Vol. 4 1954–1956)

"In The Wee Small Hours Of The Morning"
Frank Sinatra (In The Wee Small Hours)
"Take Five"
The Dave Brubeck Quartet (Time Out)
"You're Driving Me Crazy"
Art Pepper (The Capitol Vault Jazz Series)
"You Can Depend On Me"
Nat King Cole (The Complete Recordings Of The Nat King Cole Trio)
"Yesterdays"
The Four Freshmen (Our Latin Vibes)
"Fin De L'Affaire"
Hank Mobley (Hank Mobley Quintet)
"How Long Has This Been Going On?"
Tommy Flanagan, John Coltrane, Kenny Burrell (The Cats)
"My Shining Hour"
Chris Connor (A Jazz Date With Chris Connor)
"If You Could See Me Now"
Chet Baker (Chet)
"They Say It's Wonderful"
Johnny Mathis (Heavenly)
"Pent-Up House"
Sonny Rollins, Clifford Brown, Max Roach, Richie Powell, George Morrow (Plus Four)
"Trav'lin' Light"
Gerry Mulligan, Chet Baker (Reunion With Chet Baker)
"Solitude"
Tony Bennett (Jazz)

"Something I Dreamed Last Night"
Miles Davis Quintet (Steamin' With The Miles Davis Quintet)
"Too Close For Comfort"
Mel Tormé, The Marty Paich Orchestra (Mel Tormé: Swings Shubert Alley)
"Trouble In Mind"
Dinah Washington, Ben Webster (The Best In Blues)
"All My Tomorrows"
Frank Sinatra (Nothing But The Best)
"Mack The Knife"
Bobby Darin (The Ultimate Bobby Darin)
"Mambocito Mio"
Illinois Jacquet, (The Kid And The Brute)
"Stormy Weather"
Billie Holiday (An Evening With Billie Holiday)
"Fever"
Peggy Lee (All Aglow Again!)
"Portrait Of Jenny"
Clifford Brown (Clifford Brown With Strings)
"I'm A Fool To Want You"
Lee Morgan (Here's Lee Morgan)
"Ain't Misbehavin'"
Ray Charles (The Genius After Hours)
"My Little Brown Book"
Duke Ellington, John Coltrane (Duke Ellington & John Coltrane)
"You Do Something To Me"
Sonny Rollins (The Bridge)
"Alone Together"
Kenny Dorham (Quiet Kenny)

"Why Was I Born?"
Judy Garland (The London Sessions: The Best Of
The Capitol Masters)
"You'd Be So Nice To Come Home To"
Joe Stafford (Jo + Jazz)
"Twisted"
Lambert, Hendricks & Ross (The Hottest New
Group In Jazz)
"I've Got The World On A String"
Peggy Lee (Sugar 'N' Spice)
"Have You Met Miss Jones?"
Louis Armstrong (Louis Under The Stars)
"Isn't It Romantic?"
Ella Fitzgerald (Ella Fitzgerald Sings The Rodgers
And Hart Song Book)
"I'm Old Fashioned"
Chet Baker (Plays For Lovers)
"Don't Explain"
Billie Holiday (The Decca Singles Vol. 1: 1945–
1949)
"Let's Get Lost"
Chet Baker (Chet Baker Sings And Plays)
"Goodbye"
Julie London (Julie... At Home)
"Someone To Watch Over Me"
Sarah Vaughan (Sarah Vaughan Sings George
Gershwin)
"We'll Be Together Again"
Johnny Hartmann (Songs From The Heart)

Steven Ramirez is the award-winning American author of thriller, supernatural, and literary fiction. A former screenwriter, he's written about man-made plagues and idyllic towns infested with ghosts and demons. His latest novel is *Let's Get Lost*, a modern fairy tale. Steven lives in Los Angeles.

AUTHOR WEBSITE
stevenramirez.com

instagram.com/byStevenRamirez

goodreads.com/byStevenRamirez

bookbub.com/authors/steven-ramirez

www.ingramcontent.com/pod-product-compliance
Lightning Source LLC
Chambersburg PA
CBHW031437200726
48289CB00002BA/424